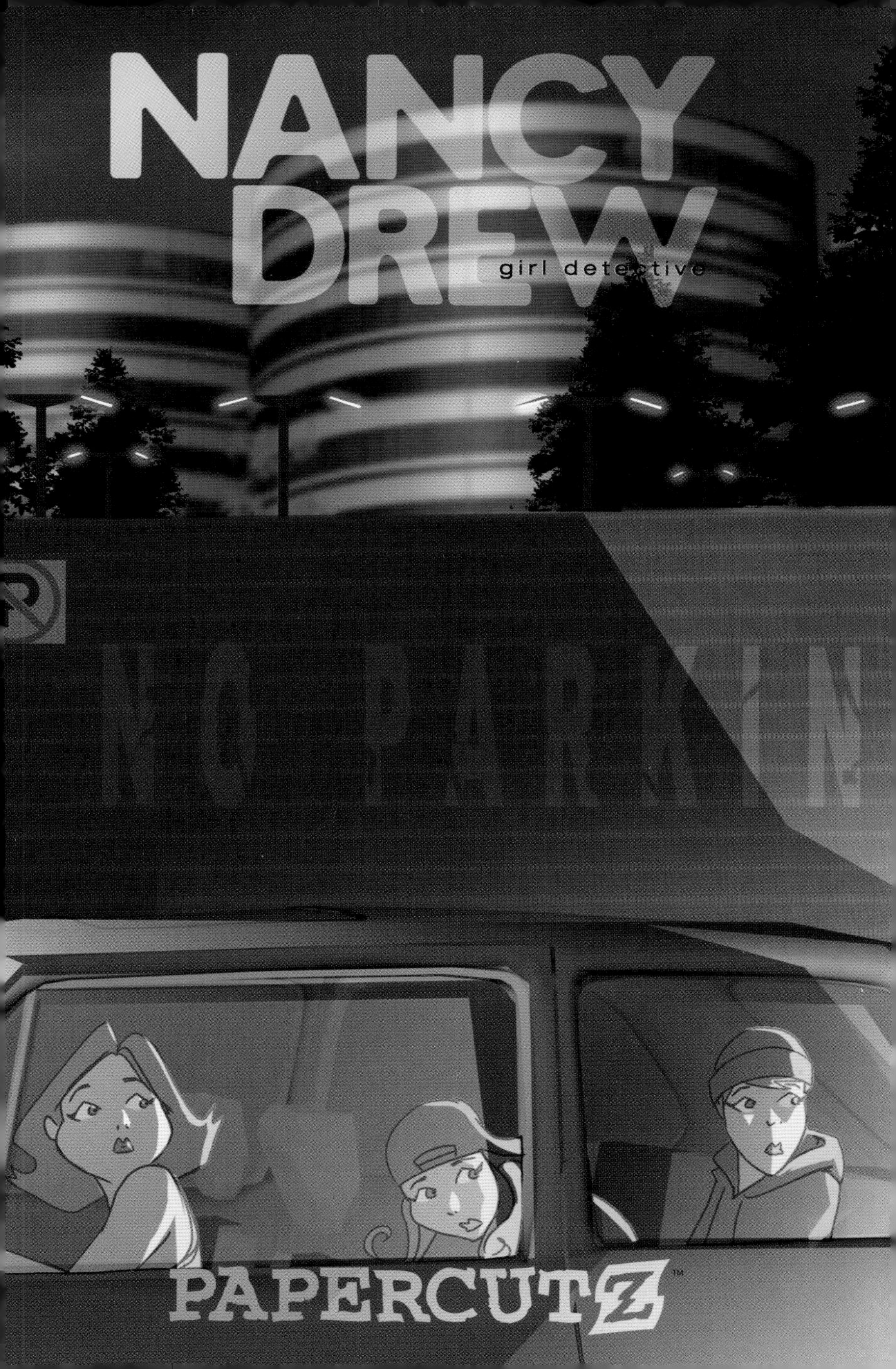
NANCY DREW
girl detective
NO PARKIN
PAPERCUTZ™

NANCY DREW
girl detective ®

Graphic Novel #1
"The Demon of
River Heights"

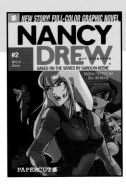

Graphic Novel #2
"Writ In Stone"

Graphic Novel #3
"The Haunted Dollhouse"

Graphic Novel #4
"The Girl Who Wasn't There"

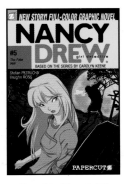

Graphic Novel #5
"The Fake Heir"

Graphic Novel #6
"Mr. Cheeters Is Missing"

Graphic Novel #7
"The Charmed Bracelet"

Coming in February
Graphic Novel #8
"Global Warning"

NANCY DREW
girl detective ®

#7

The Charmed Bracelet

STEFAN PETRUCHA • Writer
DANIEL VAUGHN ROSS • Artist
with 3D CG elements by LUIS LUNDGREN
Preview pages, and art direction by SHO MURASE
Based on the series by
CAROLYN KEENE

New York

The Charmed Bracelet
STEFAN PETRUCHA – Writer
DANIEL VAUGHN ROSS – Artist
with 3D CG elements by LUIS LUNDGREN
BRYAN SENKA – Letterer
CARLOS JOSE GUZMAN – Colorist
JIM SALICRUP
Editor-in-Chief

ISBN 10: 1-59707-036-X paperback edition
ISBN 13: 978-1-59707-036-2 paperback edition
ISBN 10: 1-59707-037-8 hardcover edition
ISBN 13: 978-1-59707-037-9 hardcover edition

Printed in China.
Distributed by Holtzbrinck Publishers.

10 9 8 7 6 5 4 3 2 1

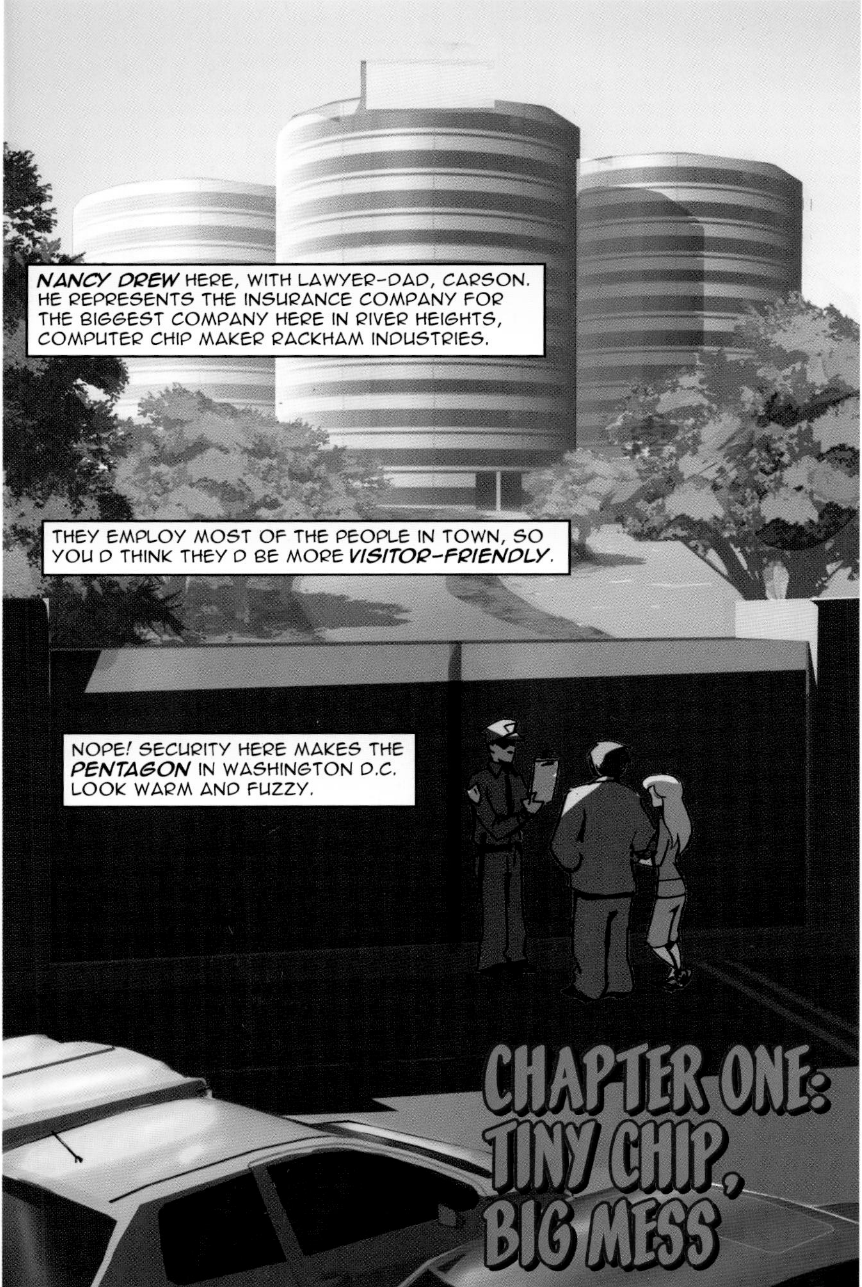
NANCY DREW HERE, WITH LAWYER-DAD, CARSON. HE REPRESENTS THE INSURANCE COMPANY FOR THE BIGGEST COMPANY HERE IN RIVER HEIGHTS, COMPUTER CHIP MAKER RACKHAM INDUSTRIES.
THEY EMPLOY MOST OF THE PEOPLE IN TOWN, SO YOU'D THINK THEY'D BE MORE VISITOR-FRIENDLY.
NOPE! SECURITY HERE MAKES THE PENTAGON IN WASHINGTON D.C. LOOK WARM AND FUZZY.
CHAPTER ONE: TINY CHIP, BIG MESS

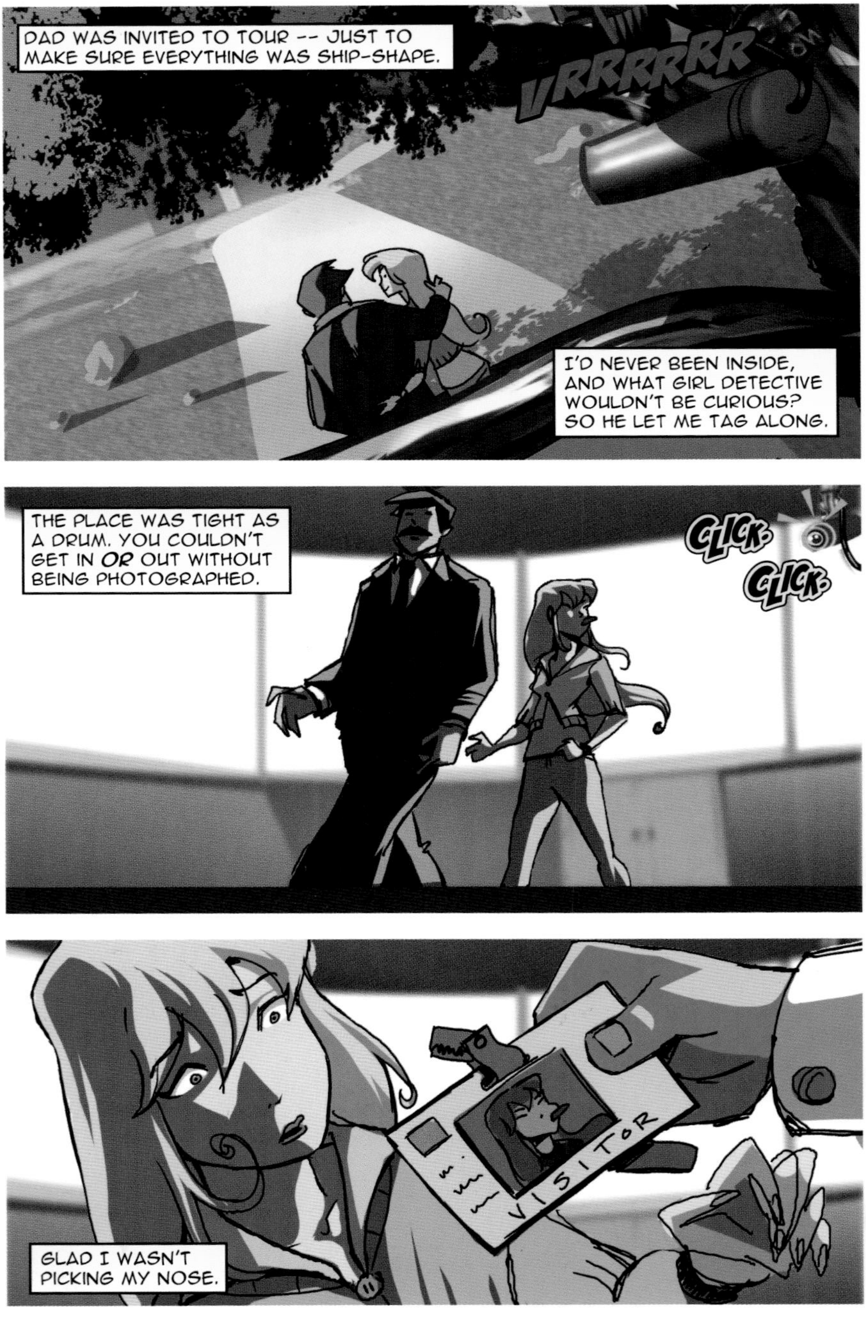

DAD WAS INVITED TO TOUR -- JUST TO MAKE SURE EVERYTHING WAS SHIP-SHAPE.
VRRRRRR
I'D NEVER BEEN INSIDE, AND WHAT GIRL DETECTIVE WOULDN'T BE CURIOUS? SO HE LET ME TAG ALONG.
THE PLACE WAS TIGHT AS A DRUM. YOU COULDN'T GET IN OR OUT WITHOUT BEING PHOTOGRAPHED.
CLICK.
CLICK.
VISITOR
GLAD I WASN'T PICKING MY NOSE.

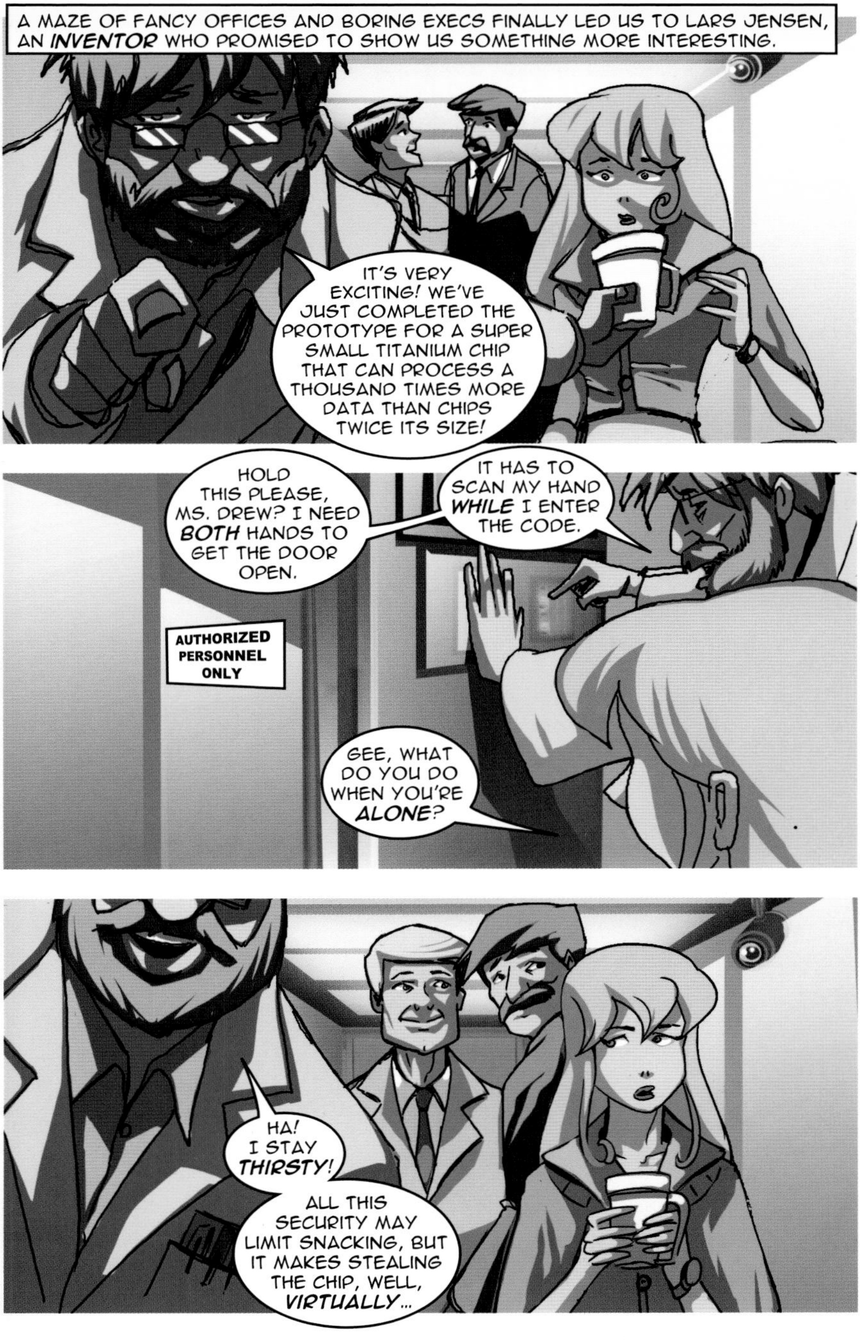

A MAZE OF FANCY OFFICES AND BORING EXECS FINALLY LED US TO LARS JENSEN, AN *INVENTOR* WHO PROMISED TO SHOW US SOMETHING MORE INTERESTING.
IT'S VERY EXCITING! WE'VE JUST COMPLETED THE PROTOTYPE FOR A SUPER SMALL TITANIUM CHIP THAT CAN PROCESS A THOUSAND TIMES MORE DATA THAN CHIPS TWICE ITS SIZE!
HOLD THIS PLEASE, MS. DREW? I NEED *BOTH* HANDS TO GET THE DOOR OPEN.
IT HAS TO SCAN MY HAND *WHILE* I ENTER THE CODE.
AUTHORIZED PERSONNEL ONLY
GEE, WHAT DO YOU DO WHEN YOU'RE *ALONE*?
HA! I STAY *THIRSTY*!
ALL THIS SECURITY MAY LIMIT SNACKING, BUT IT MAKES STEALING THE CHIP, WELL, *VIRTUALLY*...

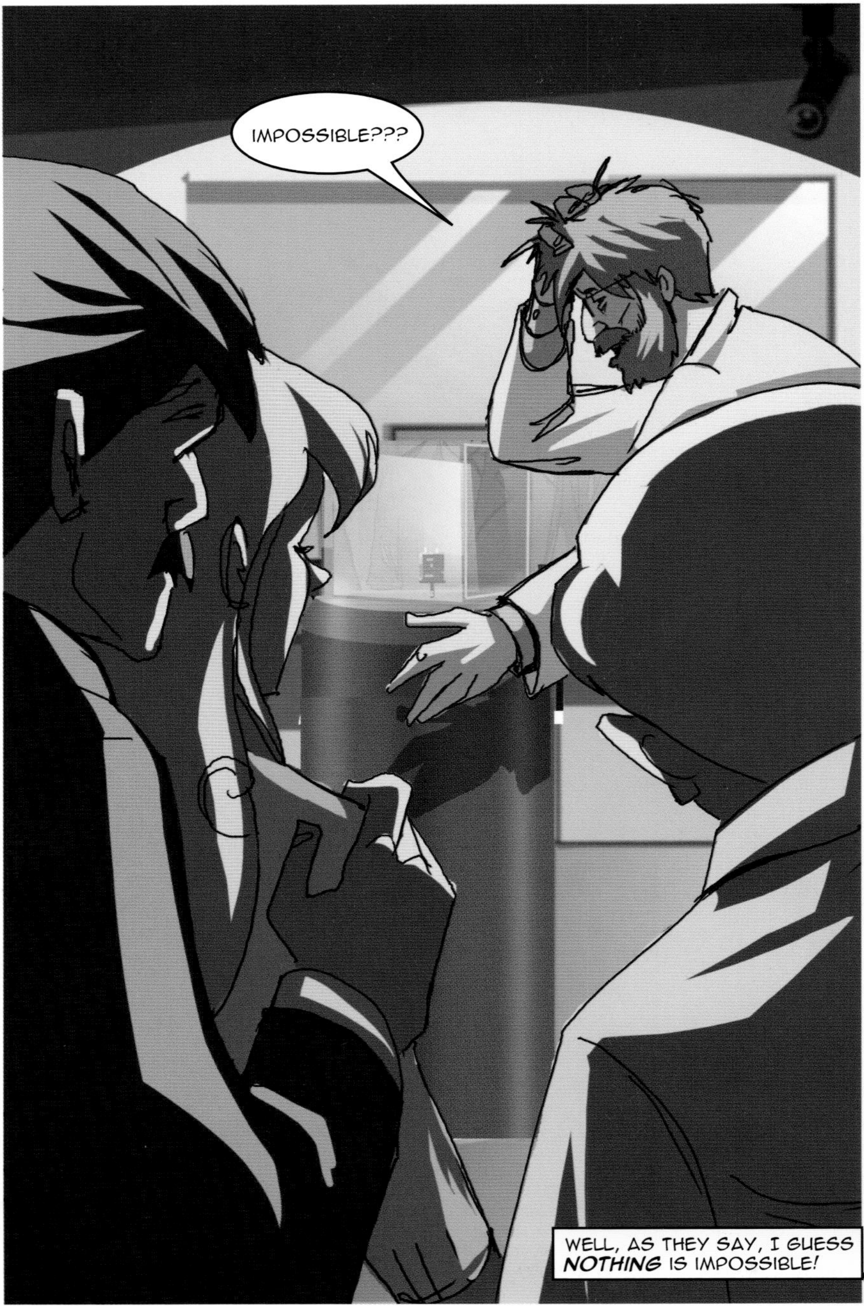
IMPOSSIBLE???
WELL, AS THEY SAY, I GUESS *NOTHING* IS IMPOSSIBLE!

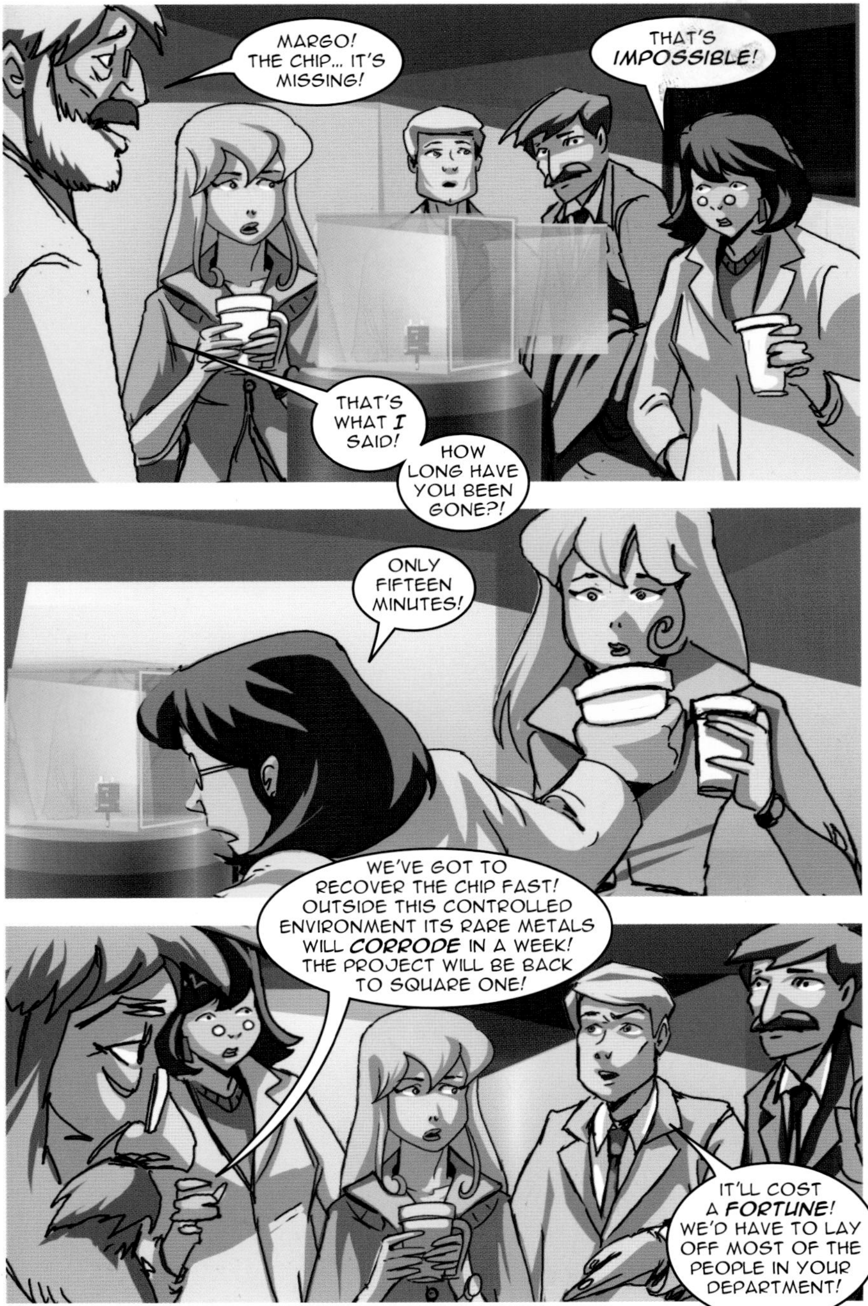
MARGO! THE CHIP... IT'S MISSING!
THAT'S IMPOSSIBLE!
THAT'S WHAT I SAID!
HOW LONG HAVE YOU BEEN GONE?!
ONLY FIFTEEN MINUTES!
WE'VE GOT TO RECOVER THE CHIP FAST! OUTSIDE THIS CONTROLLED ENVIRONMENT ITS RARE METALS WILL CORRODE IN A WEEK! THE PROJECT WILL BE BACK TO SQUARE ONE!
IT'LL COST A FORTUNE! WE'D HAVE TO LAY OFF MOST OF THE PEOPLE IN YOUR DEPARTMENT!

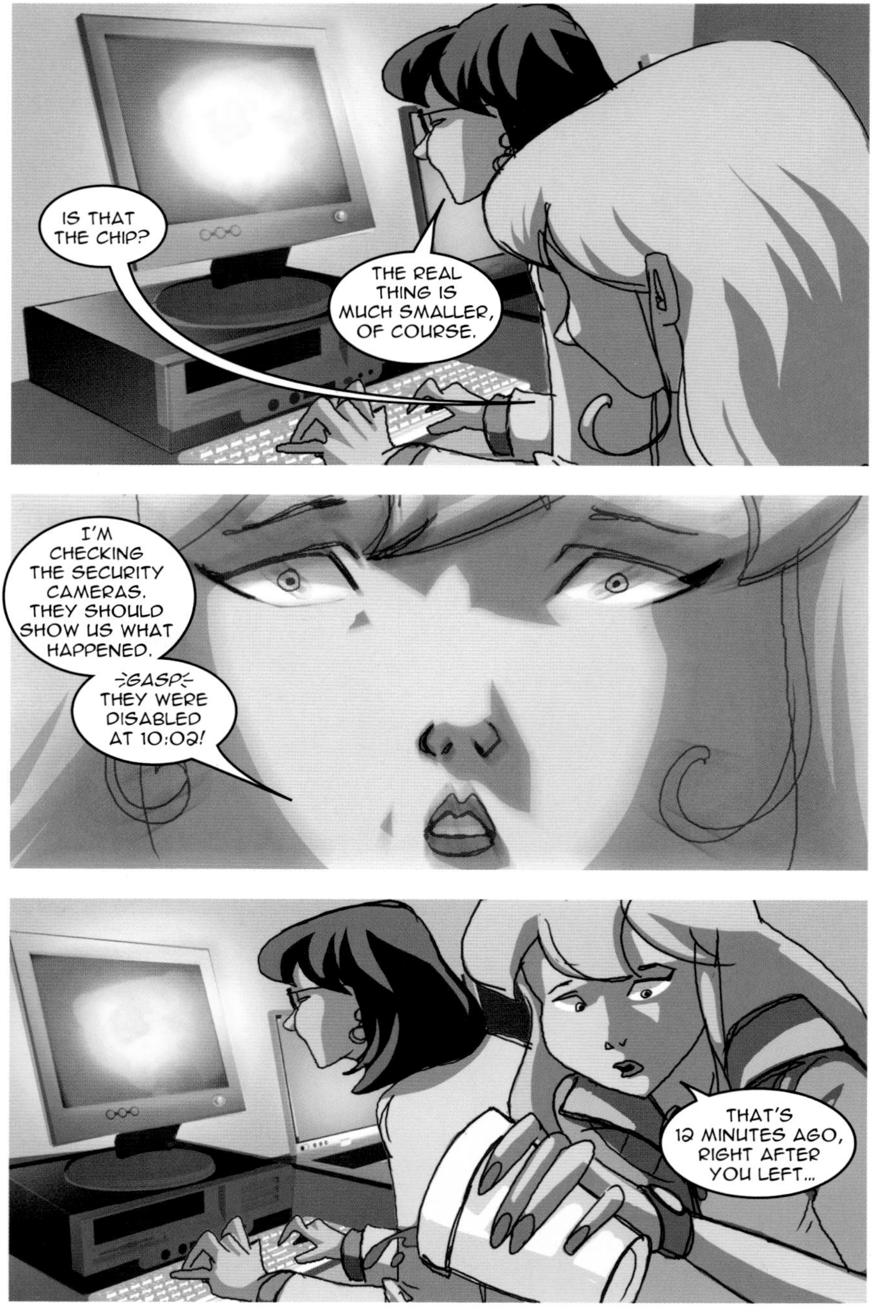
IS THAT THE CHIP?
THE REAL THING IS MUCH SMALLER, OF COURSE.
I'M CHECKING THE SECURITY CAMERAS. THEY SHOULD SHOW US WHAT HAPPENED.
GASP THEY WERE DISABLED AT 10:02!
THAT'S 12 MINUTES AGO, RIGHT AFTER YOU LEFT...

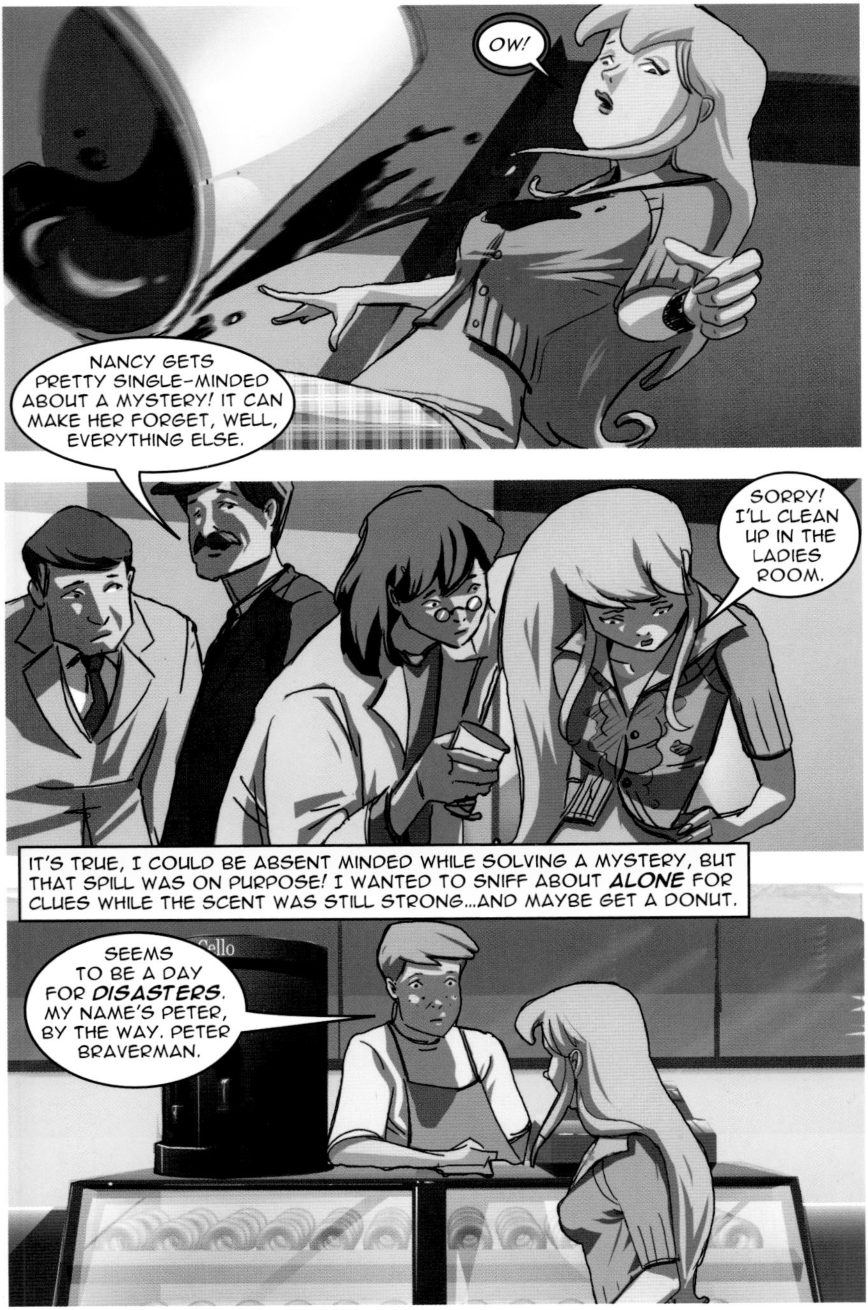
OW!
NANCY GETS PRETTY SINGLE-MINDED ABOUT A MYSTERY! IT CAN MAKE HER FORGET, WELL, EVERYTHING ELSE.
SORRY! I'LL CLEAN UP IN THE LADIES ROOM.
IT'S TRUE, I COULD BE ABSENT MINDED WHILE SOLVING A MYSTERY, BUT THAT SPILL WAS ON PURPOSE! I WANTED TO SNIFF ABOUT ***ALONE*** FOR CLUES WHILE THE SCENT WAS STILL STRONG...AND MAYBE GET A DONUT.
SEEMS TO BE A DAY FOR ***DISASTERS***. MY NAME'S PETER, BY THE WAY. PETER BRAVERMAN.

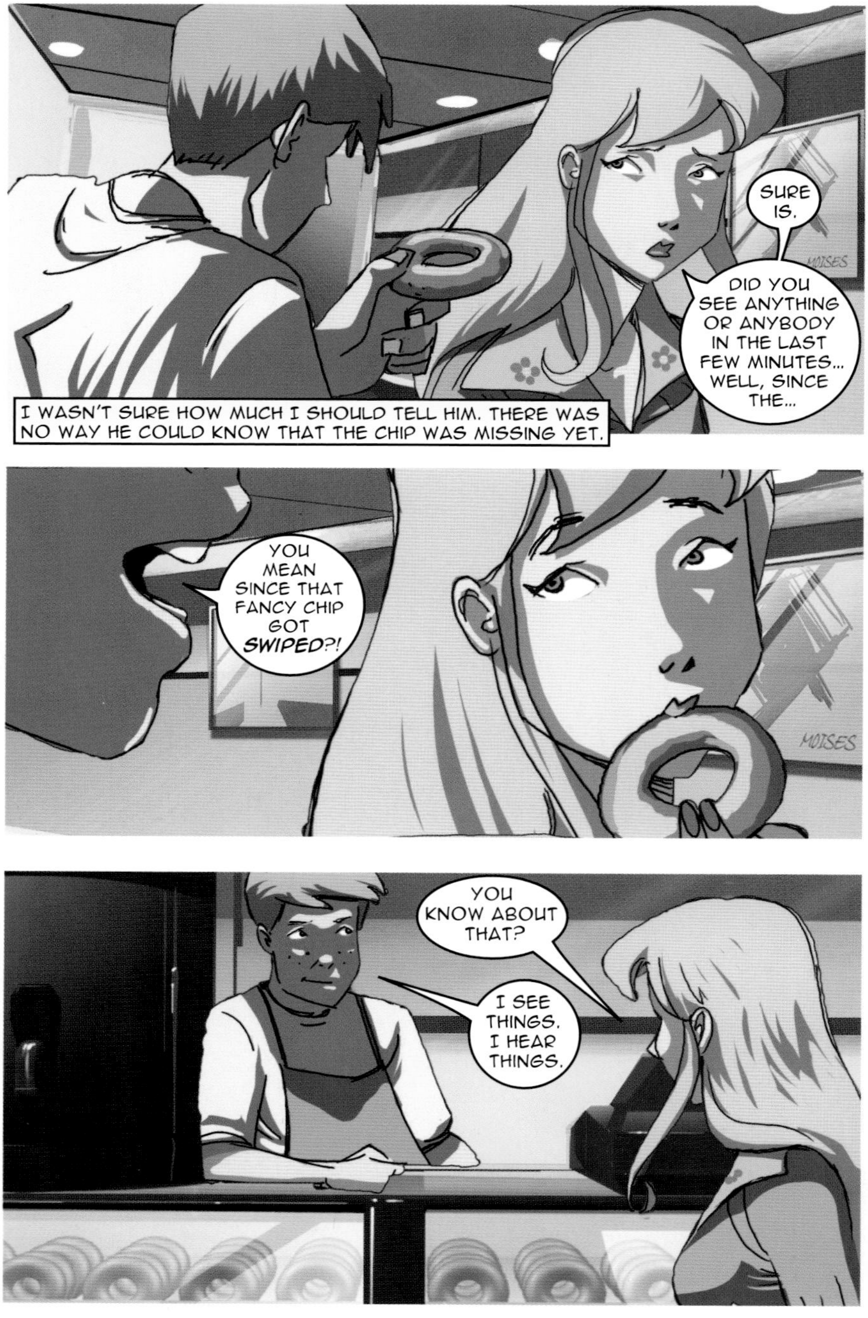
SURE IS.
DID YOU SEE ANYTHING OR ANYBODY IN THE LAST FEW MINUTES... WELL, SINCE THE...
I WASN'T SURE HOW MUCH I SHOULD TELL HIM. THERE WAS NO WAY HE COULD KNOW THAT THE CHIP WAS MISSING YET.
MOISES
YOU MEAN SINCE THAT FANCY CHIP GOT SWIPED?!
MOISES
YOU KNOW ABOUT THAT?
I SEE THINGS. I HEAR THINGS.

"LIKE I KNOW FOR INSTANCE THAT SOME JEALOUS EXEC THINKS THE CHIP IS TOO RISKY AND EXPENSIVE. THEY'D *LOVE* TO SEE THE PROJECT JUST GO AWAY."

"THAT CHIP SUCKED UP ALL THE MONEY THAT COULD BE GOING TO *THEIR* PROJECTS."

SORRY, WALTER.

WALTER REACH PROJECT
NO FUNDING

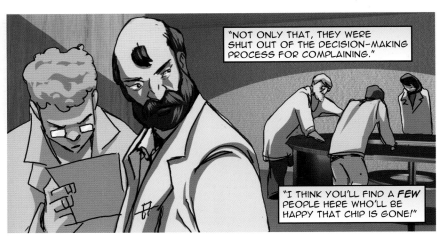

"NOT ONLY THAT, THEY WERE SHUT OUT OF THE DECISION-MAKING PROCESS FOR COMPLAINING."

"I THINK YOU'LL FIND A *FEW* PEOPLE HERE WHO'LL BE HAPPY THAT CHIP IS GONE!"

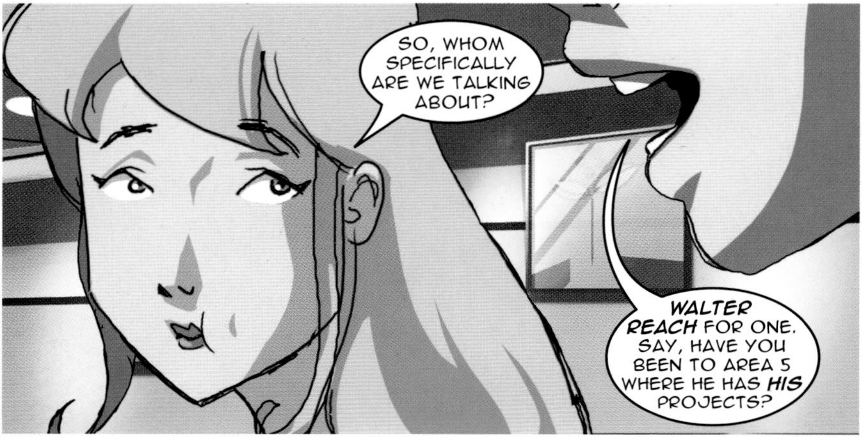
SO, WHOM SPECIFICALLY ARE WE TALKING ABOUT?
WALTER REACH FOR ONE. SAY, HAVE YOU BEEN TO AREA 5 WHERE HE HAS HIS PROJECTS?

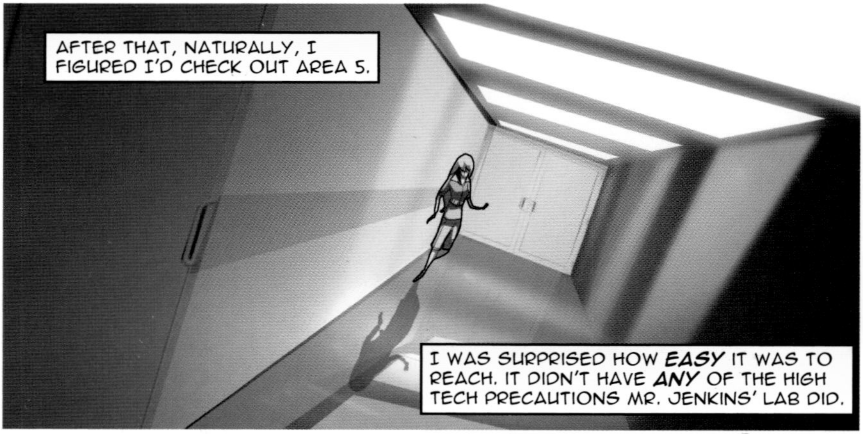
AFTER THAT, NATURALLY, I FIGURED I'D CHECK OUT AREA 5.
I WAS SURPRISED HOW EASY IT WAS TO REACH. IT DIDN'T HAVE ANY OF THE HIGH TECH PRECAUTIONS MR. JENKINS' LAB DID.

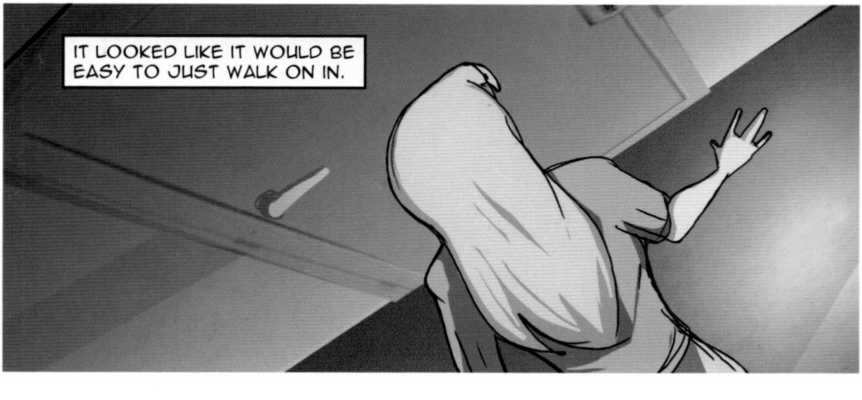
IT LOOKED LIKE IT WOULD BE EASY TO JUST WALK ON IN.

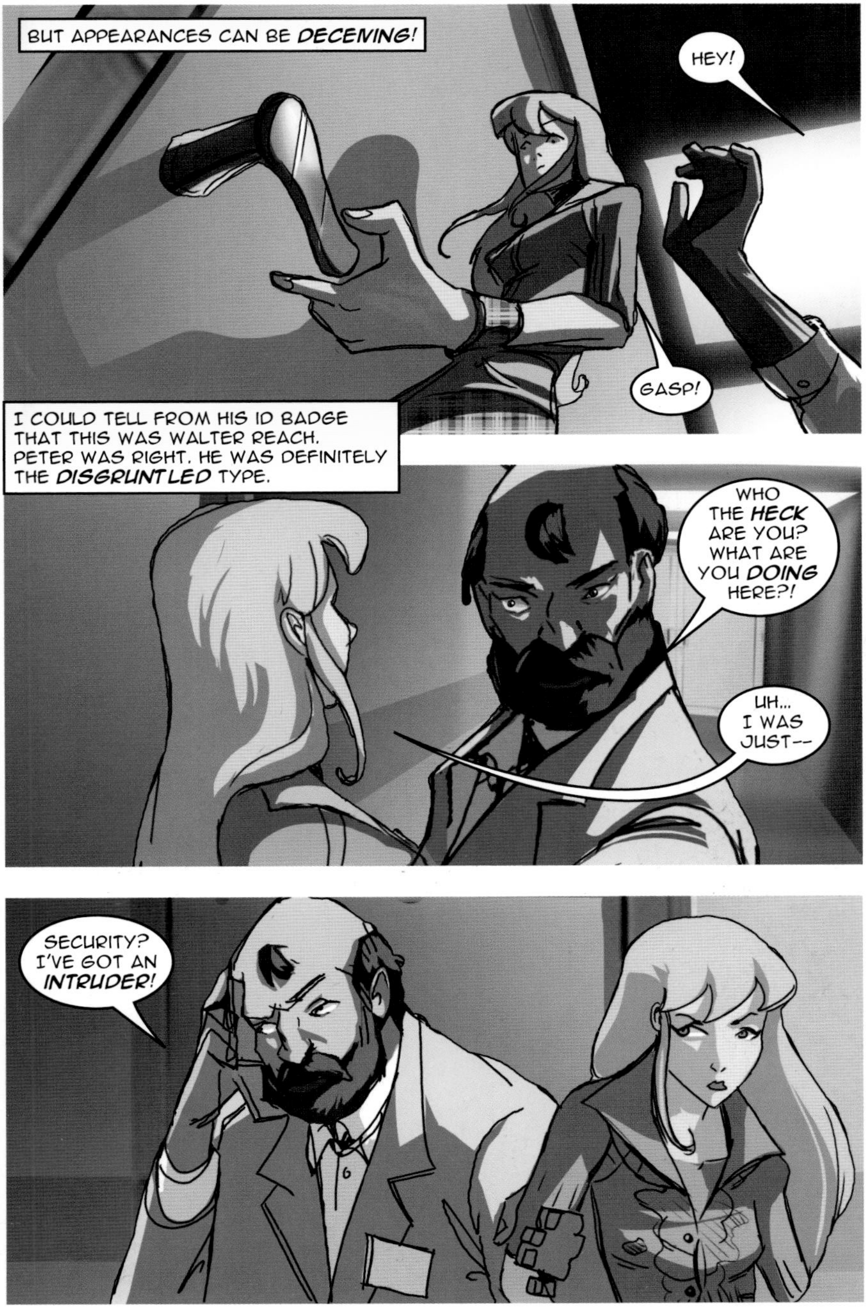

BUT APPEARANCES CAN BE DECEIVING!
HEY!
GASP!
I COULD TELL FROM HIS ID BADGE THAT THIS WAS WALTER REACH. PETER WAS RIGHT. HE WAS DEFINITELY THE DISGRUNTLED TYPE.
WHO THE HECK ARE YOU? WHAT ARE YOU DOING HERE?!
UH... I WAS JUST--
SECURITY? I'VE GOT AN INTRUDER!

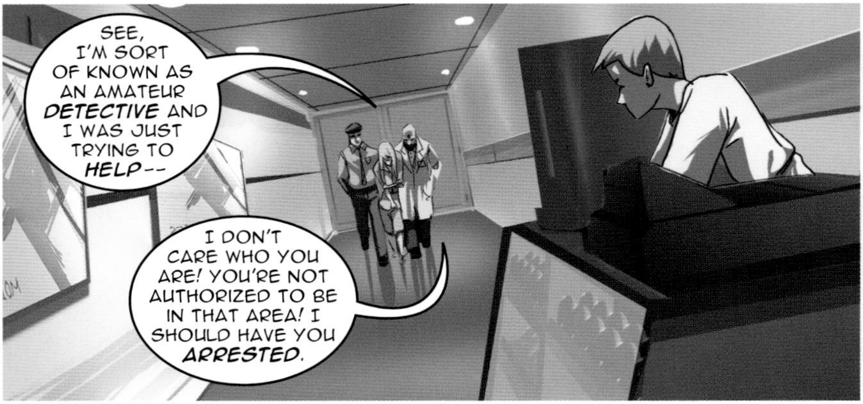
SEE, I'M SORT OF KNOWN AS AN AMATEUR DETECTIVE AND I WAS JUST TRYING TO HELP--
I DON'T CARE WHO YOU ARE! YOU'RE NOT AUTHORIZED TO BE IN THAT AREA! I SHOULD HAVE YOU ARRESTED.

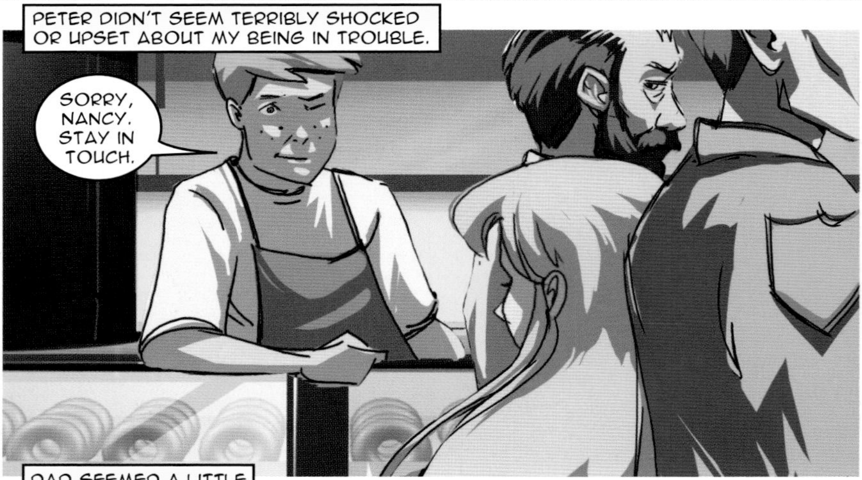
PETER DIDN'T SEEM TERRIBLY SHOCKED OR UPSET ABOUT MY BEING IN TROUBLE.
SORRY, NANCY. STAY IN TOUCH.

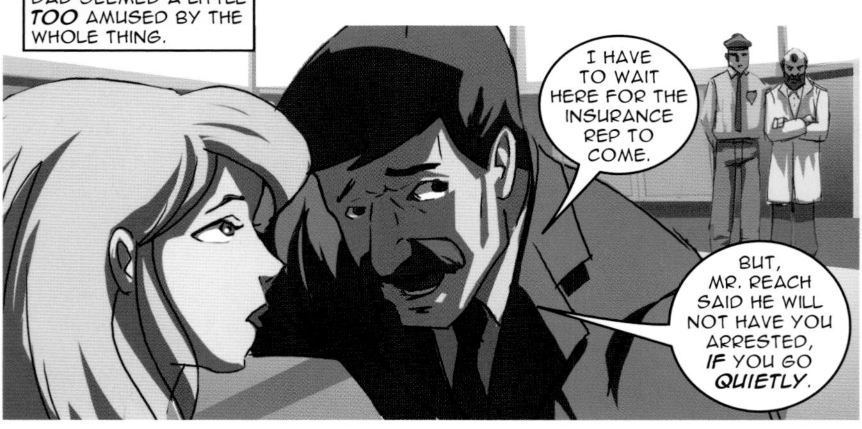
DAD SEEMED A LITTLE TOO AMUSED BY THE WHOLE THING.
I HAVE TO WAIT HERE FOR THE INSURANCE REP TO COME.
BUT, MR. REACH SAID HE WILL NOT HAVE YOU ARRESTED, IF YOU GO QUIETLY.

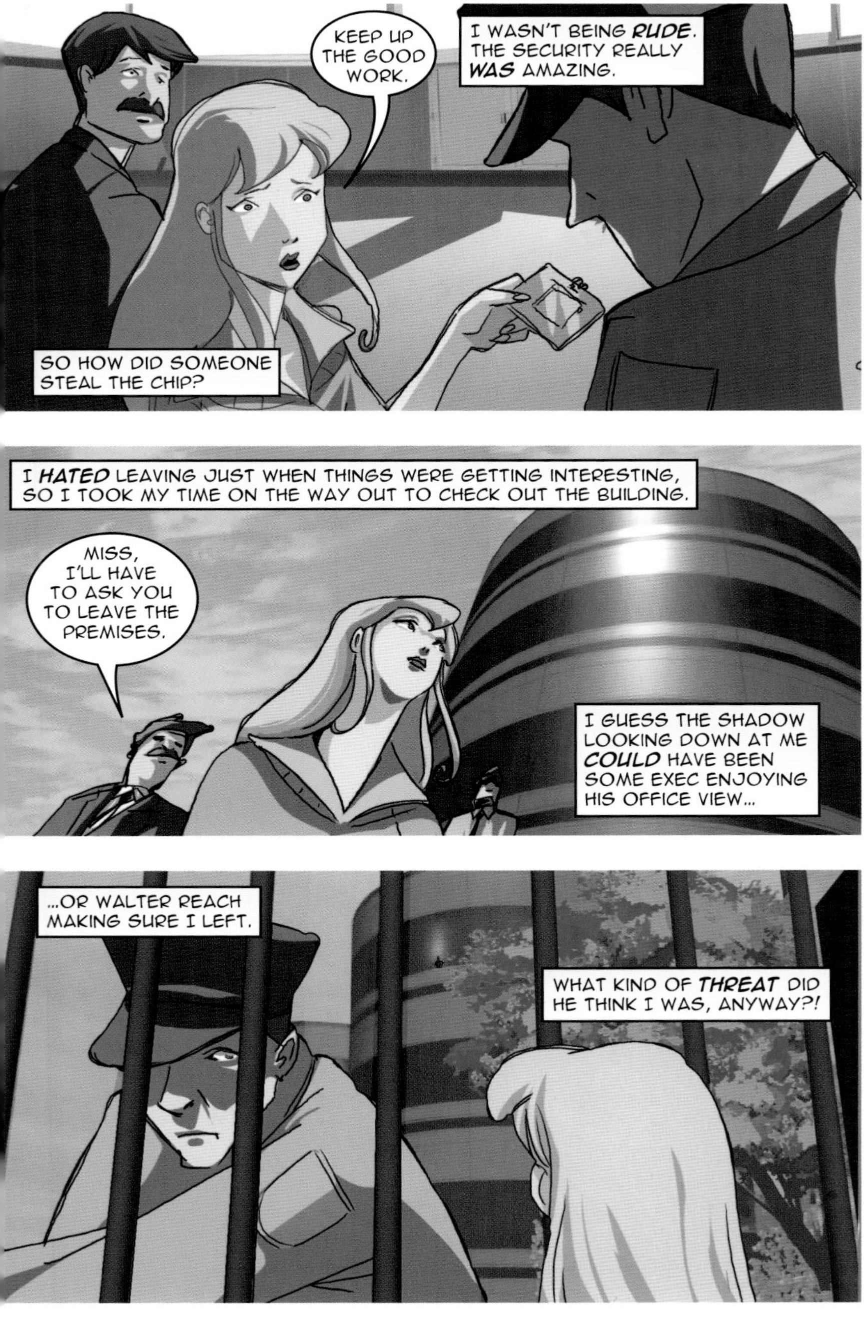
KEEP UP THE GOOD WORK.
I WASN'T BEING RUDE. THE SECURITY REALLY WAS AMAZING.
SO HOW DID SOMEONE STEAL THE CHIP?
I HATED LEAVING JUST WHEN THINGS WERE GETTING INTERESTING, SO I TOOK MY TIME ON THE WAY OUT TO CHECK OUT THE BUILDING.
MISS, I'LL HAVE TO ASK YOU TO LEAVE THE PREMISES.
I GUESS THE SHADOW LOOKING DOWN AT ME COULD HAVE BEEN SOME EXEC ENJOYING HIS OFFICE VIEW...
...OR WALTER REACH MAKING SURE I LEFT.
WHAT KIND OF THREAT DID HE THINK I WAS, ANYWAY?!

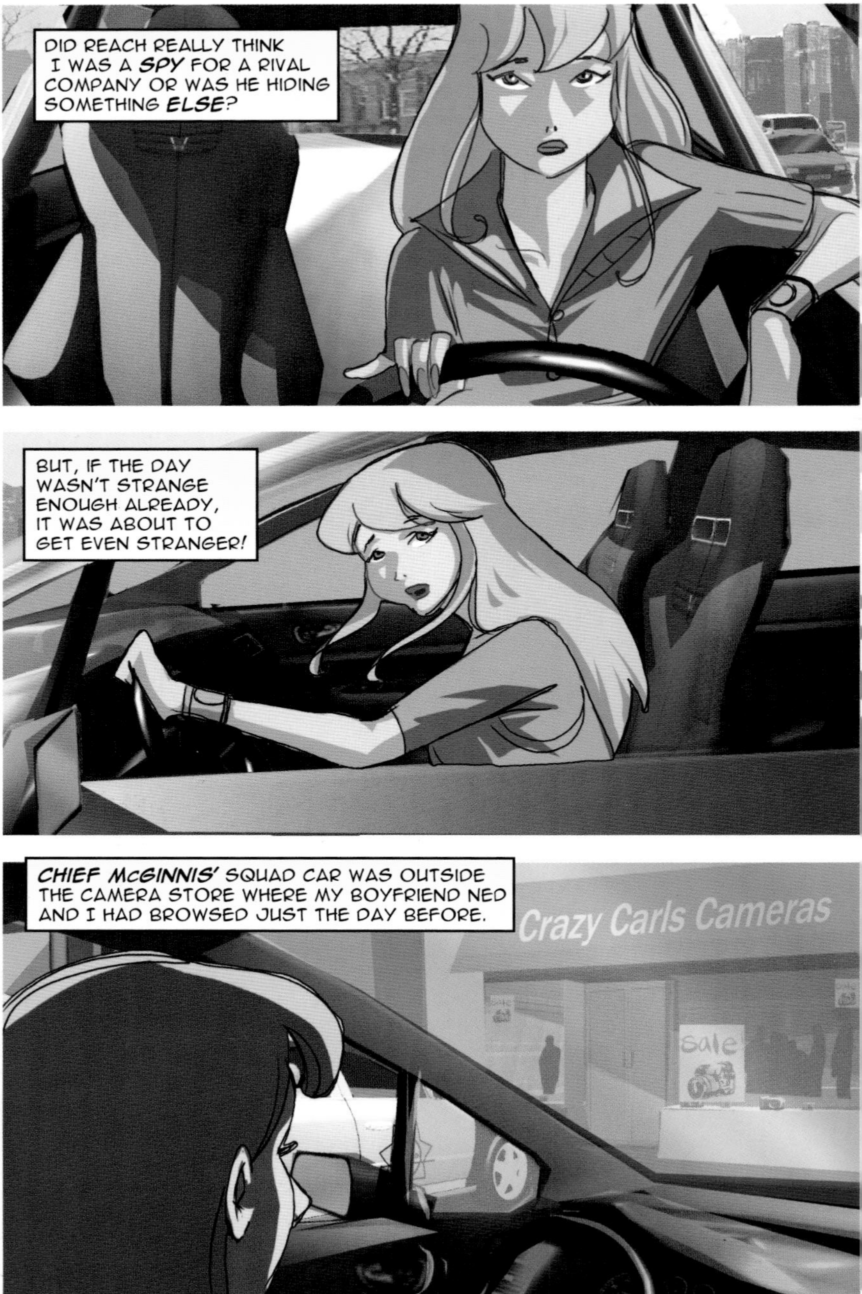
DID REACH REALLY THINK I WAS A SPY FOR A RIVAL COMPANY OR WAS HE HIDING SOMETHING ELSE?
BUT, IF THE DAY WASN'T STRANGE ENOUGH ALREADY, IT WAS ABOUT TO GET EVEN STRANGER!
CHIEF McGINNIS' SQUAD CAR WAS OUTSIDE THE CAMERA STORE WHERE MY BOYFRIEND NED AND I HAD BROWSED JUST THE DAY BEFORE.
Crazy Carls Cameras
Sale

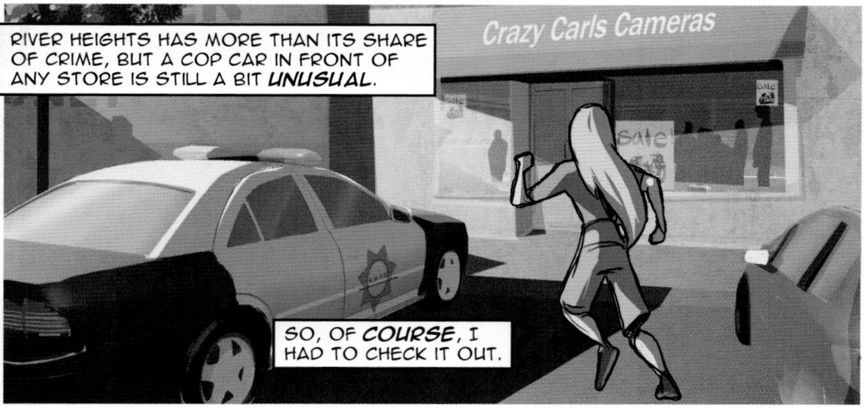
RIVER HEIGHTS HAS MORE THAN ITS SHARE OF CRIME, BUT A COP CAR IN FRONT OF ANY STORE IS STILL A BIT UNUSUAL.
Crazy Carls Cameras
SO, OF COURSE, I HAD TO CHECK IT OUT.

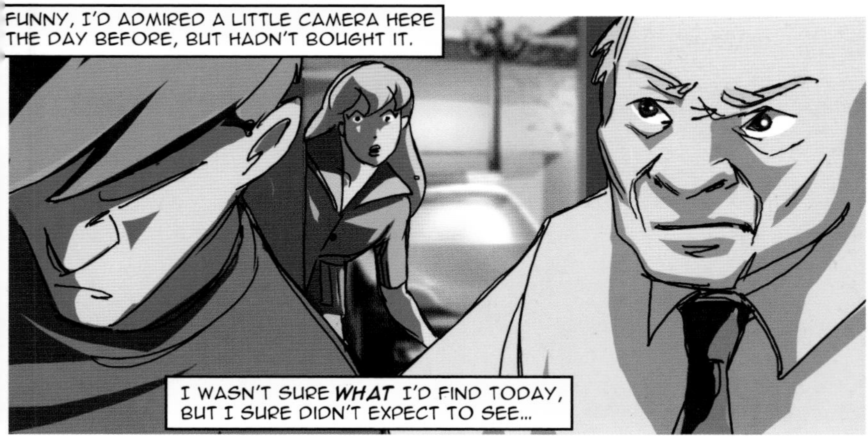
FUNNY, I'D ADMIRED A LITTLE CAMERA HERE THE DAY BEFORE, BUT HADN'T BOUGHT IT.
I WASN'T SURE WHAT I'D FIND TODAY, BUT I SURE DIDN'T EXPECT TO SEE...

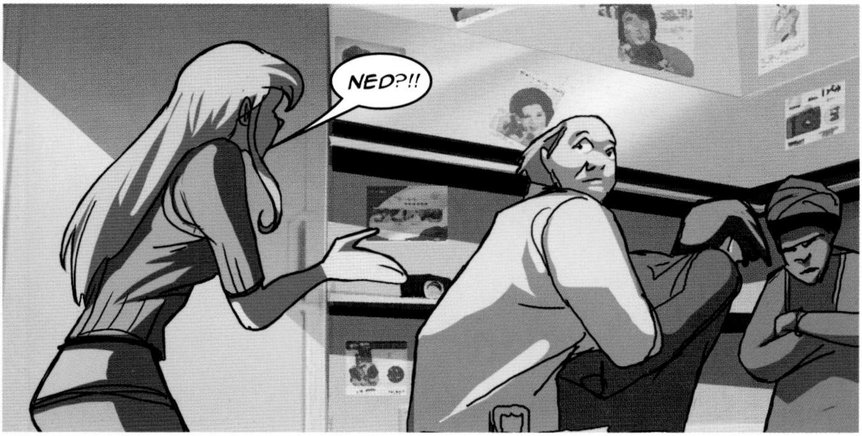
NED?!!

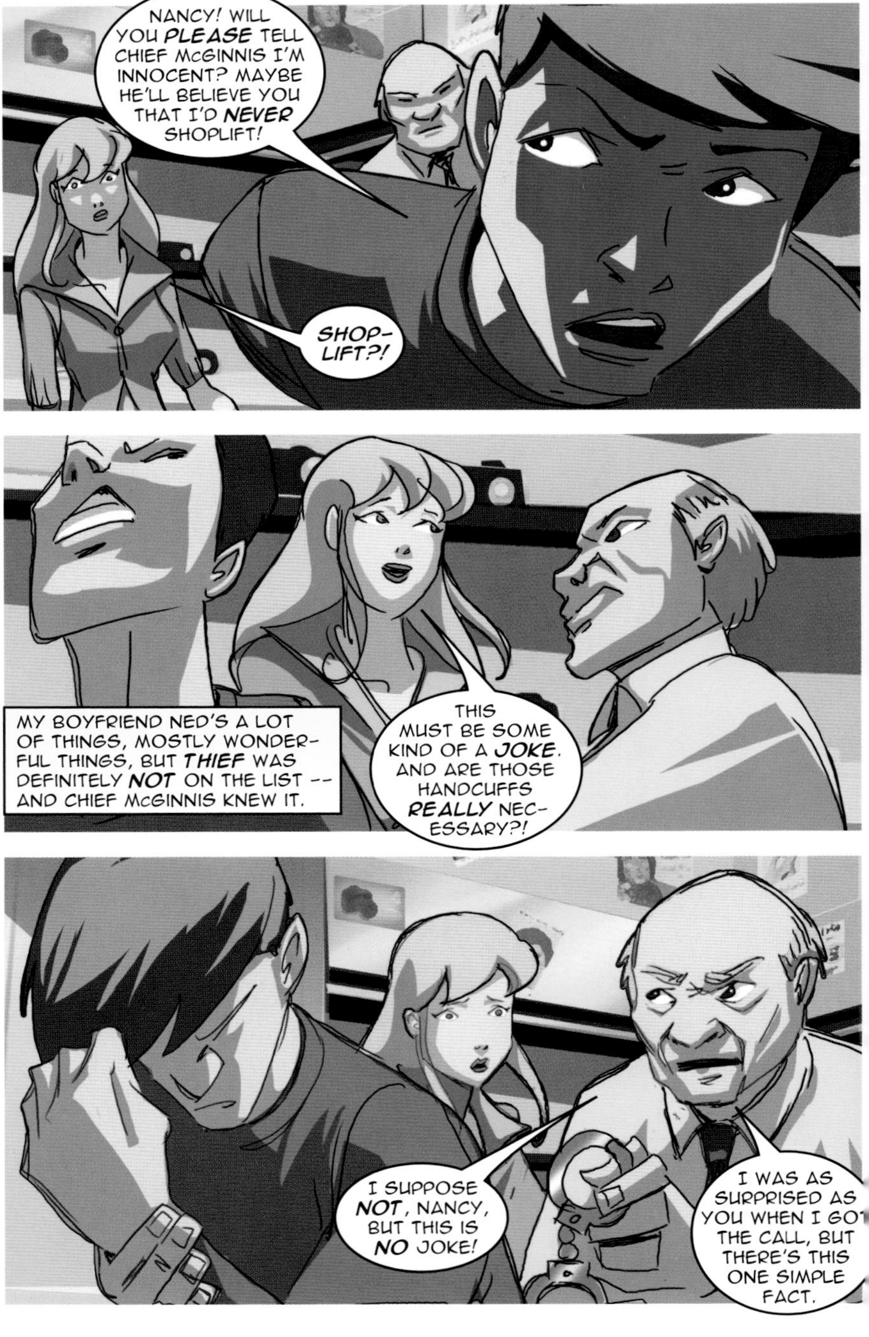
NANCY! WILL YOU **PLEASE** TELL CHIEF McGINNIS I'M INNOCENT? MAYBE HE'LL BELIEVE YOU THAT I'D **NEVER** SHOPLIFT!
SHOP-LIFT?!
MY BOYFRIEND NED'S A LOT OF THINGS, MOSTLY WONDERFUL THINGS, BUT **THIEF** WAS DEFINITELY **NOT** ON THE LIST -- AND CHIEF McGINNIS KNEW IT.
THIS MUST BE SOME KIND OF A **JOKE**. AND ARE THOSE HANDCUFFS **REALLY** NECESSARY?!
I SUPPOSE **NOT**, NANCY, BUT THIS IS **NO** JOKE!
I WAS AS SURPRISED AS YOU WHEN I GOT THE CALL, BUT THERE'S THIS ONE SIMPLE FACT.

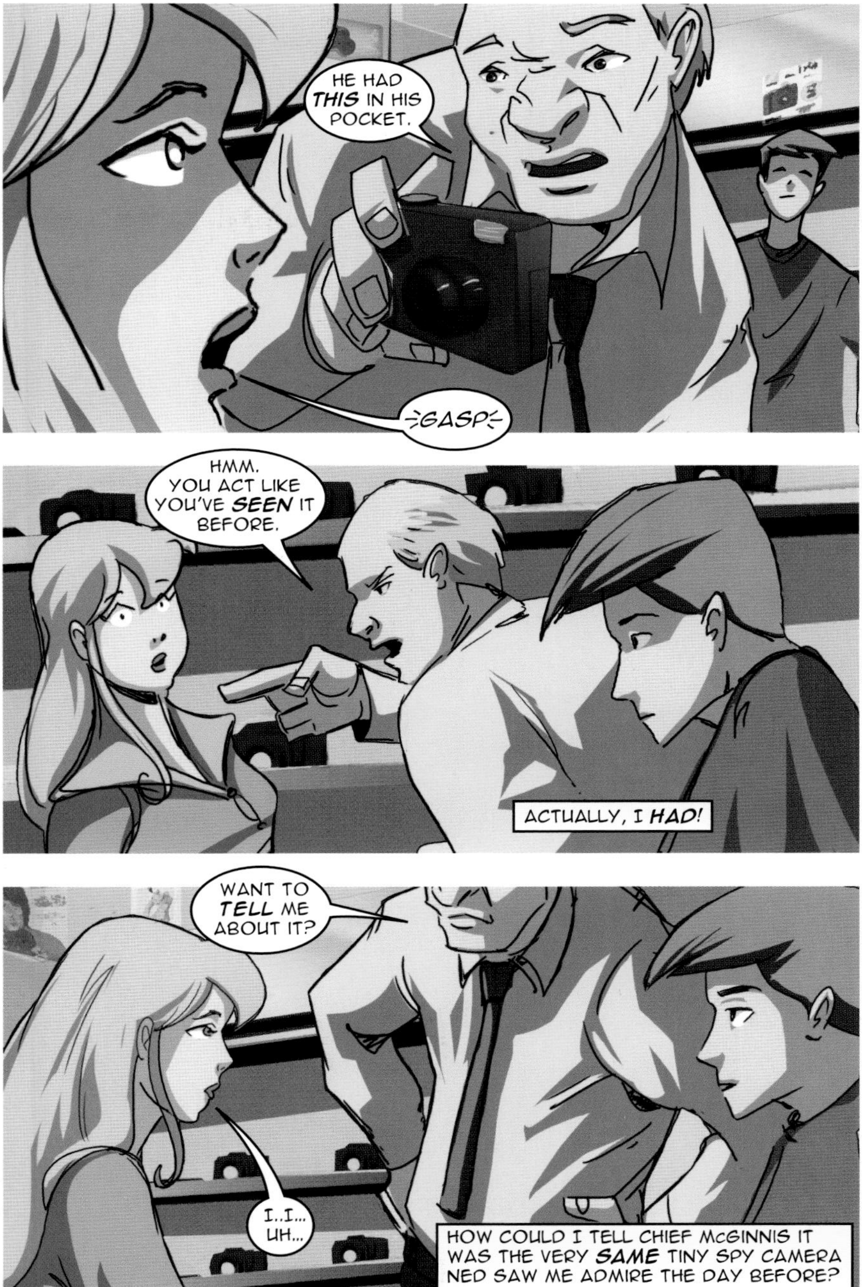
HE HAD THIS IN HIS POCKET.
GASP
HMM. YOU ACT LIKE YOU'VE SEEN IT BEFORE.
ACTUALLY, I HAD!
WANT TO TELL ME ABOUT IT?
I...I... UH...
HOW COULD I TELL CHIEF McGINNIS IT WAS THE VERY SAME TINY SPY CAMERA NED SAW ME ADMIRE THE DAY BEFORE?

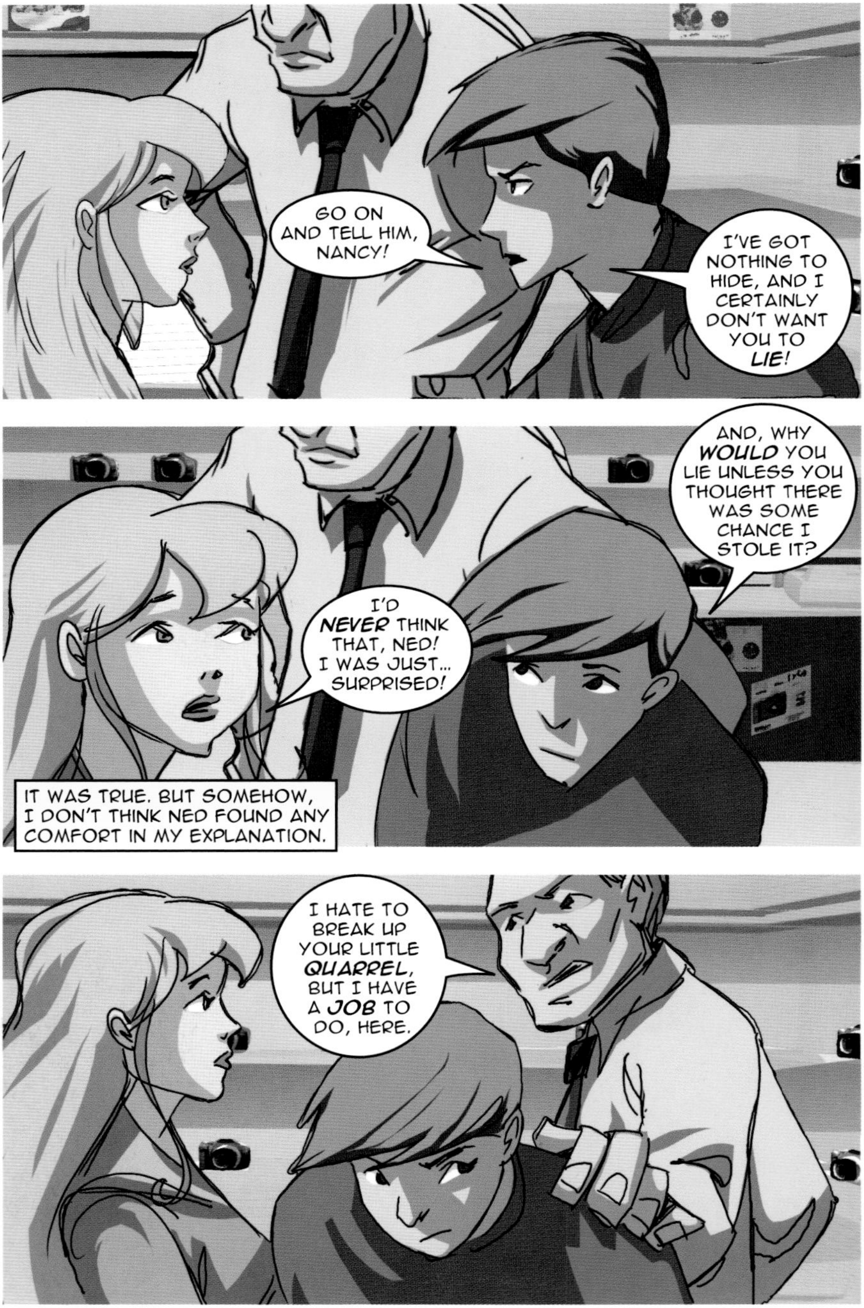

GO ON AND TELL HIM, NANCY!
I'VE GOT NOTHING TO HIDE, AND I CERTAINLY DON'T WANT YOU TO LIE!
AND, WHY WOULD YOU LIE UNLESS YOU THOUGHT THERE WAS SOME CHANCE I STOLE IT?
I'D NEVER THINK THAT, NED! I WAS JUST... SURPRISED!
IT WAS TRUE. BUT SOMEHOW, I DON'T THINK NED FOUND ANY COMFORT IN MY EXPLANATION.
I HATE TO BREAK UP YOUR LITTLE QUARREL, BUT I HAVE A JOB TO DO, HERE.

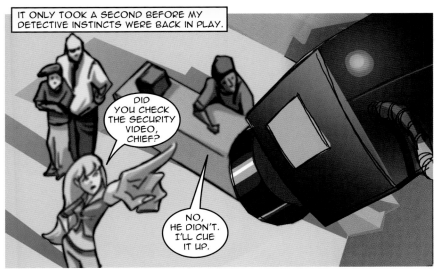

IT ONLY TOOK A SECOND BEFORE MY DETECTIVE INSTINCTS WERE BACK IN PLAY.

DID YOU CHECK THE SECURITY VIDEO, CHIEF?

NO, HE DIDN'T. I'LL CUE IT UP.

THIS OUGHT TO CLEAR EVERYTHING UP!

OR *NOT*.

IT CAN'T BE!

THE CAMERA SEEMED TO SHOW *NED* TAKING THE CAMERA!

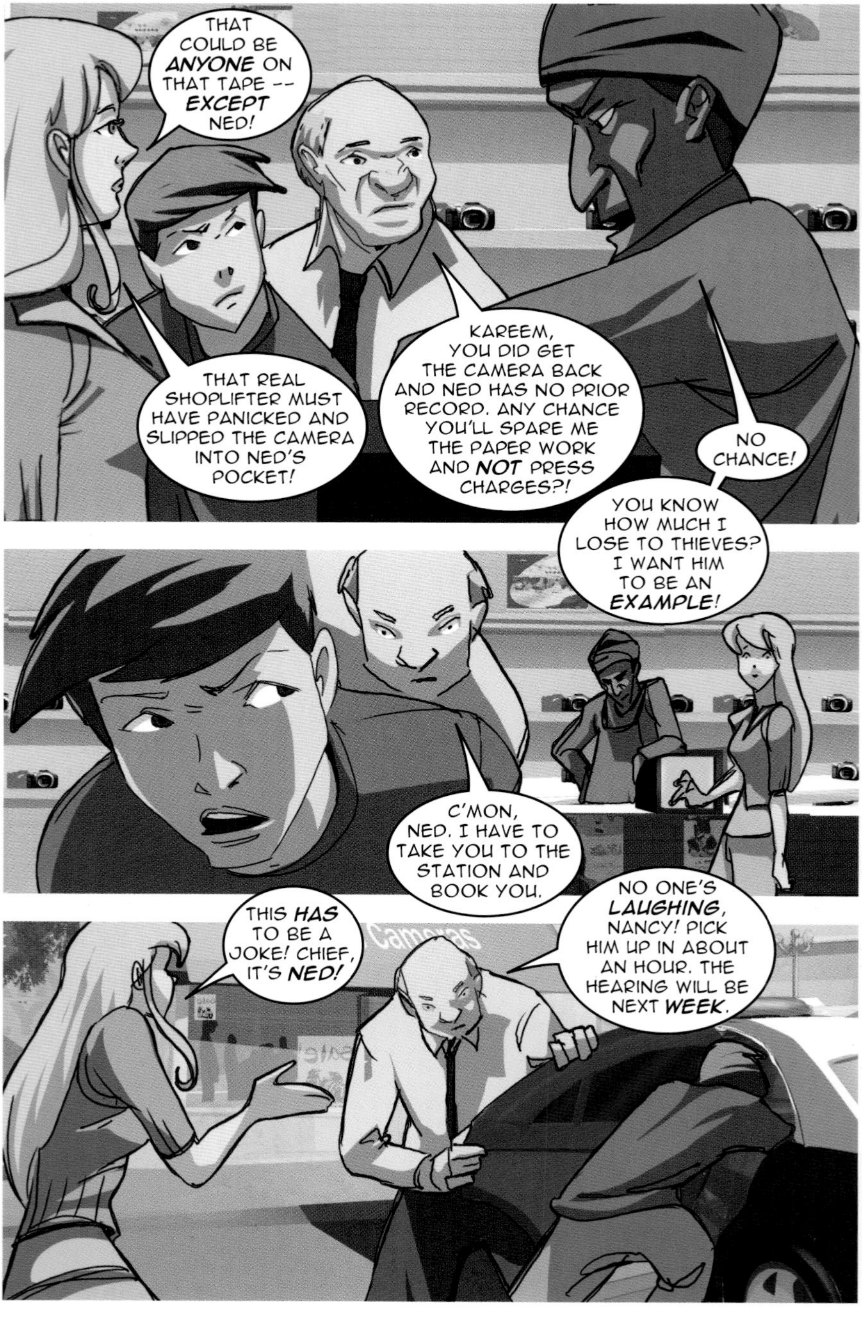
THAT COULD BE ANYONE ON THAT TAPE -- EXCEPT NED!
THAT REAL SHOPLIFTER MUST HAVE PANICKED AND SLIPPED THE CAMERA INTO NED'S POCKET!
KAREEM, YOU DID GET THE CAMERA BACK AND NED HAS NO PRIOR RECORD. ANY CHANCE YOU'LL SPARE ME THE PAPER WORK AND NOT PRESS CHARGES?!
NO CHANCE!
YOU KNOW HOW MUCH I LOSE TO THIEVES? I WANT HIM TO BE AN EXAMPLE!
C'MON, NED. I HAVE TO TAKE YOU TO THE STATION AND BOOK YOU.
THIS HAS TO BE A JOKE! CHIEF, IT'S NED!
NO ONE'S LAUGHING, NANCY! PICK HIM UP IN ABOUT AN HOUR. THE HEARING WILL BE NEXT WEEK.

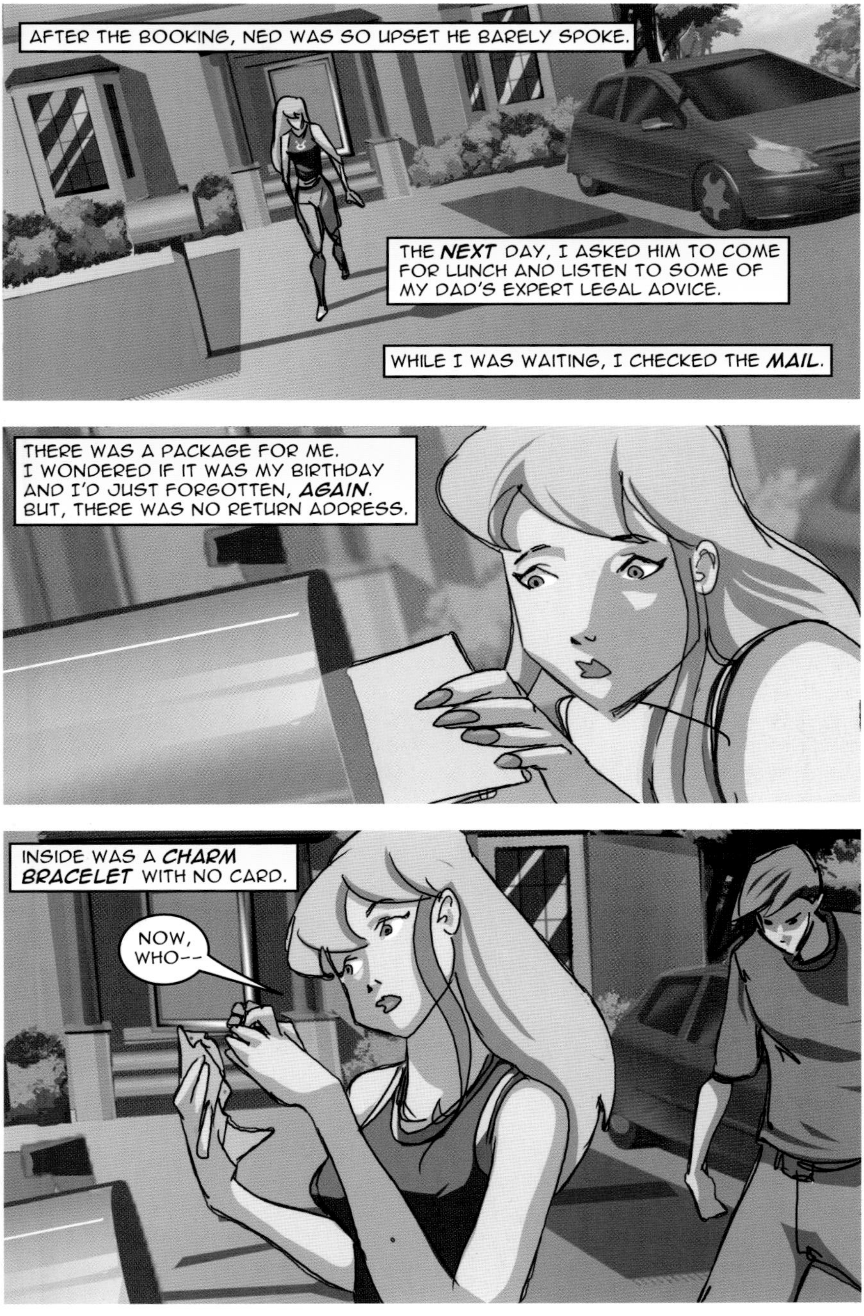
AFTER THE BOOKING, NED WAS SO UPSET HE BARELY SPOKE.
THE NEXT DAY, I ASKED HIM TO COME FOR LUNCH AND LISTEN TO SOME OF MY DAD'S EXPERT LEGAL ADVICE.
WHILE I WAS WAITING, I CHECKED THE MAIL.
THERE WAS A PACKAGE FOR ME. I WONDERED IF IT WAS MY BIRTHDAY AND I'D JUST FORGOTTEN, AGAIN. BUT, THERE WAS NO RETURN ADDRESS.
INSIDE WAS A CHARM BRACELET WITH NO CARD.
NOW, WHO--

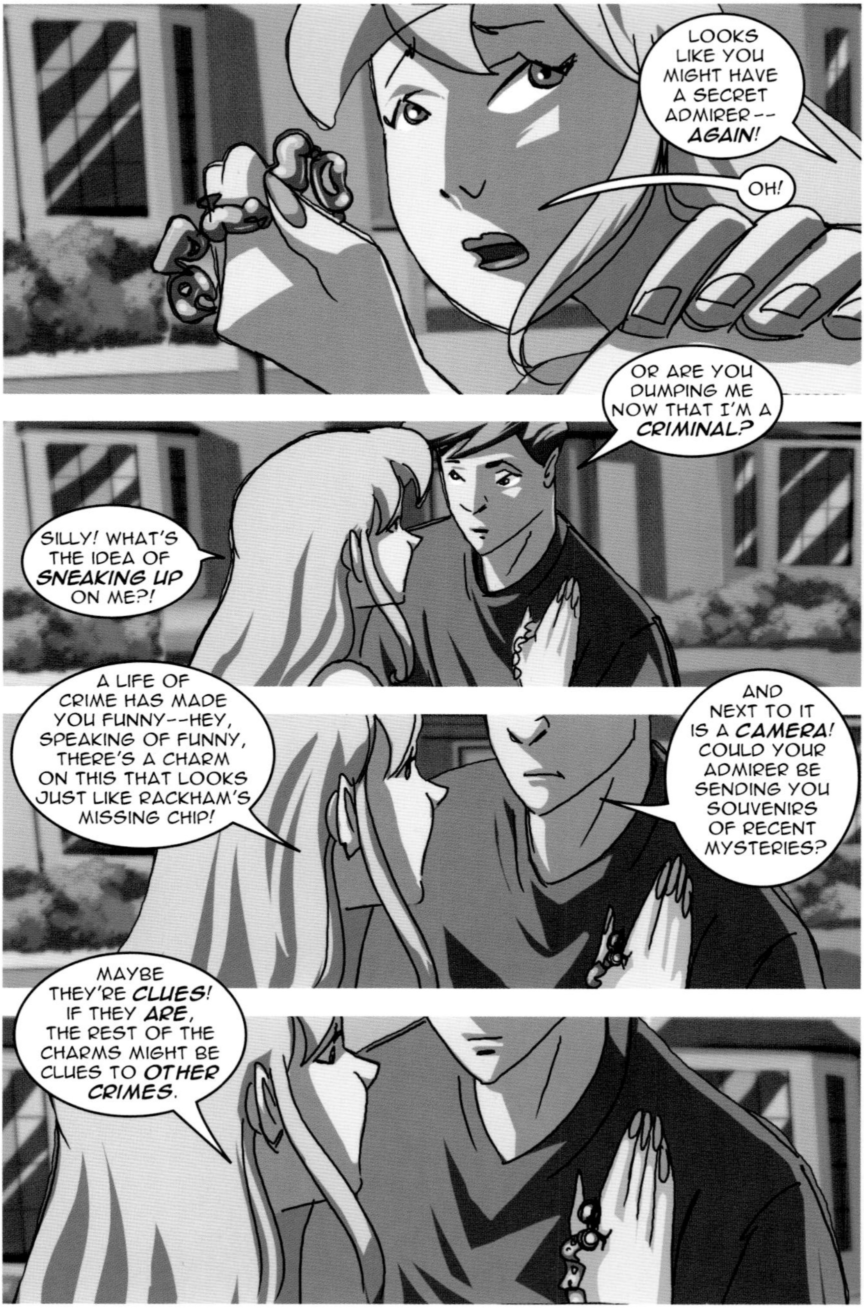
LOOKS LIKE YOU MIGHT HAVE A SECRET ADMIRER-- AGAIN!
OH!
OR ARE YOU DUMPING ME NOW THAT I'M A CRIMINAL?
SILLY! WHAT'S THE IDEA OF SNEAKING UP ON ME?!
A LIFE OF CRIME HAS MADE YOU FUNNY--HEY, SPEAKING OF FUNNY, THERE'S A CHARM ON THIS THAT LOOKS JUST LIKE RACKHAM'S MISSING CHIP!
AND NEXT TO IT IS A CAMERA! COULD YOUR ADMIRER BE SENDING YOU SOUVENIRS OF RECENT MYSTERIES?
MAYBE THEY'RE CLUES! IF THEY ARE, THE REST OF THE CHARMS MIGHT BE CLUES TO OTHER CRIMES.

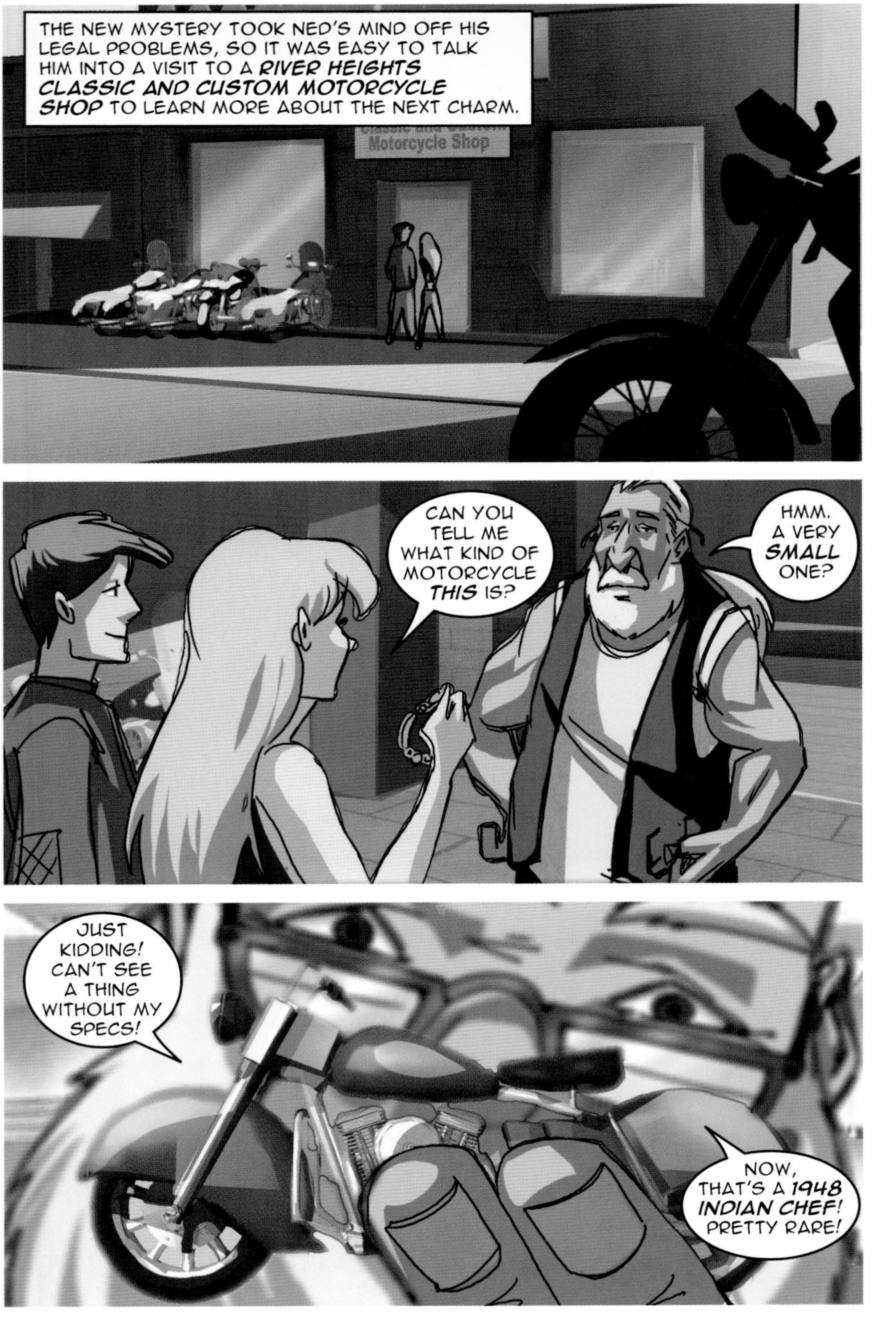
THE NEW MYSTERY TOOK NED'S MIND OFF HIS LEGAL PROBLEMS, SO IT WAS EASY TO TALK HIM INTO A VISIT TO A *RIVER HEIGHTS CLASSIC AND CUSTOM MOTORCYCLE SHOP* TO LEARN MORE ABOUT THE NEXT CHARM.
Motorcycle Shop
CAN YOU TELL ME WHAT KIND OF MOTORCYCLE *THIS* IS?
HMM. A VERY *SMALL* ONE?
JUST KIDDING! CAN'T SEE A THING WITHOUT MY SPECS!
NOW, THAT'S A *1948 INDIAN CHEF*! PRETTY RARE!

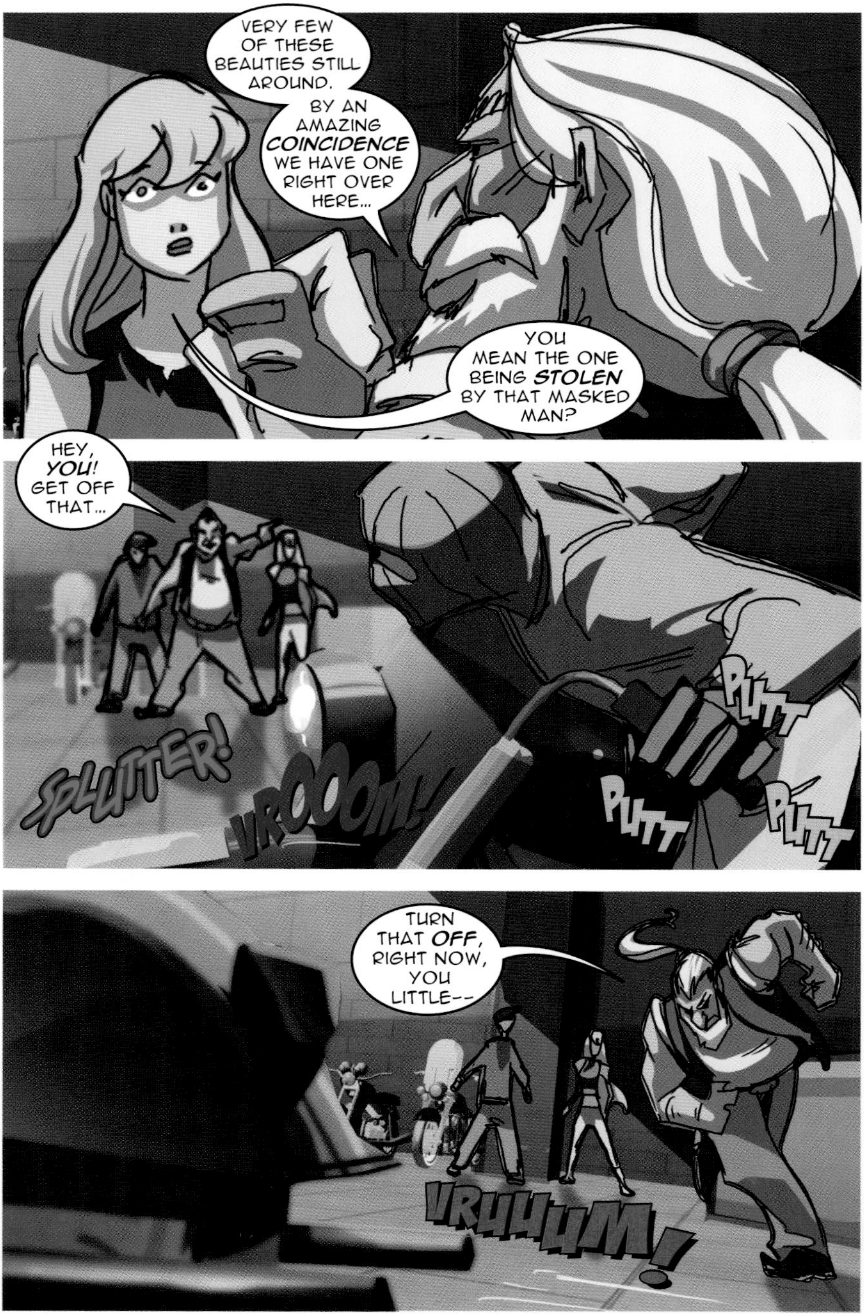
VERY FEW OF THESE BEAUTIES STILL AROUND.
BY AN AMAZING *COINCIDENCE* WE HAVE ONE RIGHT OVER HERE...
YOU MEAN THE ONE BEING *STOLEN* BY THAT MASKED MAN?
HEY, *YOU*! GET OFF THAT...
SPLUTTER!
VROOOOM!
PUTT
PUTT
PUTT
TURN THAT *OFF*, RIGHT NOW, YOU LITTLE--
VRUUUUM!

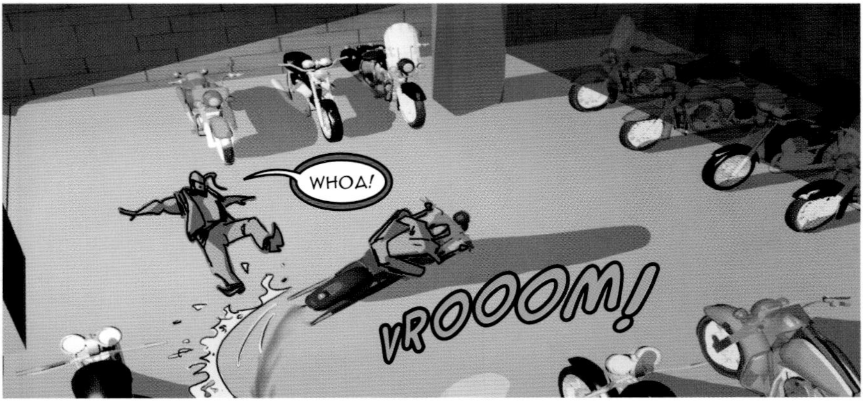
WHOA!
VROOOM!

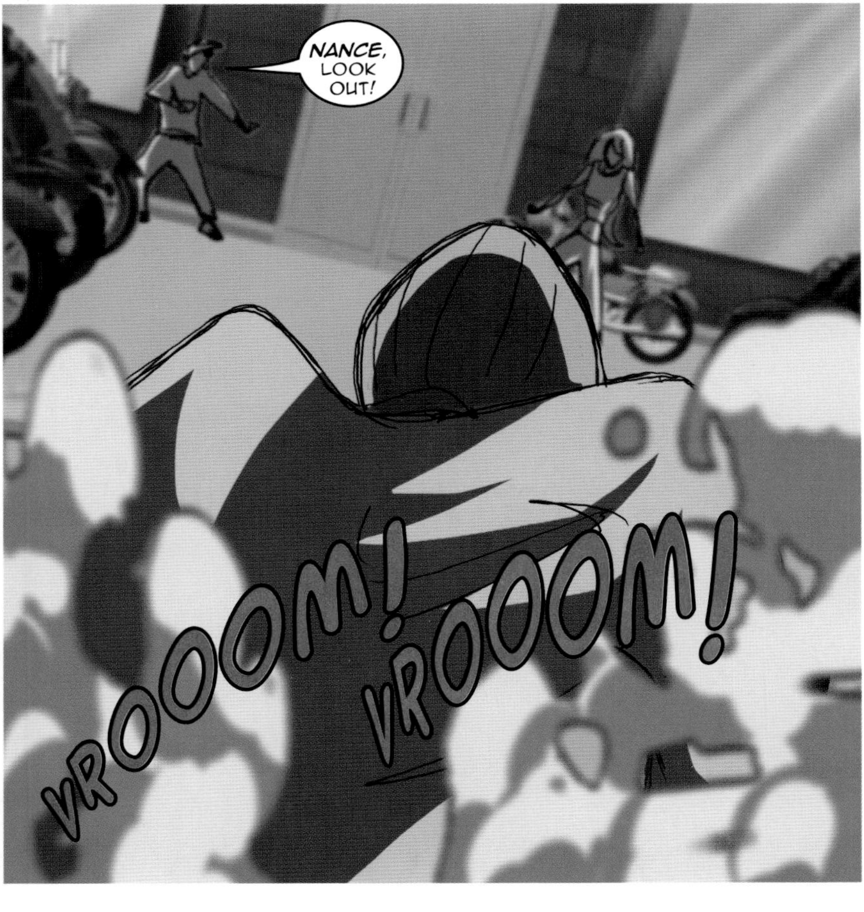
NANCE, LOOK OUT!
VROOOM!
VROOOM!

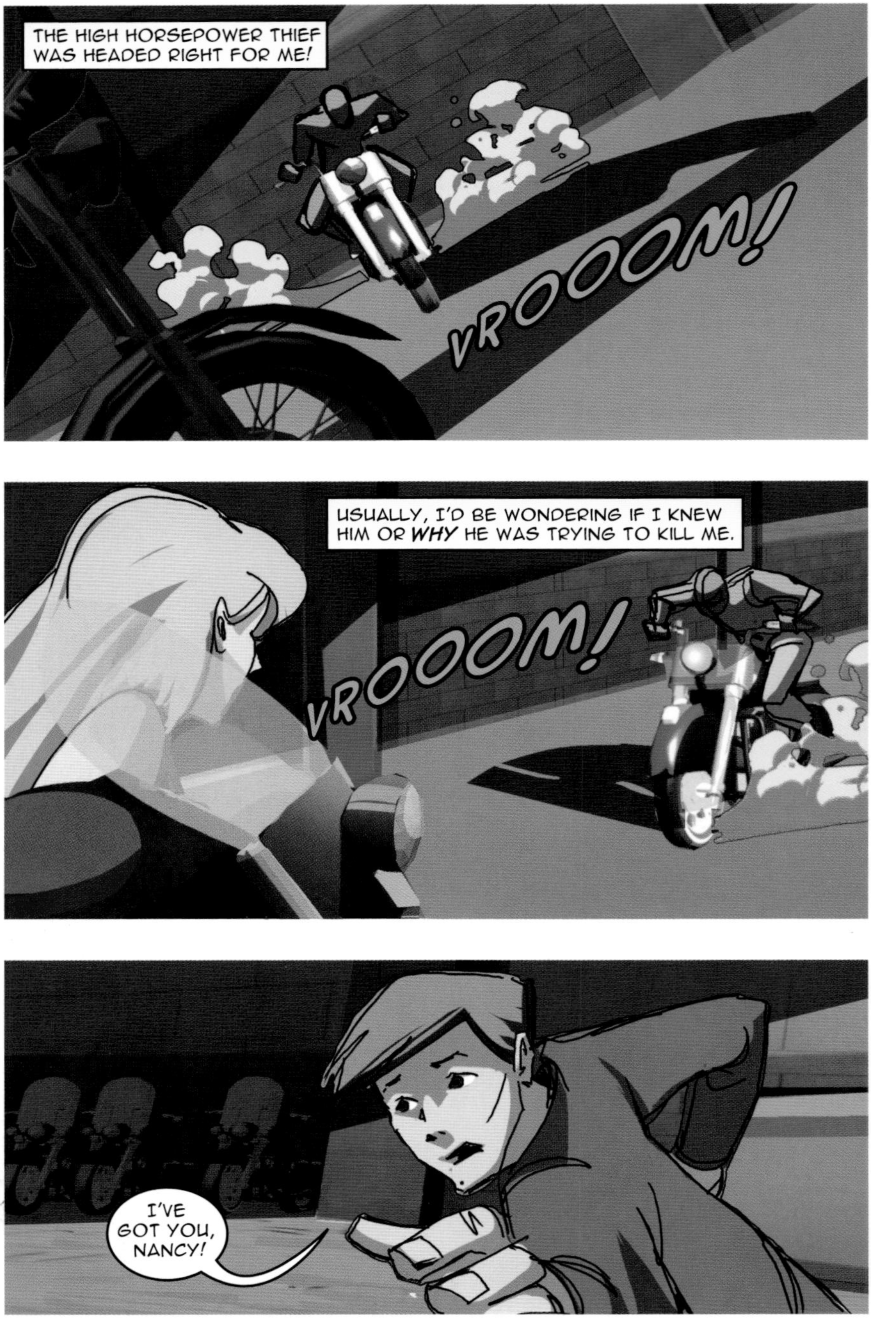
THE HIGH HORSEPOWER THIEF WAS HEADED RIGHT FOR ME!
VROOOM!
USUALLY, I'D BE WONDERING IF I KNEW HIM OR WHY HE WAS TRYING TO KILL ME.
VROOOM!
I'VE GOT YOU, NANCY!

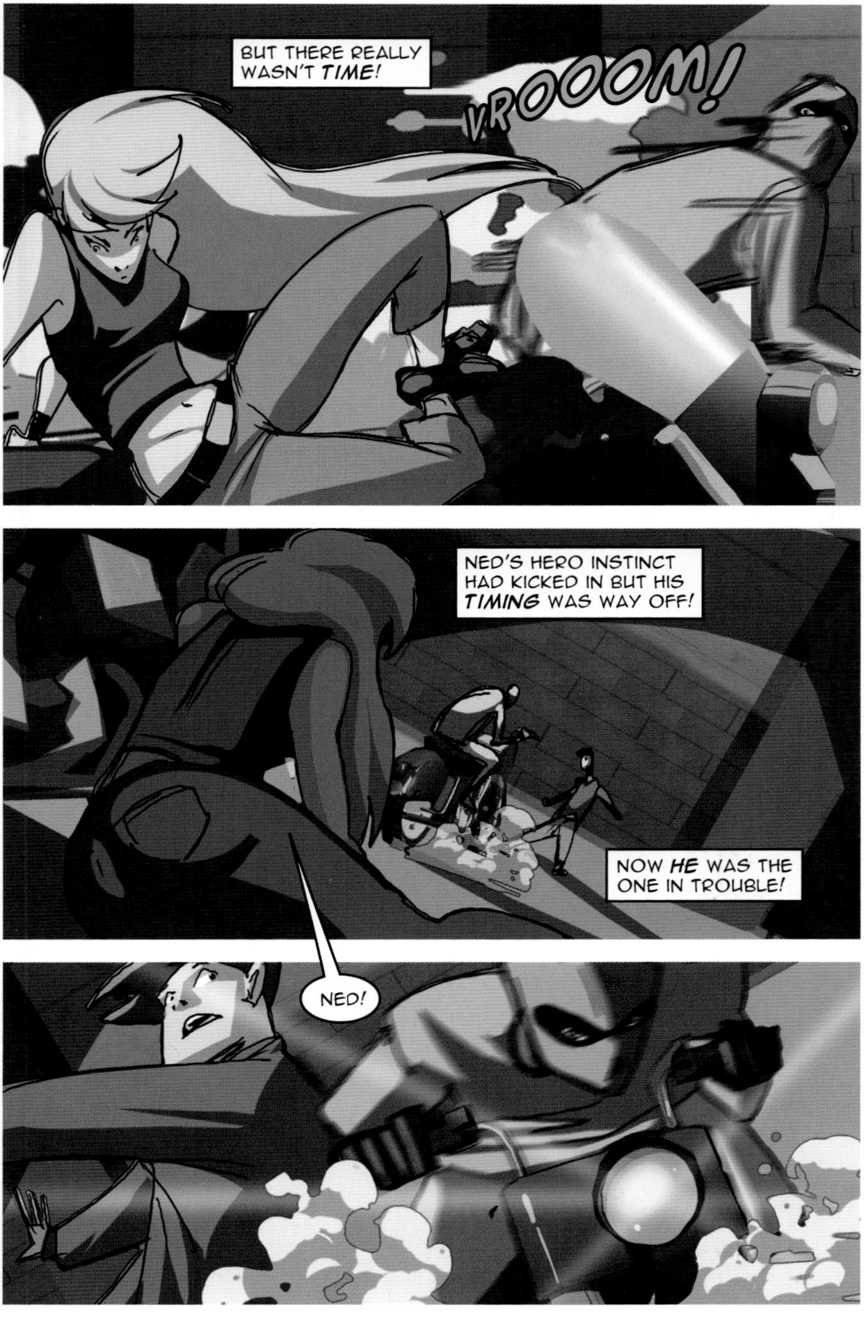
BUT THERE REALLY WASN'T TIME!
VROOOM!
NED'S HERO INSTINCT HAD KICKED IN BUT HIS TIMING WAS WAY OFF!
NOW HE WAS THE ONE IN TROUBLE!
NED!

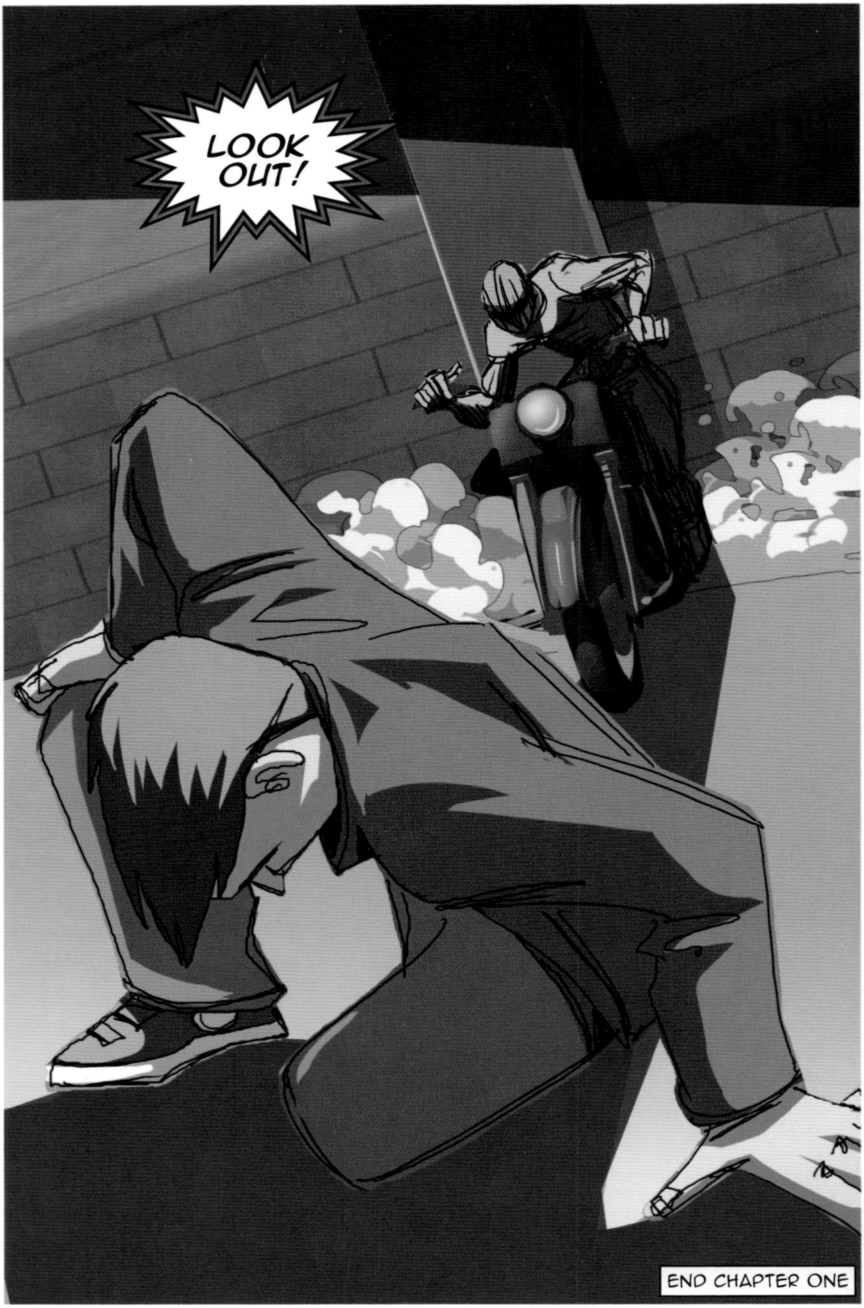
LOOK OUT!
END CHAPTER ONE

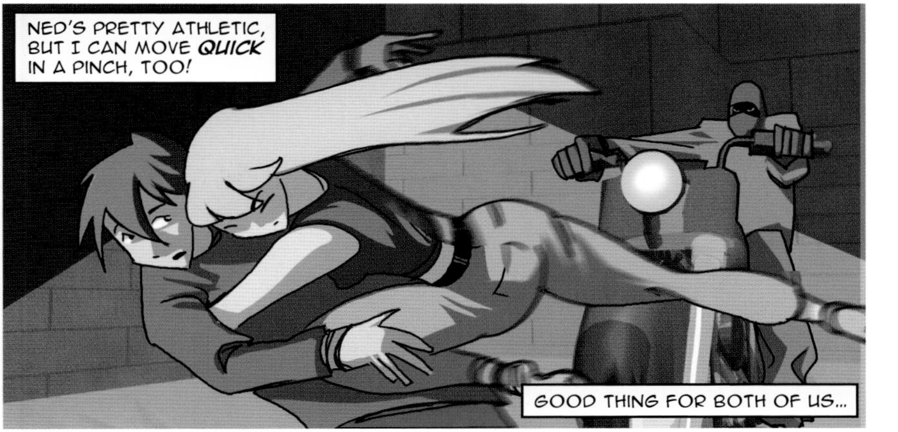
NED'S PRETTY ATHLETIC, BUT I CAN MOVE QUICK IN A PINCH, TOO!
GOOD THING FOR BOTH OF US...

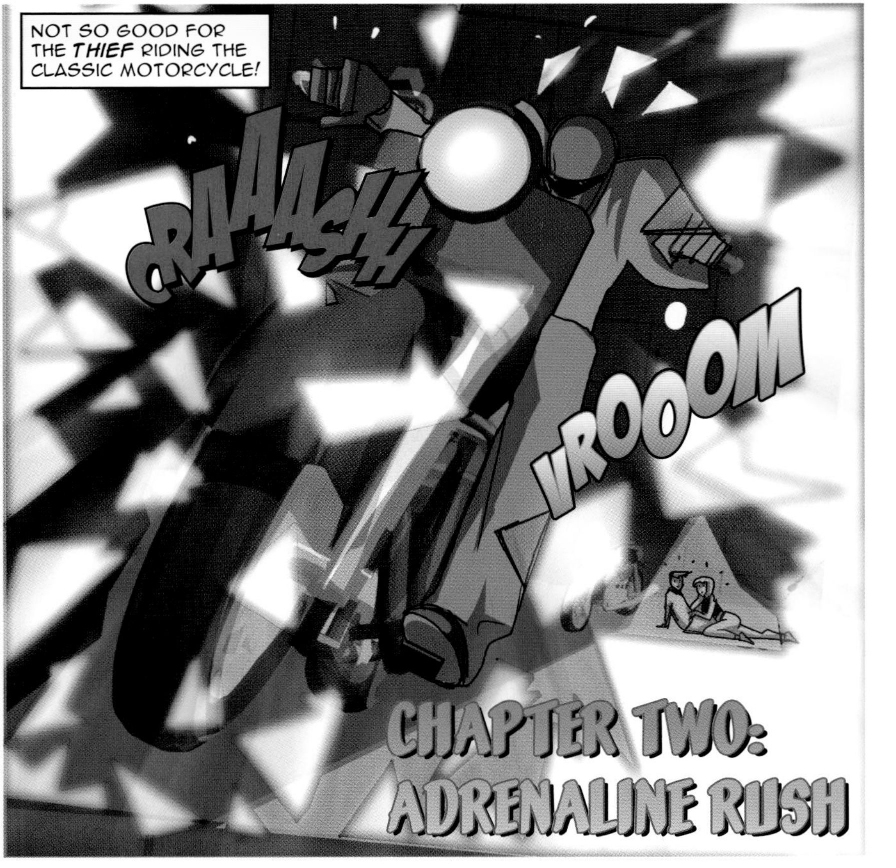
NOT SO GOOD FOR THE THIEF RIDING THE CLASSIC MOTORCYCLE!
CRAAASHH
VROOOOM
CHAPTER TWO:
ADRENALINE RUSH

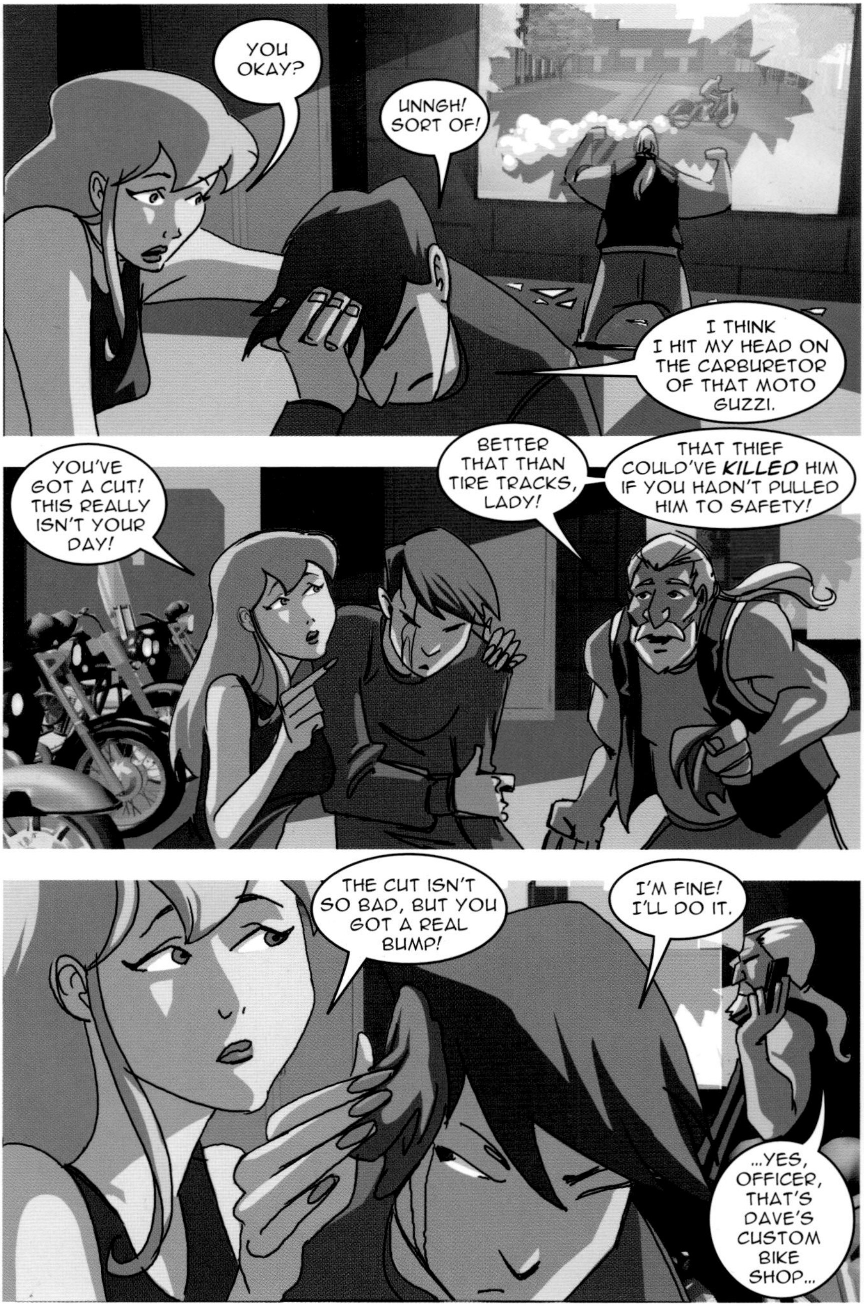
YOU OKAY?
UNNGH! SORT OF!
I THINK I HIT MY HEAD ON THE CARBURETOR OF THAT MOTO GUZZI.
YOU'VE GOT A CUT! THIS REALLY ISN'T YOUR DAY!
BETTER THAT THAN TIRE TRACKS, LADY!
THAT THIEF COULD'VE KILLED HIM IF YOU HADN'T PULLED HIM TO SAFETY!
THE CUT ISN'T SO BAD, BUT YOU GOT A REAL BUMP!
I'M FINE! I'LL DO IT.
...YES, OFFICER, THAT'S DAVE'S CUSTOM BIKE SHOP...

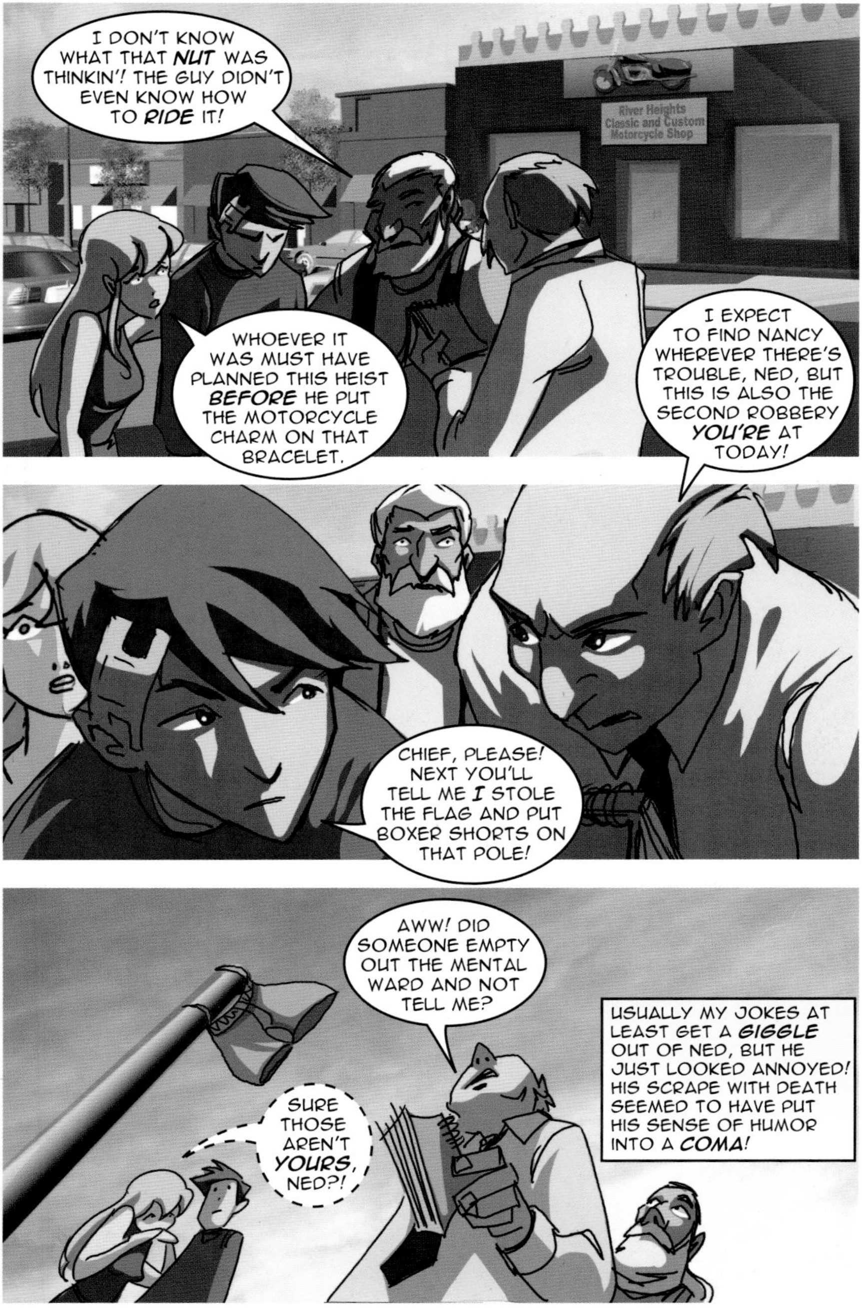
I DON'T KNOW WHAT THAT NUT WAS THINKIN'! THE GUY DIDN'T EVEN KNOW HOW TO RIDE IT!
River Heights Classic and Custom Motorcycle Shop
WHOEVER IT WAS MUST HAVE PLANNED THIS HEIST BEFORE HE PUT THE MOTORCYCLE CHARM ON THAT BRACELET.
I EXPECT TO FIND NANCY WHEREVER THERE'S TROUBLE, NED, BUT THIS IS ALSO THE SECOND ROBBERY YOU'RE AT TODAY!
CHIEF, PLEASE! NEXT YOU'LL TELL ME I STOLE THE FLAG AND PUT BOXER SHORTS ON THAT POLE!
AWW! DID SOMEONE EMPTY OUT THE MENTAL WARD AND NOT TELL ME?
USUALLY MY JOKES AT LEAST GET A GIGGLE OUT OF NED, BUT HE JUST LOOKED ANNOYED! HIS SCRAPE WITH DEATH SEEMED TO HAVE PUT HIS SENSE OF HUMOR INTO A COMA!
SURE THOSE AREN'T YOURS, NED?!

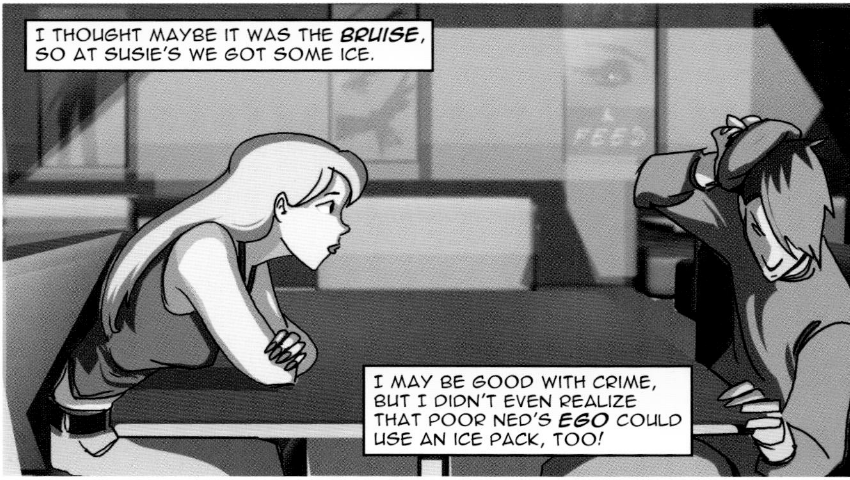
I THOUGHT MAYBE IT WAS THE **BRUISE**, SO AT SUSIE'S WE GOT SOME ICE.
I MAY BE GOOD WITH CRIME, BUT I DIDN'T EVEN REALIZE THAT POOR NED'S **EGO** COULD USE AN ICE PACK, TOO!

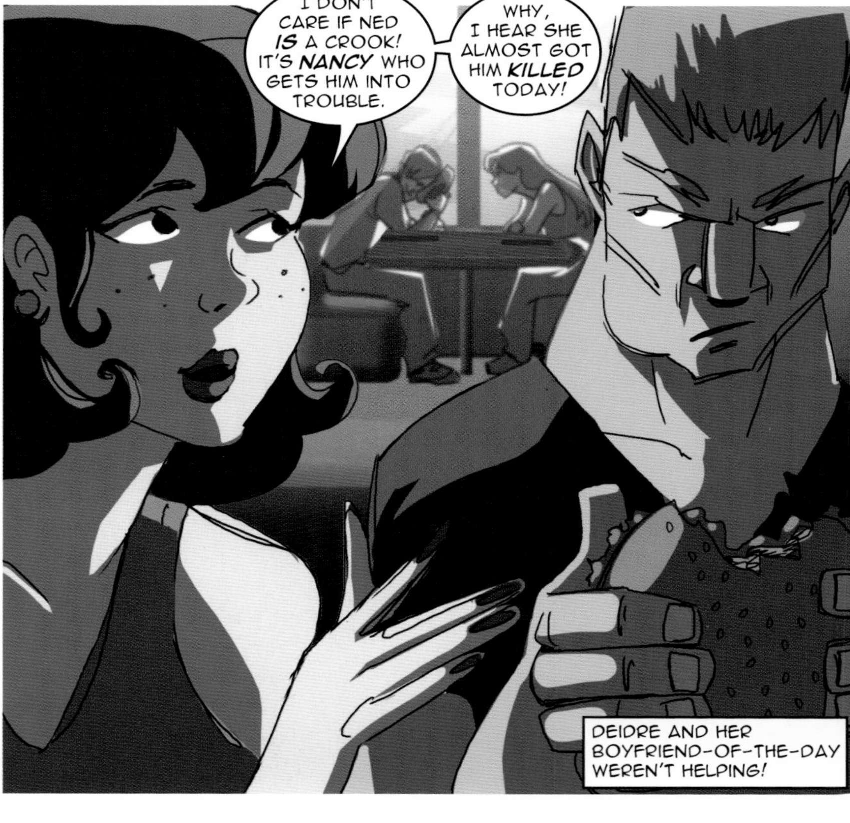
I DON'T CARE IF NED **IS** A CROOK! IT'S **NANCY** WHO GETS HIM INTO TROUBLE.
WHY, I HEAR SHE ALMOST GOT HIM **KILLED** TODAY!
DEIDRE AND HER BOYFRIEND-OF-THE-DAY WEREN'T HELPING!

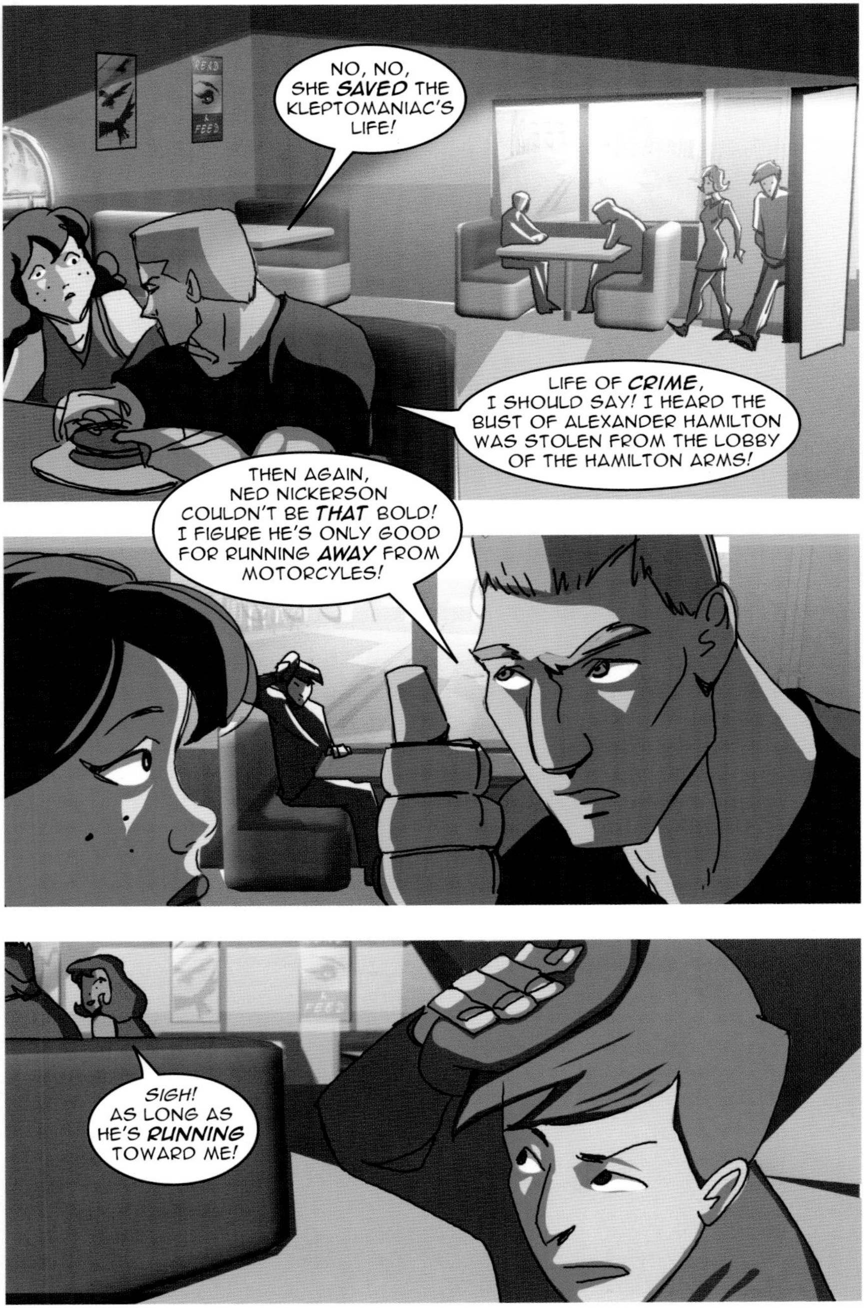
READ & FEED
NO, NO, SHE SAVED THE KLEPTOMANIAC'S LIFE!
LIFE OF CRIME, I SHOULD SAY! I HEARD THE BUST OF ALEXANDER HAMILTON WAS STOLEN FROM THE LOBBY OF THE HAMILTON ARMS!
THEN AGAIN, NED NICKERSON COULDN'T BE THAT BOLD! I FIGURE HE'S ONLY GOOD FOR RUNNING AWAY FROM MOTORCYLES!
SIGH! AS LONG AS HE'S RUNNING TOWARD ME!

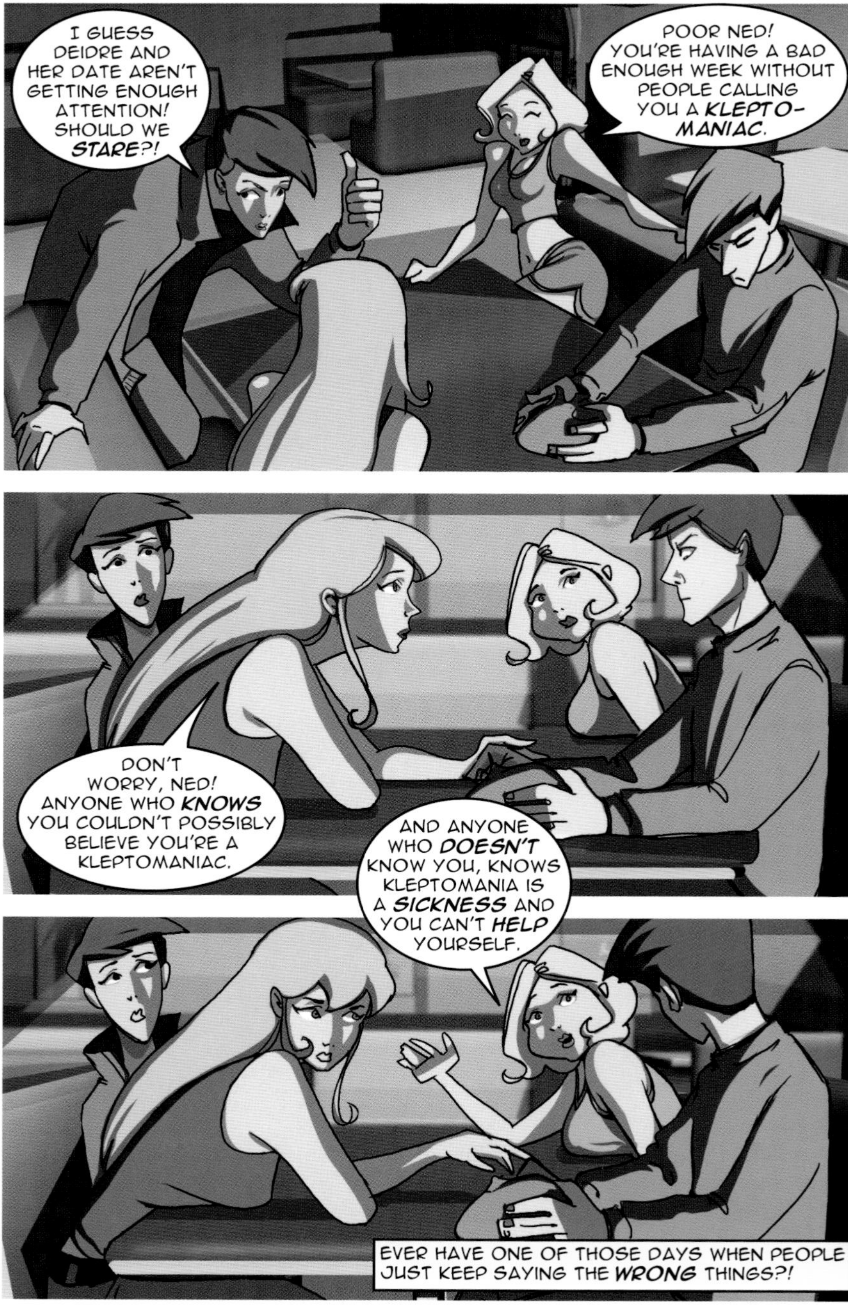
I GUESS DEIDRE AND HER DATE AREN'T GETTING ENOUGH ATTENTION! SHOULD WE STARE?!
POOR NED! YOU'RE HAVING A BAD ENOUGH WEEK WITHOUT PEOPLE CALLING YOU A KLEPTO-MANIAC.
DON'T WORRY, NED! ANYONE WHO KNOWS YOU COULDN'T POSSIBLY BELIEVE YOU'RE A KLEPTOMANIAC.
AND ANYONE WHO DOESN'T KNOW YOU, KNOWS KLEPTOMANIA IS A SICKNESS AND YOU CAN'T HELP YOURSELF.
EVER HAVE ONE OF THOSE DAYS WHEN PEOPLE JUST KEEP SAYING THE WRONG THINGS?!

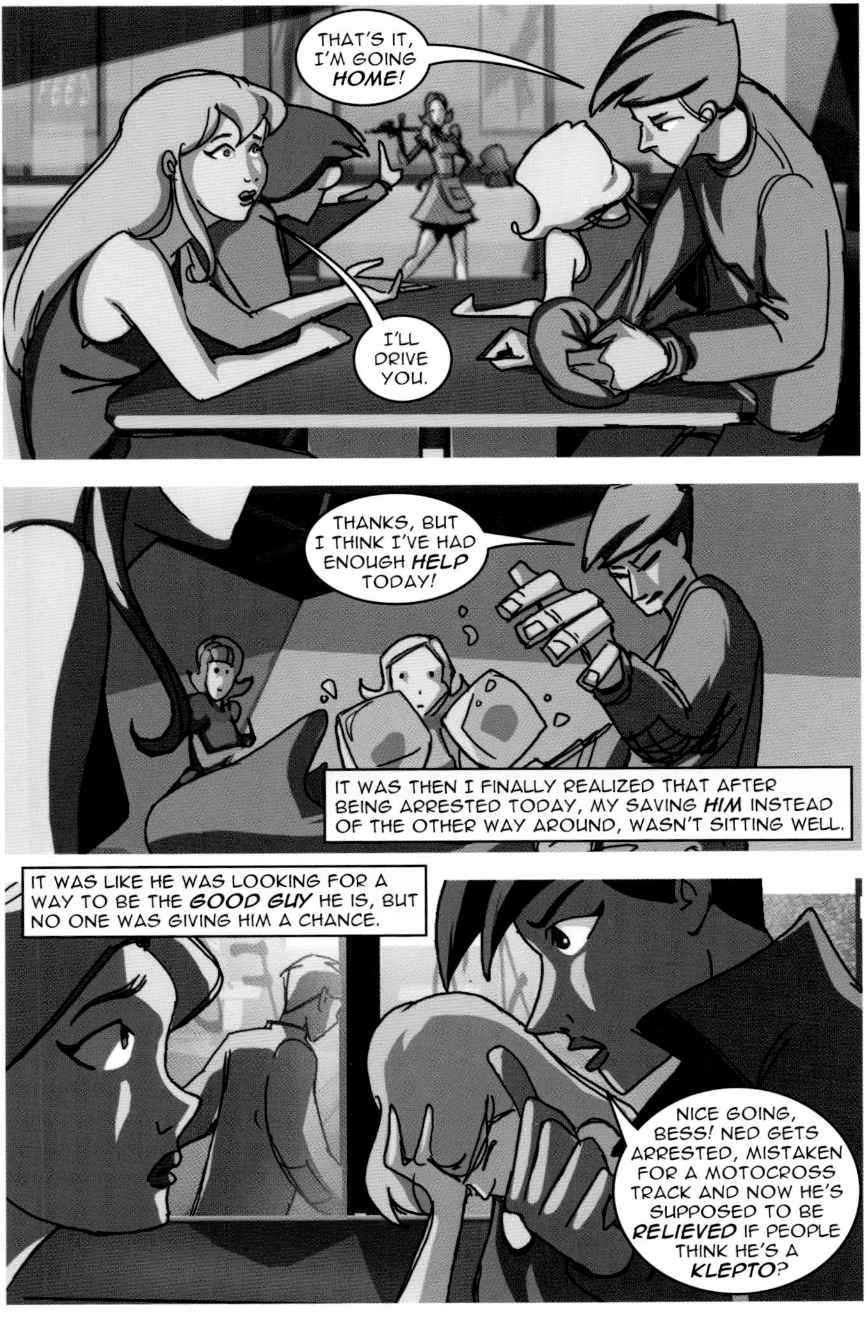
THAT'S IT, I'M GOING HOME!
I'LL DRIVE YOU.
THANKS, BUT I THINK I'VE HAD ENOUGH HELP TODAY!
IT WAS THEN I FINALLY REALIZED THAT AFTER BEING ARRESTED TODAY, MY SAVING HIM INSTEAD OF THE OTHER WAY AROUND, WASN'T SITTING WELL.
IT WAS LIKE HE WAS LOOKING FOR A WAY TO BE THE GOOD GUY HE IS, BUT NO ONE WAS GIVING HIM A CHANCE.
NICE GOING, BESS! NED GETS ARRESTED, MISTAKEN FOR A MOTOCROSS TRACK AND NOW HE'S SUPPOSED TO BE RELIEVED IF PEOPLE THINK HE'S A KLEPTO?

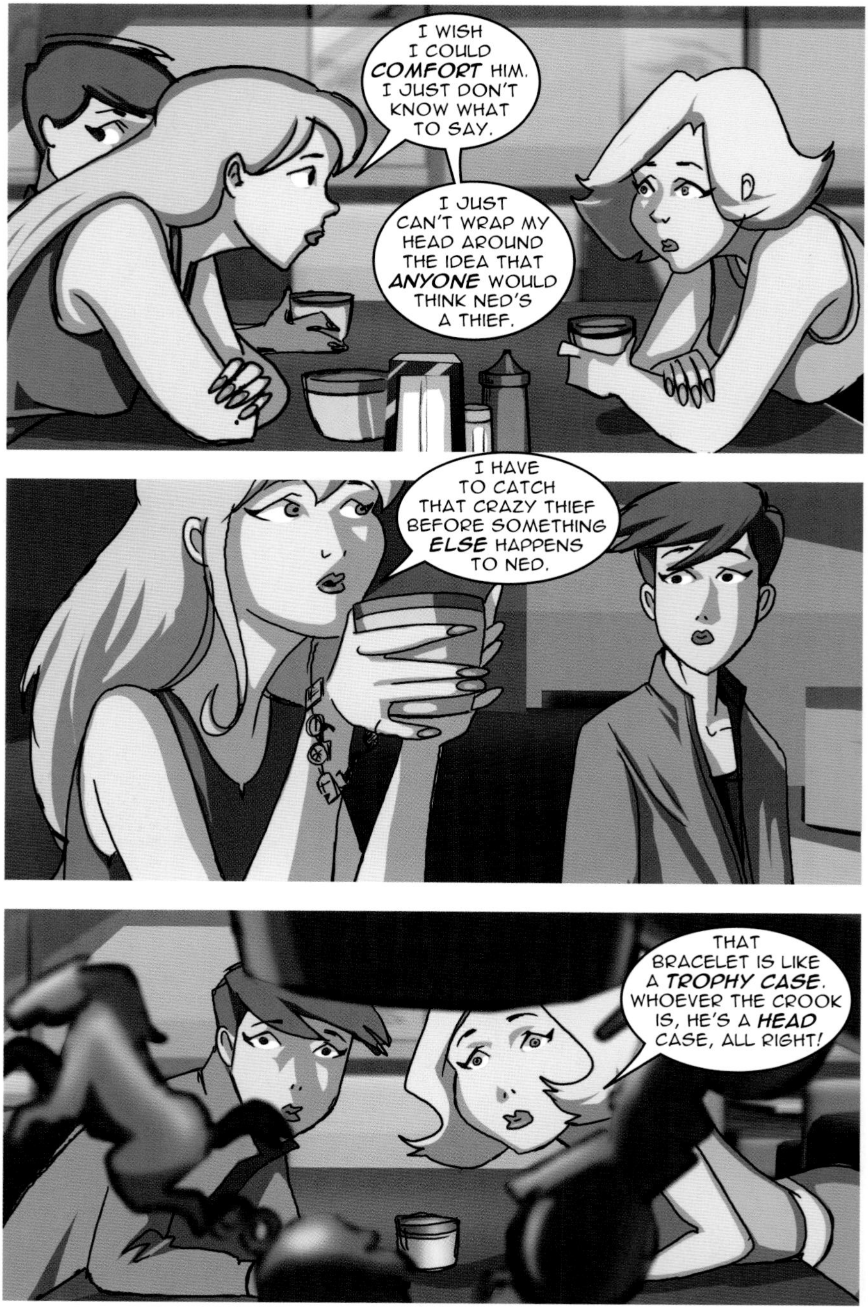
I WISH I COULD COMFORT HIM. I JUST DON'T KNOW WHAT TO SAY.
I JUST CAN'T WRAP MY HEAD AROUND THE IDEA THAT ANYONE WOULD THINK NED'S A THIEF.
I HAVE TO CATCH THAT CRAZY THIEF BEFORE SOMETHING ELSE HAPPENS TO NED.
THAT BRACELET IS LIKE A TROPHY CASE. WHOEVER THE CROOK IS, HE'S A HEAD CASE, ALL RIGHT!

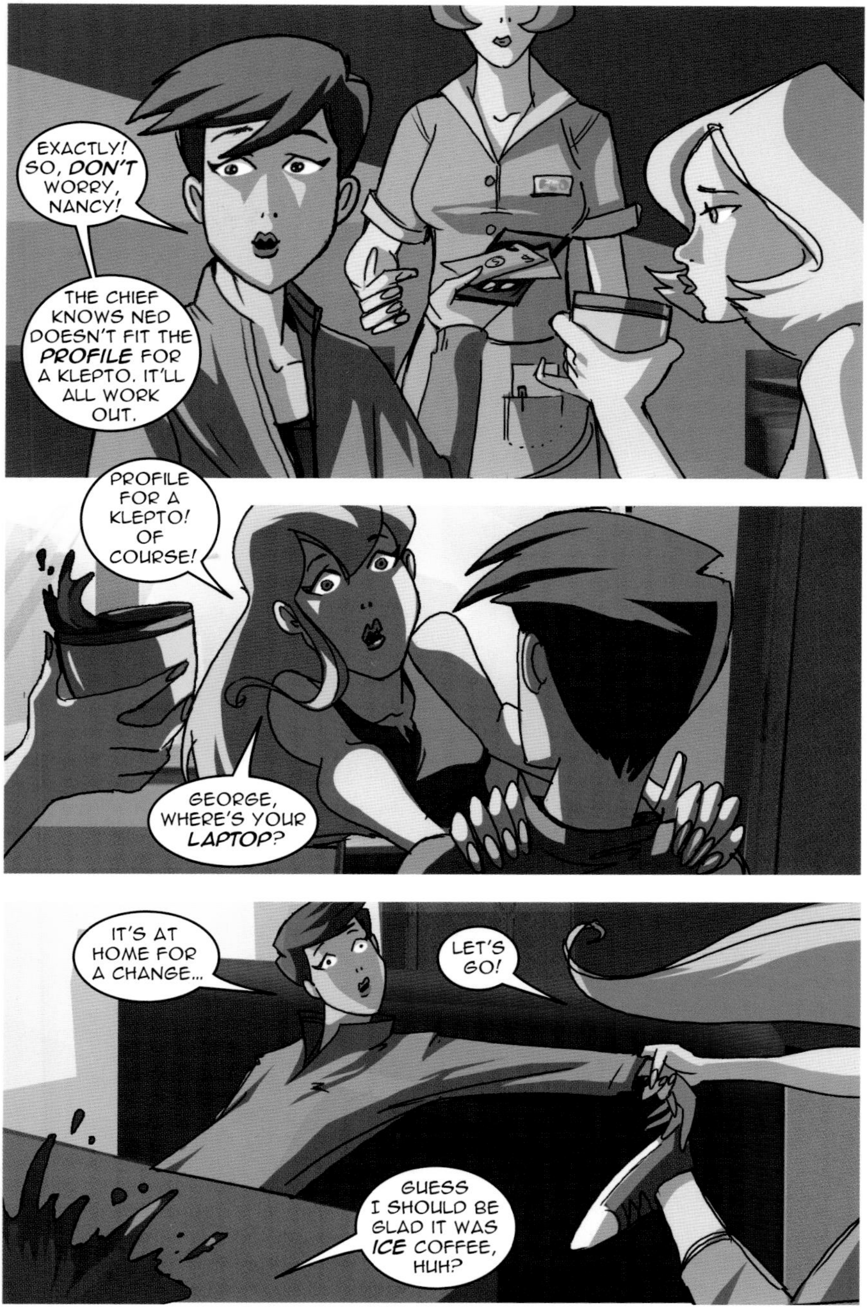
EXACTLY! SO, DON'T WORRY, NANCY!
THE CHIEF KNOWS NED DOESN'T FIT THE PROFILE FOR A KLEPTO. IT'LL ALL WORK OUT.
PROFILE FOR A KLEPTO! OF COURSE!
GEORGE, WHERE'S YOUR LAPTOP?
IT'S AT HOME FOR A CHANGE...
LET'S GO!
GUESS I SHOULD BE GLAD IT WAS ICE COFFEE, HUH?

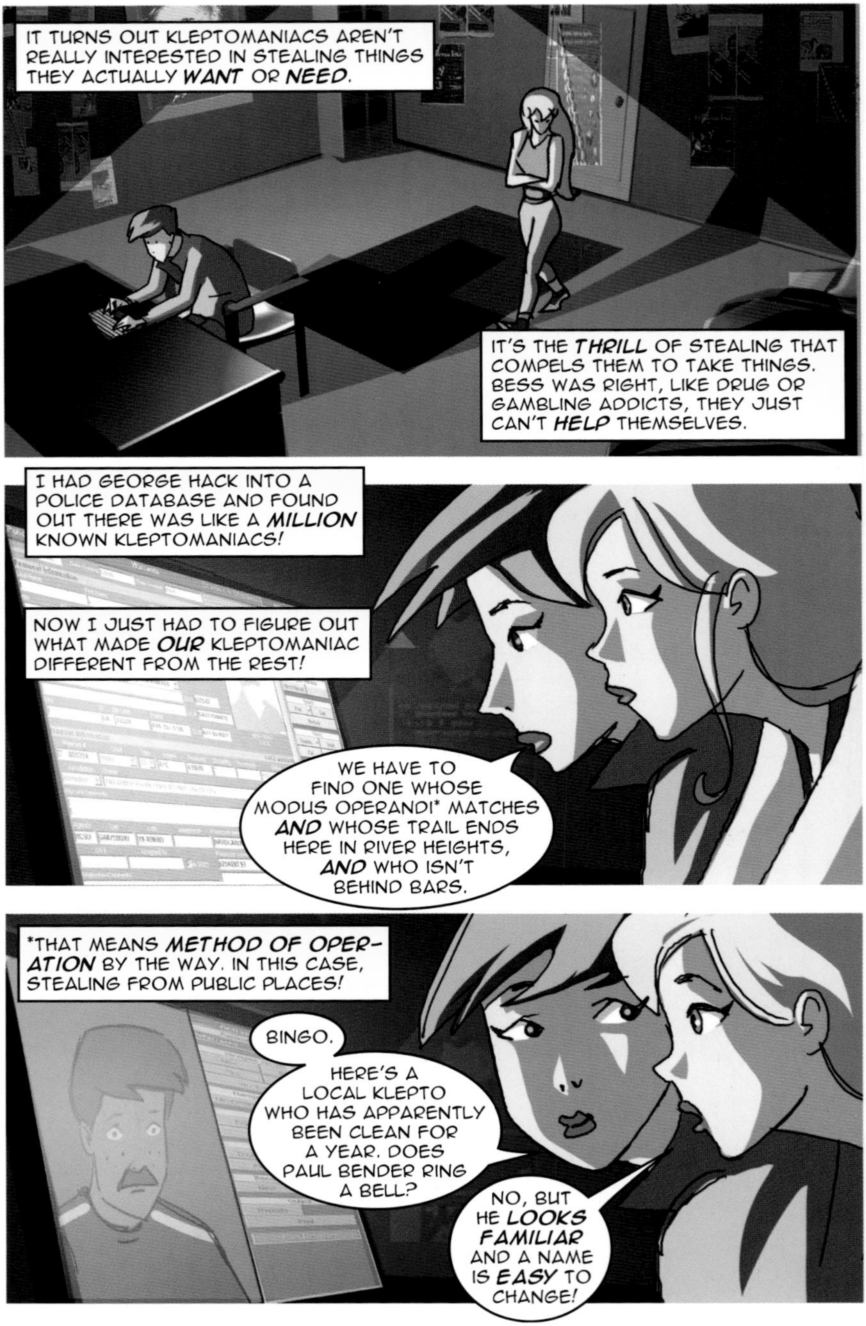
IT TURNS OUT KLEPTOMANIACS AREN'T REALLY INTERESTED IN STEALING THINGS THEY ACTUALLY WANT OR NEED.
IT'S THE THRILL OF STEALING THAT COMPELS THEM TO TAKE THINGS. BESS WAS RIGHT, LIKE DRUG OR GAMBLING ADDICTS, THEY JUST CAN'T HELP THEMSELVES.
I HAD GEORGE HACK INTO A POLICE DATABASE AND FOUND OUT THERE WAS LIKE A MILLION KNOWN KLEPTOMANIACS!
NOW I JUST HAD TO FIGURE OUT WHAT MADE OUR KLEPTOMANIAC DIFFERENT FROM THE REST!
WE HAVE TO FIND ONE WHOSE MODUS OPERANDI* MATCHES AND WHOSE TRAIL ENDS HERE IN RIVER HEIGHTS, AND WHO ISN'T BEHIND BARS.
*THAT MEANS METHOD OF OPER-ATION BY THE WAY. IN THIS CASE, STEALING FROM PUBLIC PLACES!
BINGO.
HERE'S A LOCAL KLEPTO WHO HAS APPARENTLY BEEN CLEAN FOR A YEAR. DOES PAUL BENDER RING A BELL?
NO, BUT HE LOOKS FAMILIAR AND A NAME IS EASY TO CHANGE!

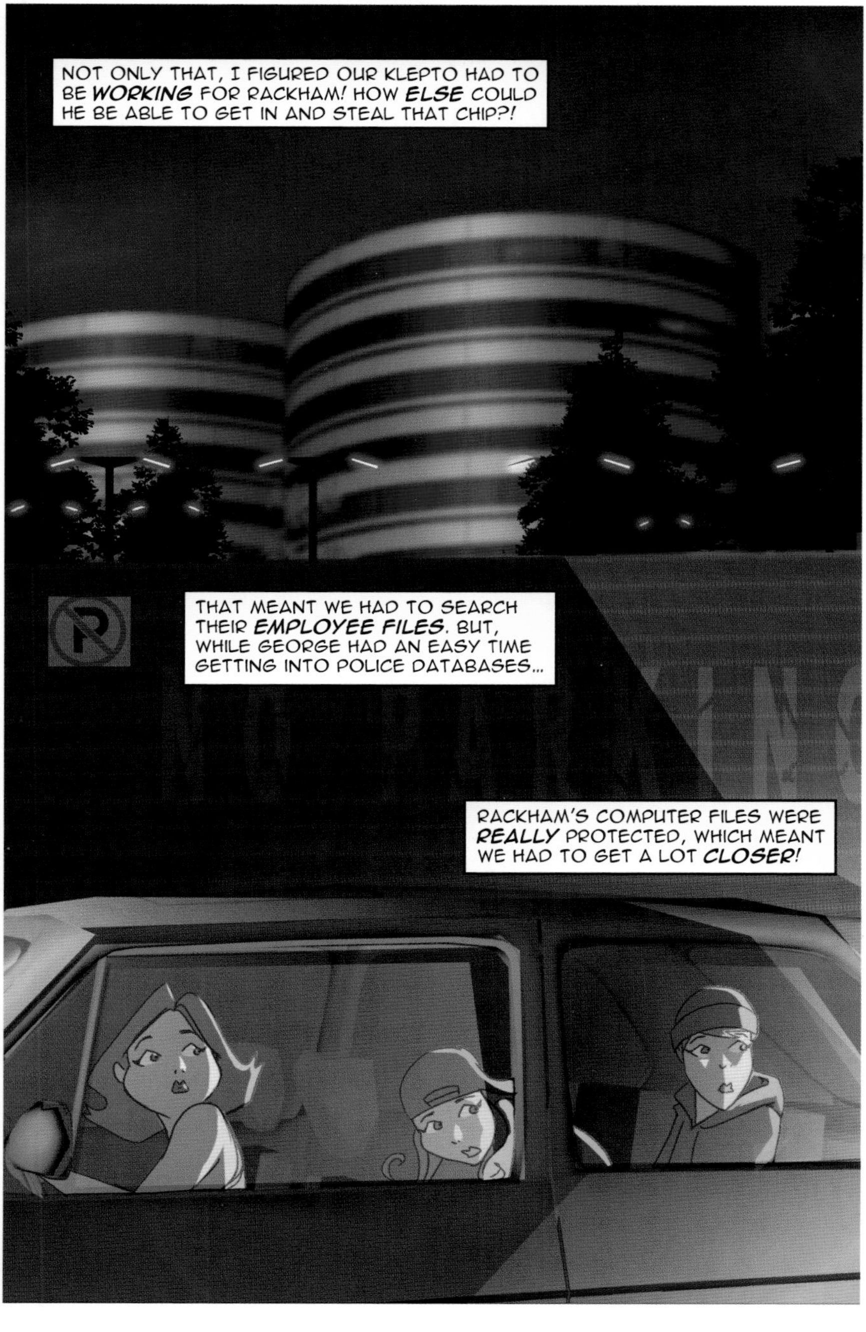
NOT ONLY THAT, I FIGURED OUR KLEPTO HAD TO BE *WORKING* FOR RACKHAM! HOW *ELSE* COULD HE BE ABLE TO GET IN AND STEAL THAT CHIP?!
THAT MEANT WE HAD TO SEARCH THEIR *EMPLOYEE FILES*. BUT, WHILE GEORGE HAD AN EASY TIME GETTING INTO POLICE DATABASES...
RACKHAM'S COMPUTER FILES WERE *REALLY* PROTECTED, WHICH MEANT WE HAD TO GET A LOT *CLOSER*!

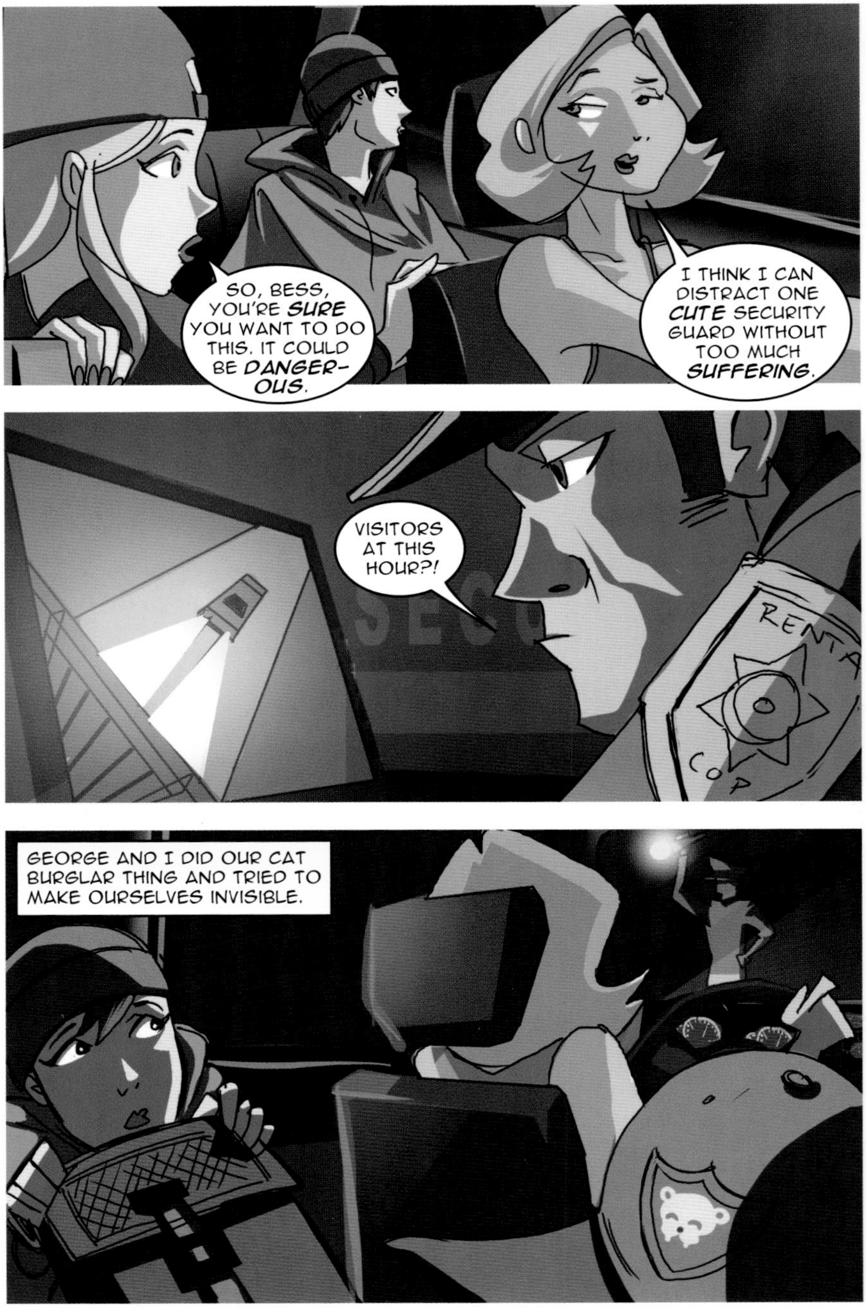
SO, BESS, YOU'RE SURE YOU WANT TO DO THIS. IT COULD BE DANGER-OUS.
I THINK I CAN DISTRACT ONE CUTE SECURITY GUARD WITHOUT TOO MUCH SUFFERING.
VISITORS AT THIS HOUR?!
RENT-A COP
GEORGE AND I DID OUR CAT BURGLAR THING AND TRIED TO MAKE OURSELVES INVISIBLE.

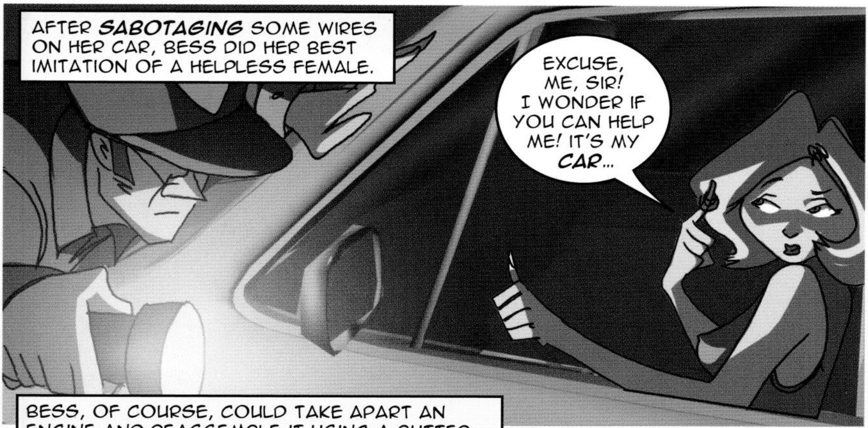
AFTER SABOTAGING SOME WIRES ON HER CAR, BESS DID HER BEST IMITATION OF A HELPLESS FEMALE.
EXCUSE, ME, SIR! I WONDER IF YOU CAN HELP ME! IT'S MY CAR...

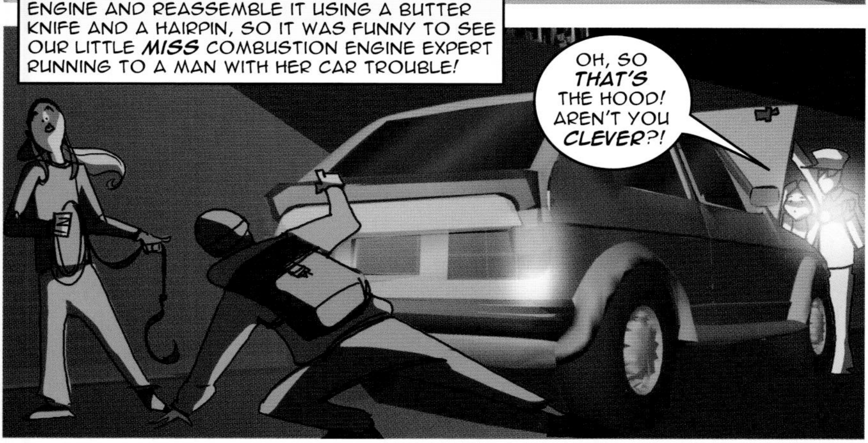
BESS, OF COURSE, COULD TAKE APART AN ENGINE AND REASSEMBLE IT USING A BUTTER KNIFE AND A HAIRPIN, SO IT WAS FUNNY TO SEE OUR LITTLE MISS COMBUSTION ENGINE EXPERT RUNNING TO A MAN WITH HER CAR TROUBLE!
OH, SO THAT'S THE HOOD! AREN'T YOU CLEVER?!

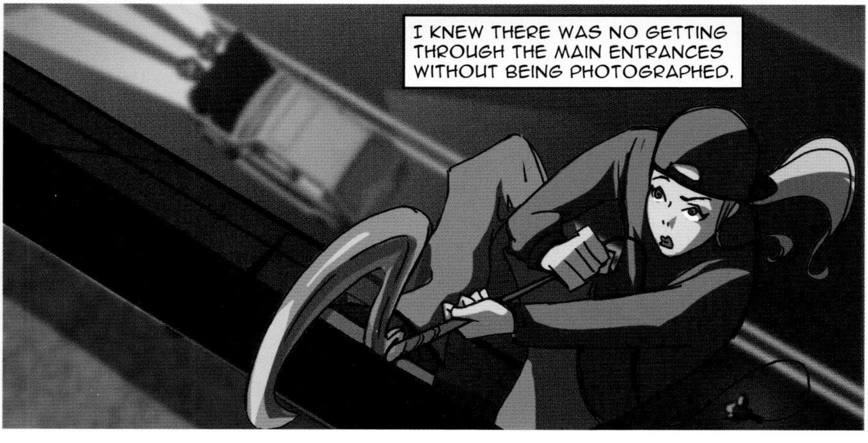
I KNEW THERE WAS NO GETTING THROUGH THE MAIN ENTRANCES WITHOUT BEING PHOTOGRAPHED.

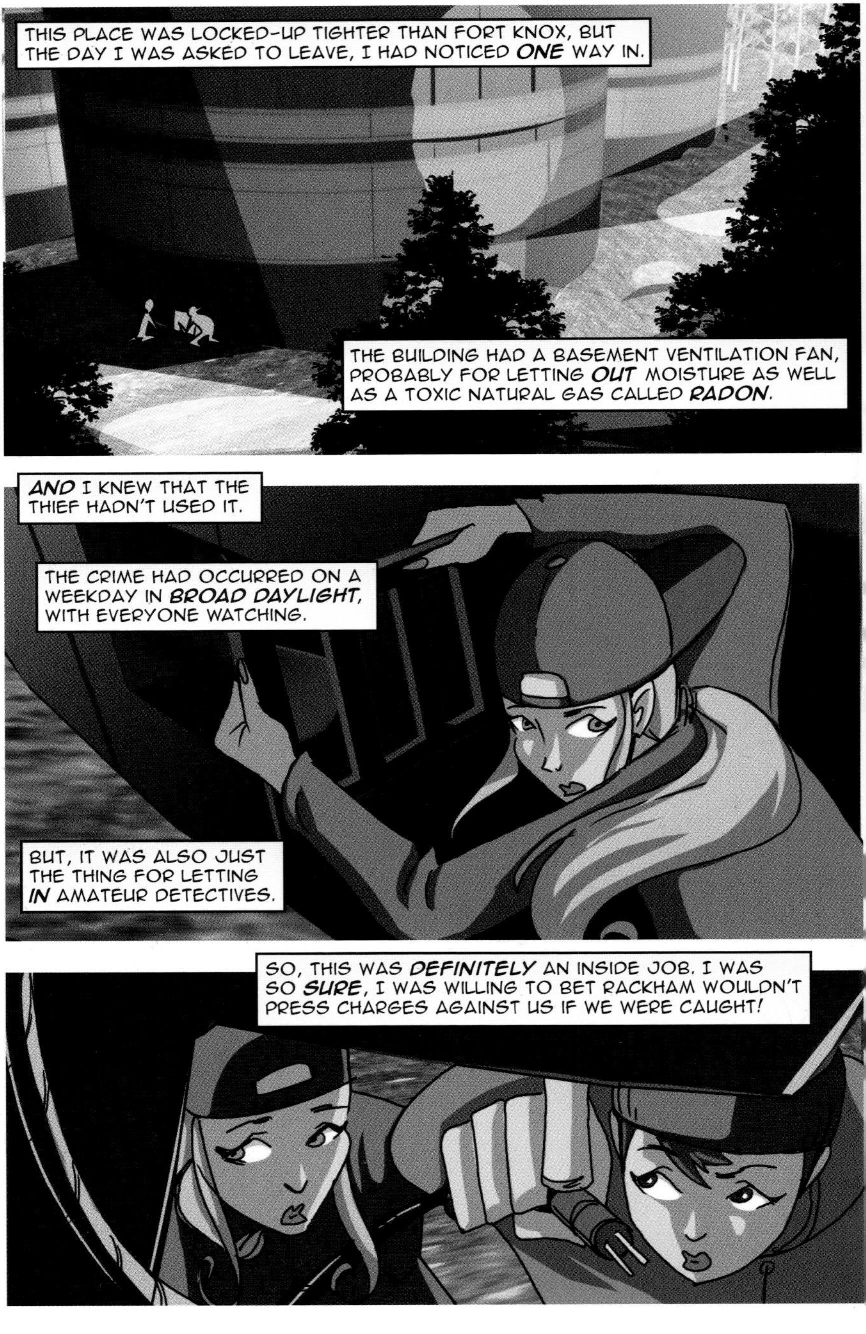
THIS PLACE WAS LOCKED-UP TIGHTER THAN FORT KNOX, BUT THE DAY I WAS ASKED TO LEAVE, I HAD NOTICED ONE WAY IN.
THE BUILDING HAD A BASEMENT VENTILATION FAN, PROBABLY FOR LETTING OUT MOISTURE AS WELL AS A TOXIC NATURAL GAS CALLED RADON.
AND I KNEW THAT THE THIEF HADN'T USED IT.
THE CRIME HAD OCCURRED ON A WEEKDAY IN BROAD DAYLIGHT, WITH EVERYONE WATCHING.
BUT, IT WAS ALSO JUST THE THING FOR LETTING IN AMATEUR DETECTIVES.
SO, THIS WAS DEFINITELY AN INSIDE JOB. I WAS SO SURE, I WAS WILLING TO BET RACKHAM WOULDN'T PRESS CHARGES AGAINST US IF WE WERE CAUGHT!

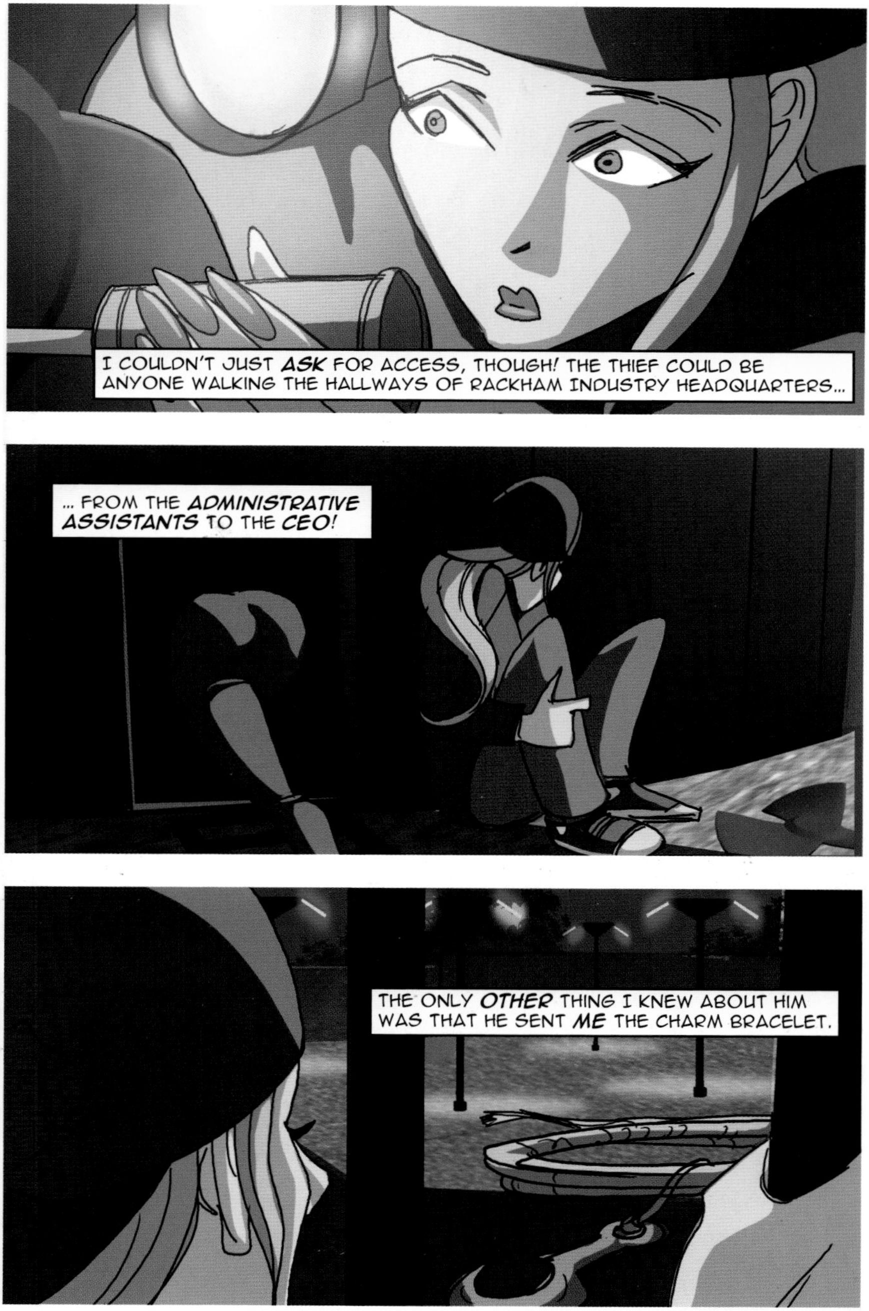
I COULDN'T JUST ASK FOR ACCESS, THOUGH! THE THIEF COULD BE ANYONE WALKING THE HALLWAYS OF RACKHAM INDUSTRY HEADQUARTERS...
... FROM THE ADMINISTRATIVE ASSISTANTS TO THE CEO!
THE ONLY OTHER THING I KNEW ABOUT HIM WAS THAT HE SENT ME THE CHARM BRACELET.

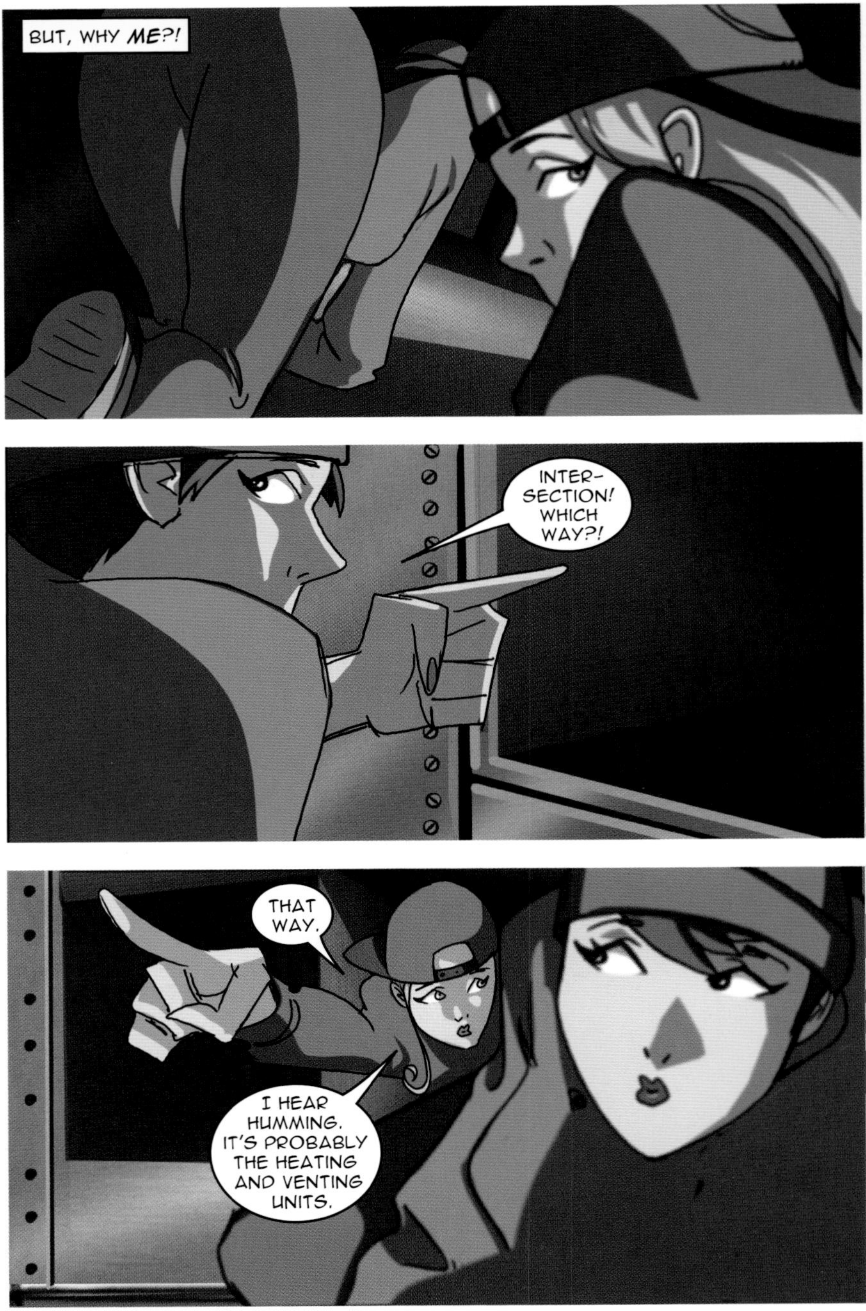
BUT, WHY *ME*?!
INTER-SECTION! WHICH WAY?!
THAT WAY.
I HEAR HUMMING. IT'S PROBABLY THE HEATING AND VENTING UNITS.

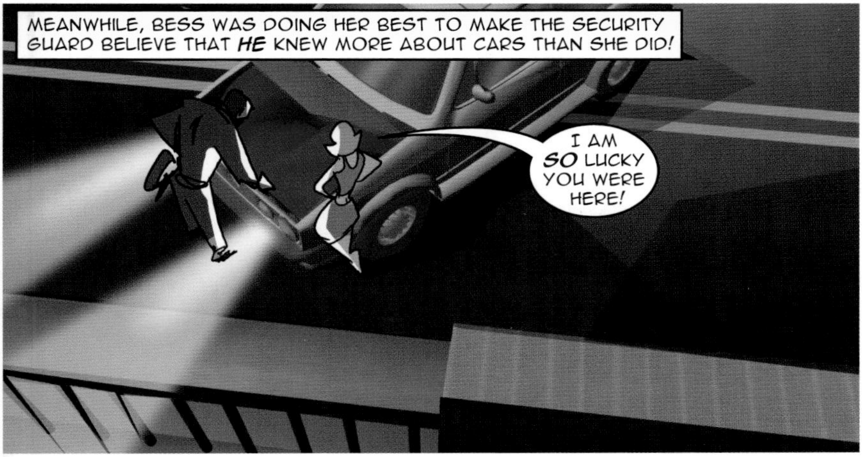

MEANWHILE, BESS WAS DOING HER BEST TO MAKE THE SECURITY GUARD BELIEVE THAT HE KNEW MORE ABOUT CARS THAN SHE DID!
I AM SO LUCKY YOU WERE HERE!

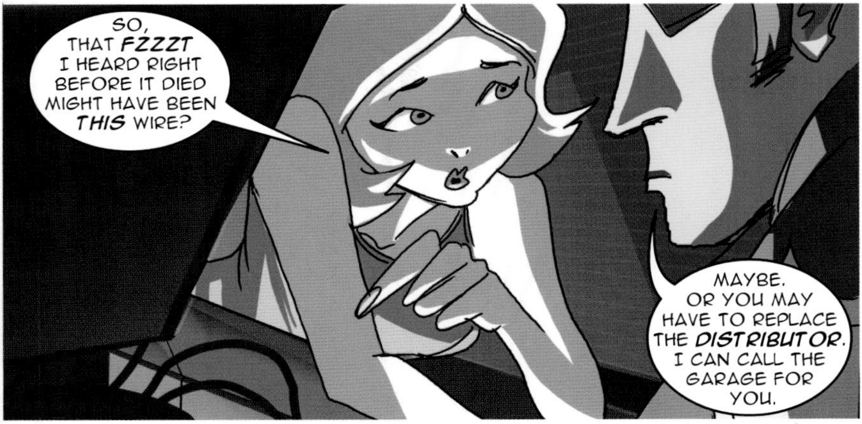

SO, THAT FZZZT I HEARD RIGHT BEFORE IT DIED MIGHT HAVE BEEN THIS WIRE?
MAYBE. OR YOU MAY HAVE TO REPLACE THE DISTRIBUTOR. I CAN CALL THE GARAGE FOR YOU.

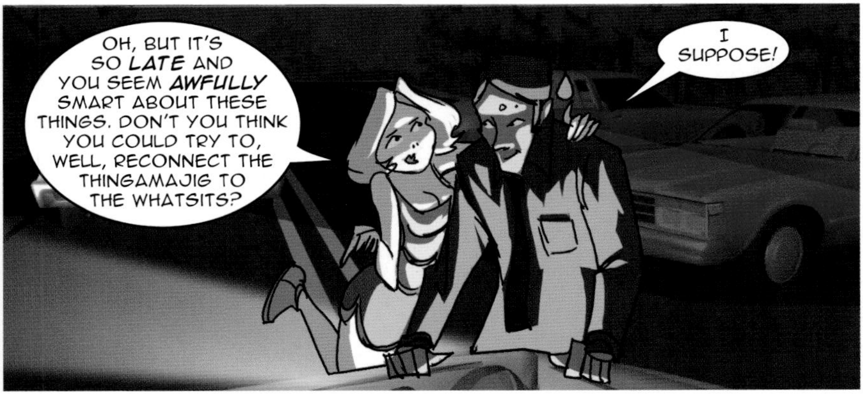

OH, BUT IT'S SO LATE AND YOU SEEM AWFULLY SMART ABOUT THESE THINGS. DON'T YOU THINK YOU COULD TRY TO, WELL, RECONNECT THE THINGAMAJIG TO THE WHATSITS?
I SUPPOSE!

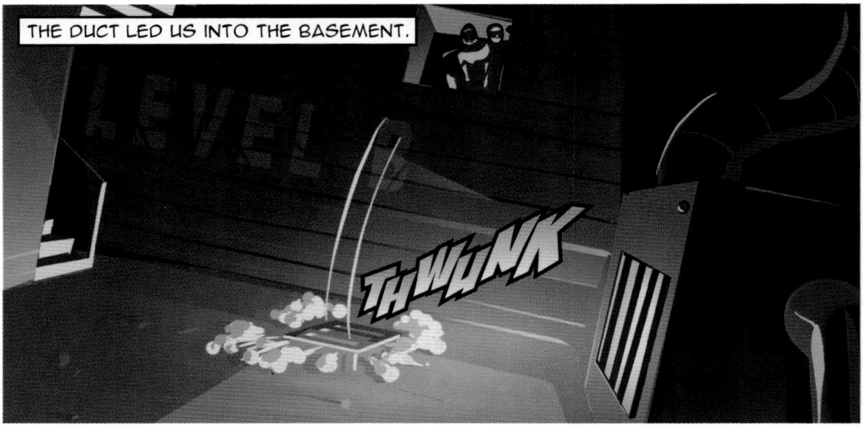
THE DUCT LED US INTO THE BASEMENT.
THWUNK

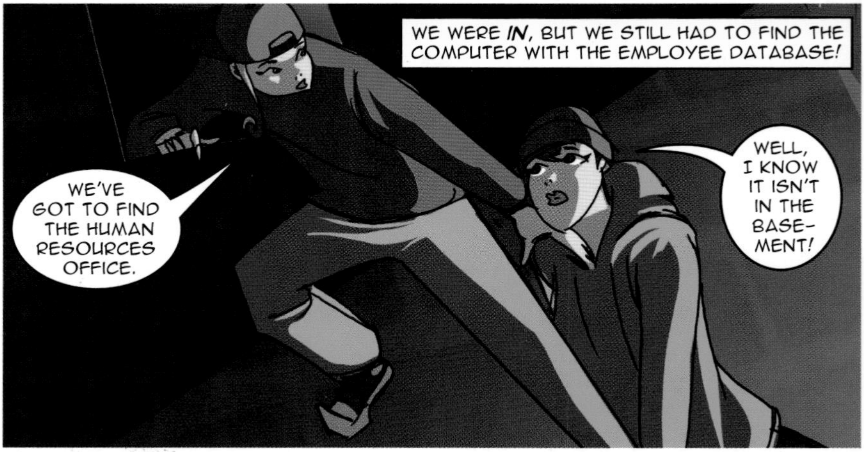
WE WERE *IN*, BUT WE STILL HAD TO FIND THE COMPUTER WITH THE EMPLOYEE DATABASE!
WE'VE GOT TO FIND THE HUMAN RESOURCES OFFICE.
WELL, I KNOW IT ISN'T IN THE BASE-MENT!

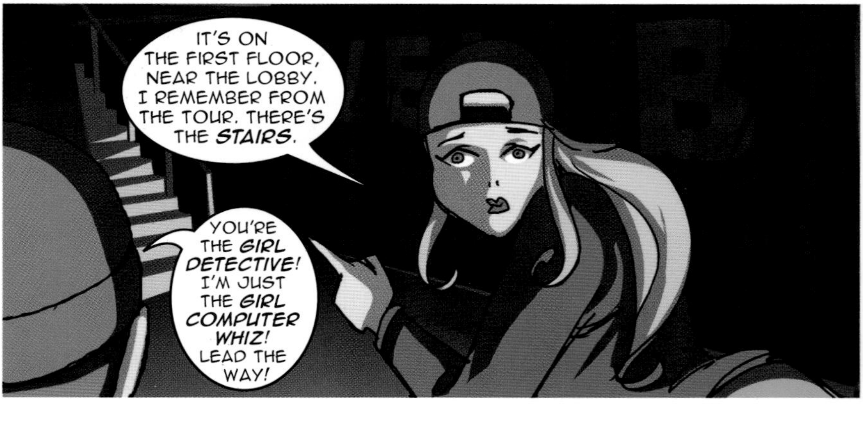
IT'S ON THE FIRST FLOOR, NEAR THE LOBBY. I REMEMBER FROM THE TOUR. THERE'S THE ***STAIRS***.
YOU'RE THE ***GIRL DETECTIVE***! I'M JUST THE ***GIRL COMPUTER WHIZ***! LEAD THE WAY!

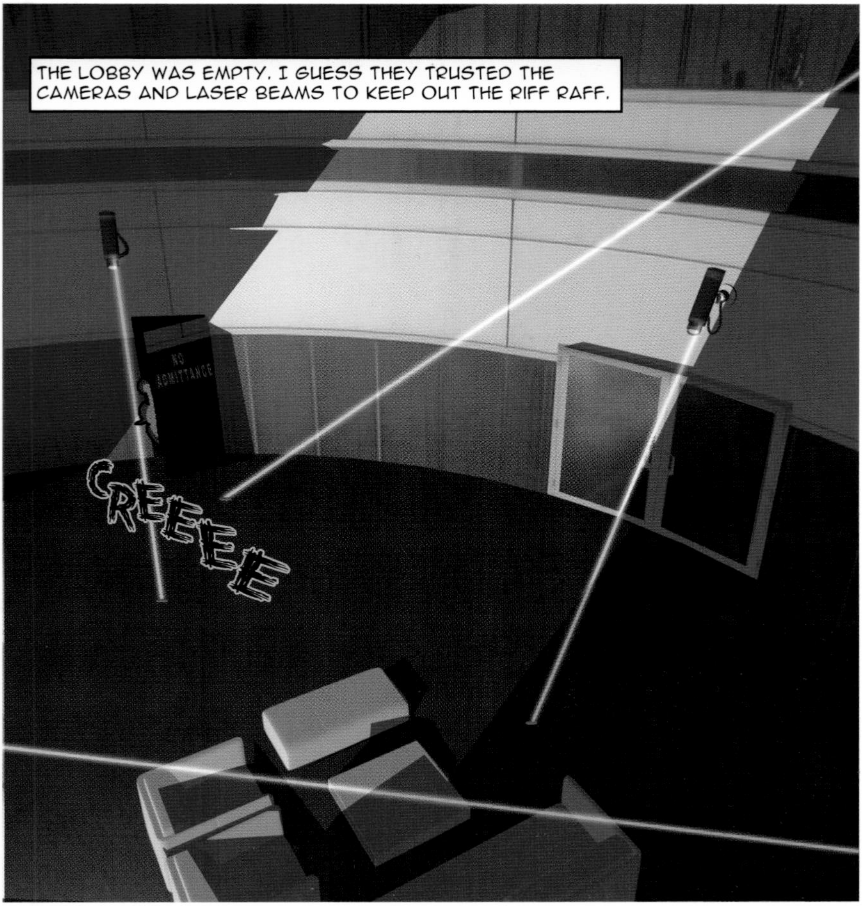
THE LOBBY WAS EMPTY. I GUESS THEY TRUSTED THE CAMERAS AND LASER BEAMS TO KEEP OUT THE RIFF RAFF.
NO ADMITTANCE
CREEEE

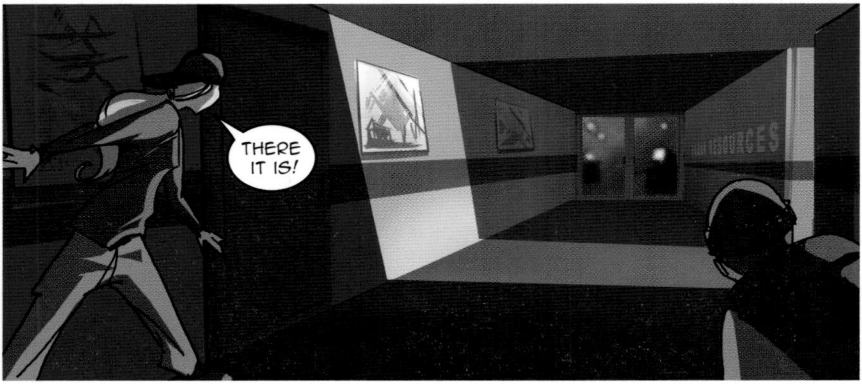
THERE IT IS!
RESOURCES

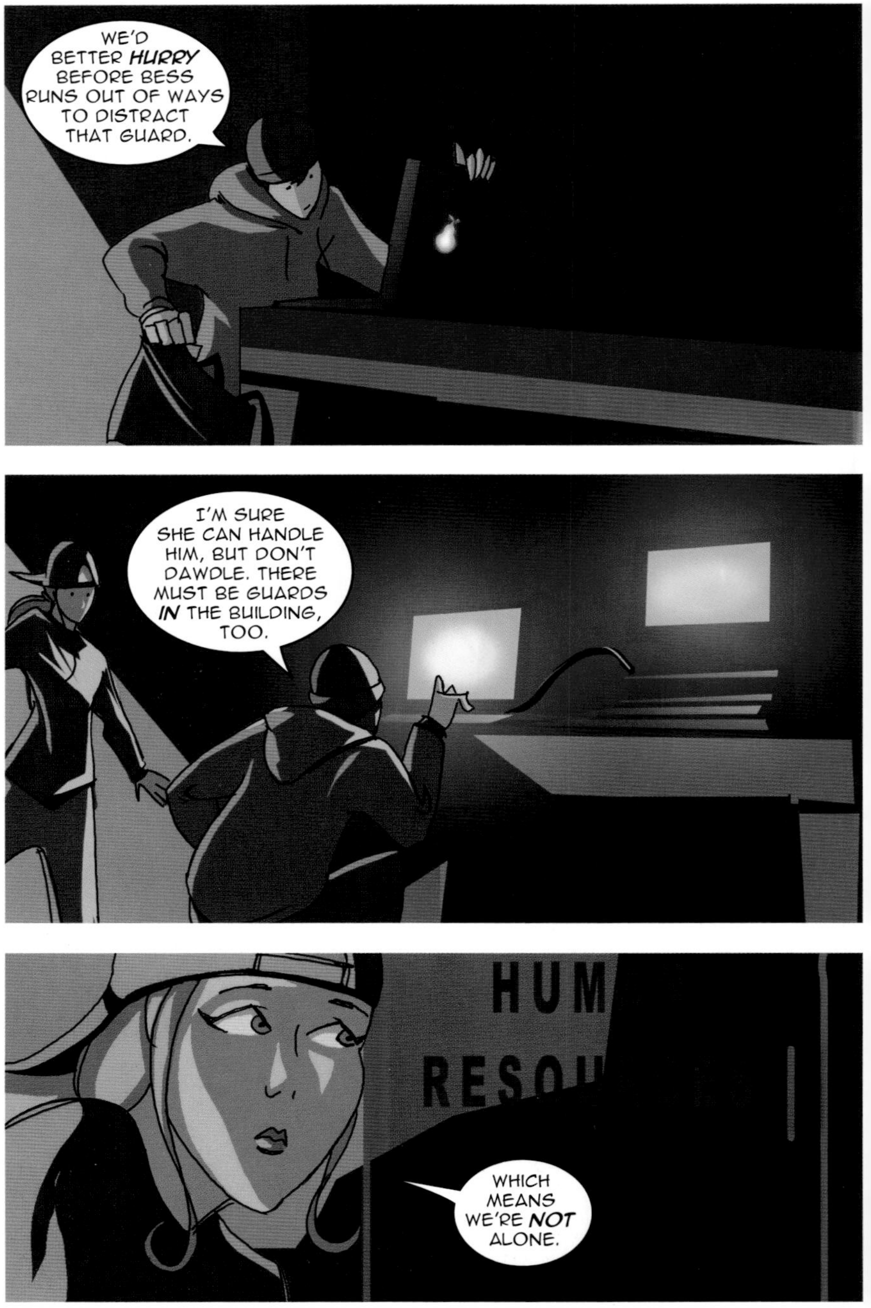
WE'D BETTER ***HURRY*** BEFORE BESS RUNS OUT OF WAYS TO DISTRACT THAT GUARD.
I'M SURE SHE CAN HANDLE HIM, BUT DON'T DAWDLE. THERE MUST BE GUARDS ***IN*** THE BUILDING, TOO.
HUM
RESO
WHICH MEANS WE'RE ***NOT*** ALONE.

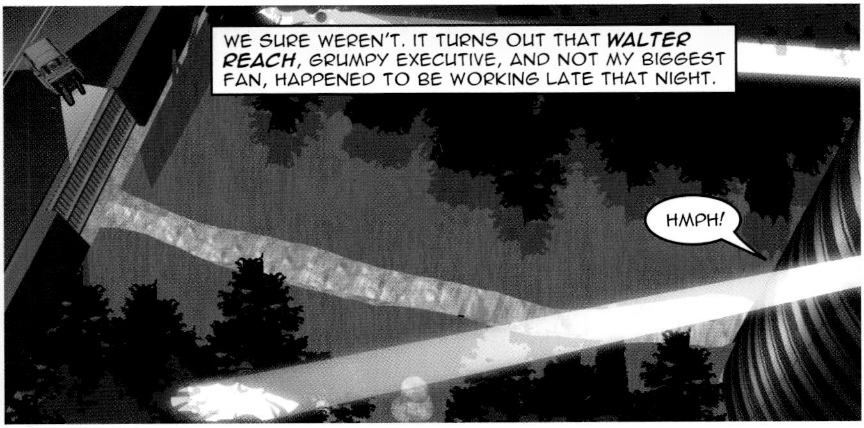
WE SURE WEREN'T. IT TURNS OUT THAT WALTER REACH, GRUMPY EXECUTIVE, AND NOT MY BIGGEST FAN, HAPPENED TO BE WORKING LATE THAT NIGHT.
HMPH!

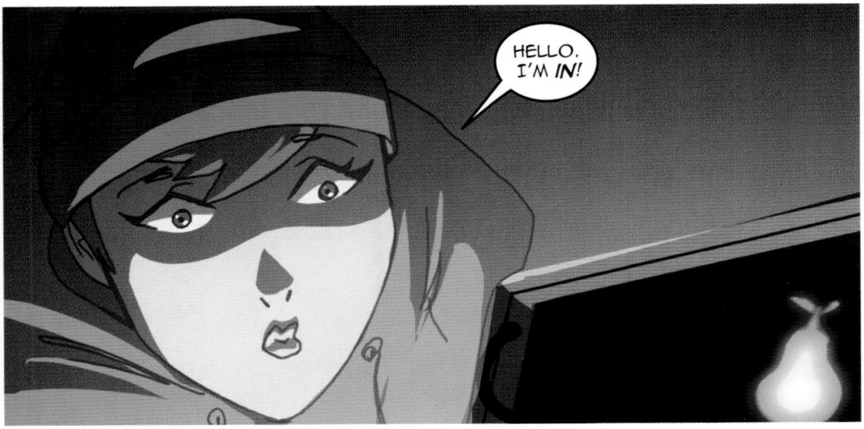
HELLO. I'M IN!

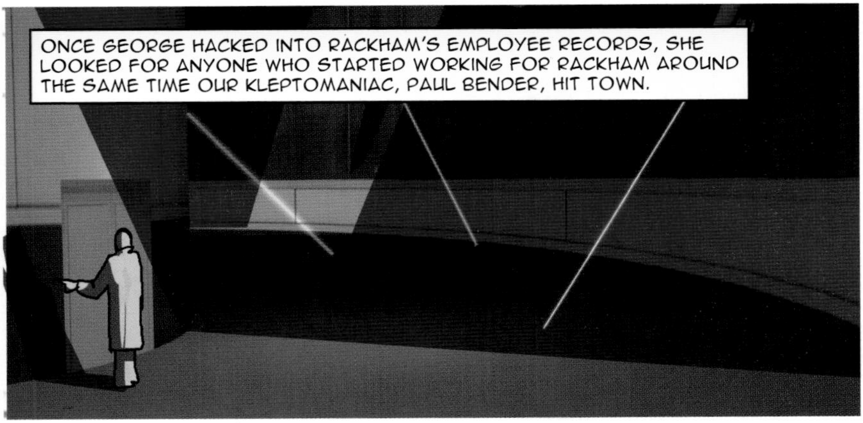
ONCE GEORGE HACKED INTO RACKHAM'S EMPLOYEE RECORDS, SHE LOOKED FOR ANYONE WHO STARTED WORKING FOR RACKHAM AROUND THE SAME TIME OUR KLEPTOMANIAC, PAUL BENDER, HIT TOWN.

THEN, WE JUST NEEDED TO SCAN THE PHOTO ID'S TO FIND ONE WHO LOOKED LIKE BINDER.

I BELIEVE WE HAVE A *WINNER!*

HAH!

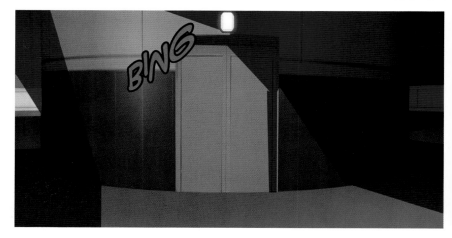

BING

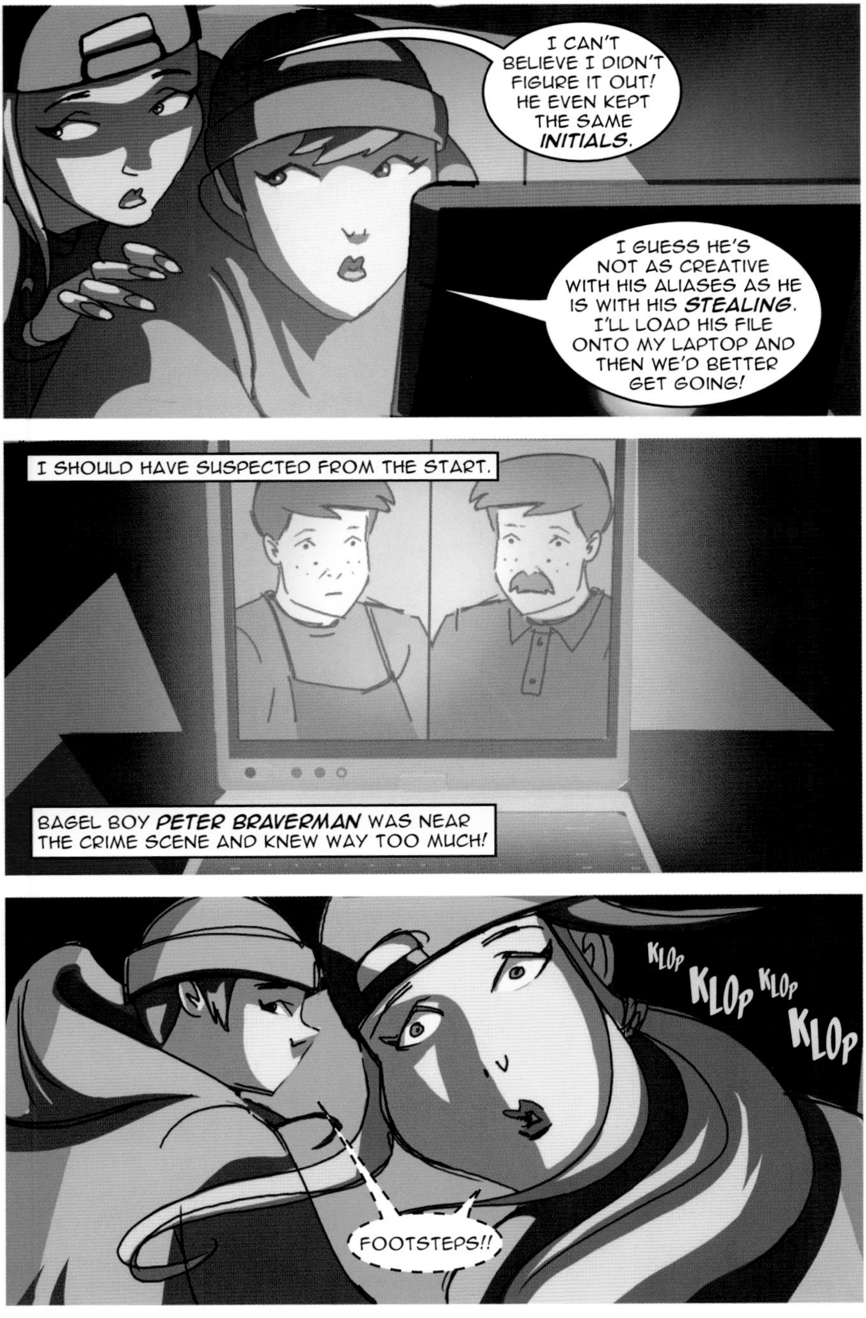
I CAN'T BELIEVE I DIDN'T FIGURE IT OUT! HE EVEN KEPT THE SAME INITIALS.
I GUESS HE'S NOT AS CREATIVE WITH HIS ALIASES AS HE IS WITH HIS STEALING. I'LL LOAD HIS FILE ONTO MY LAPTOP AND THEN WE'D BETTER GET GOING!
I SHOULD HAVE SUSPECTED FROM THE START.
BAGEL BOY PETER BRAVERMAN WAS NEAR THE CRIME SCENE AND KNEW WAY TOO MUCH!
KLOP KLOP KLOP KLOP
FOOTSTEPS!!

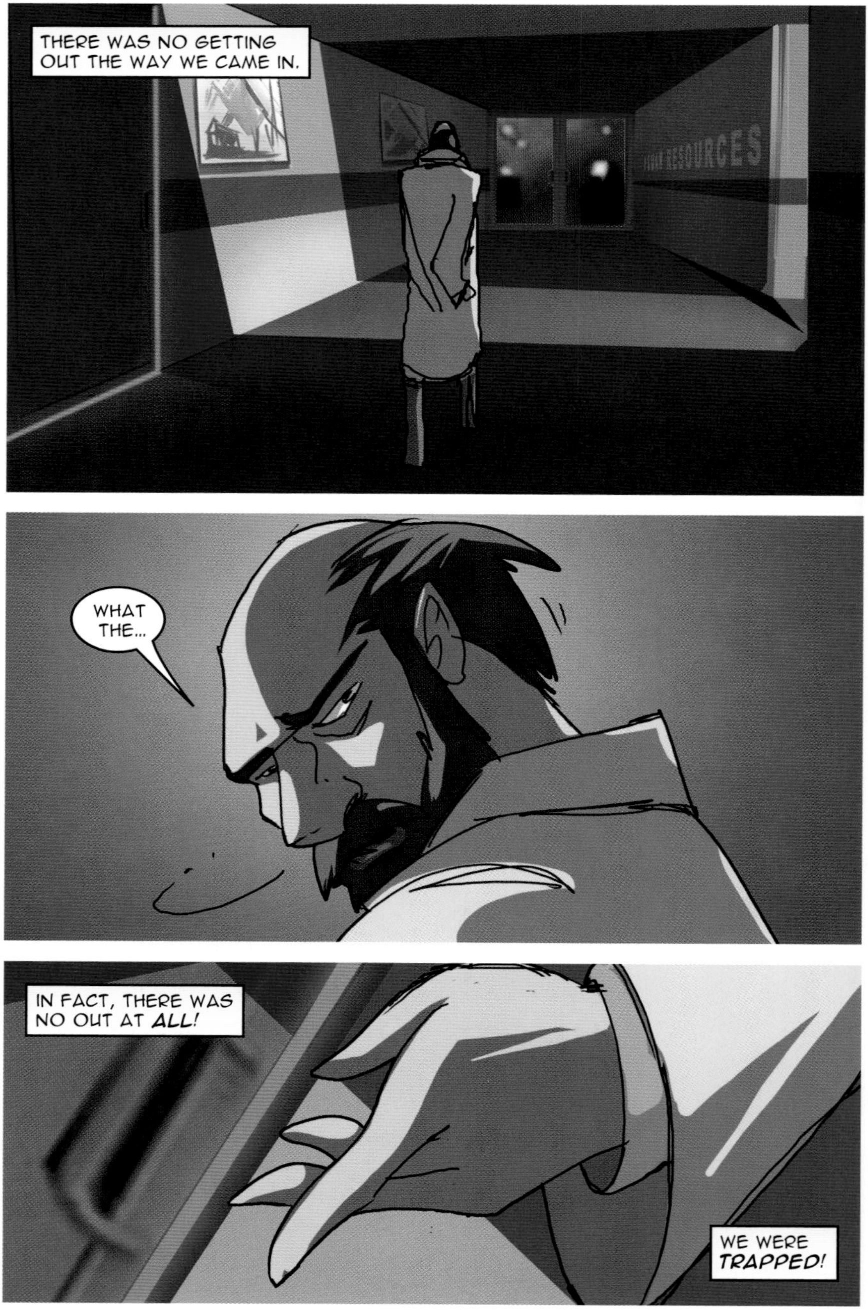
THERE WAS NO GETTING OUT THE WAY WE CAME IN.
RESOURCES
WHAT THE...
IN FACT, THERE WAS NO OUT AT ***ALL!***
WE WERE ***TRAPPED!***

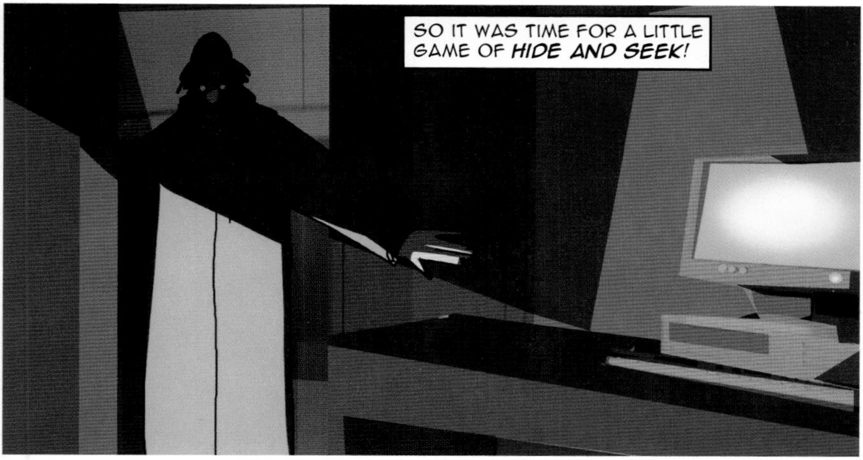
SO IT WAS TIME FOR A LITTLE GAME OF HIDE AND SEEK!

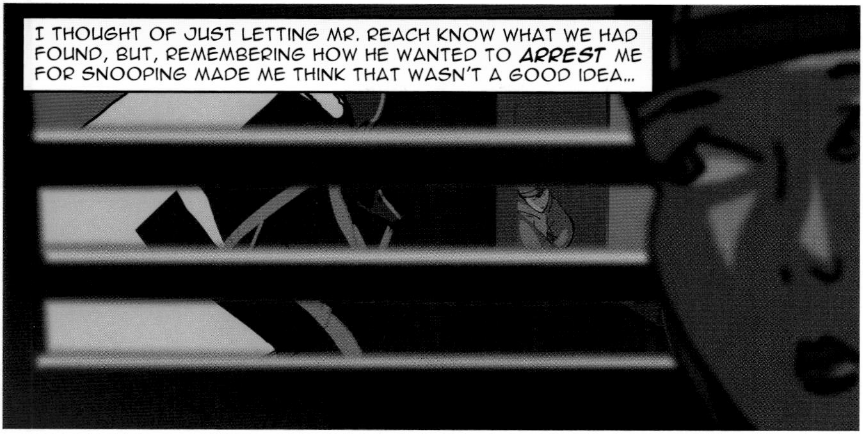
I THOUGHT OF JUST LETTING MR. REACH KNOW WHAT WE HAD FOUND, BUT, REMEMBERING HOW HE WANTED TO ARREST ME FOR SNOOPING MADE ME THINK THAT WASN'T A GOOD IDEA...

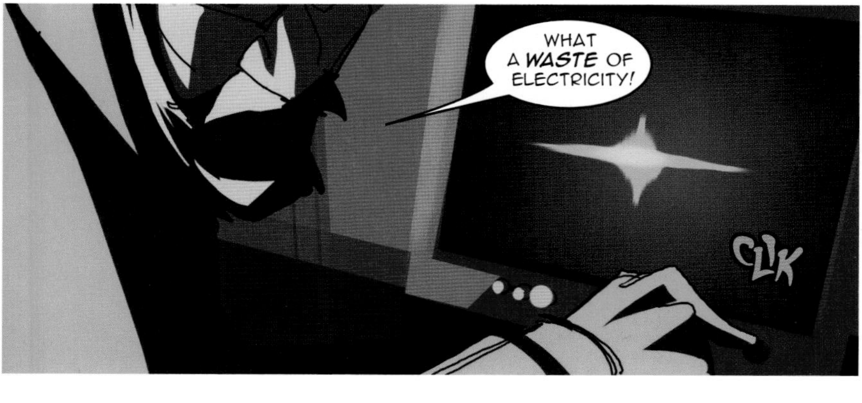
WHAT A WASTE OF ELECTRICITY!
CLIK

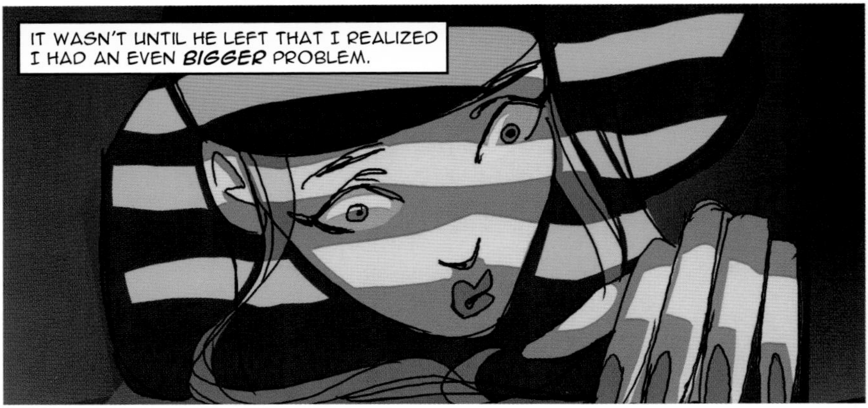
IT WASN'T UNTIL HE LEFT THAT I REALIZED I HAD AN EVEN BIGGER PROBLEM.

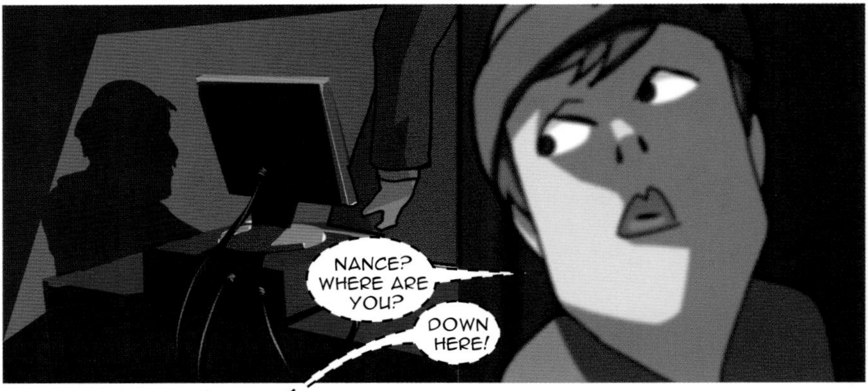
NANCE? WHERE ARE YOU?
DOWN HERE!

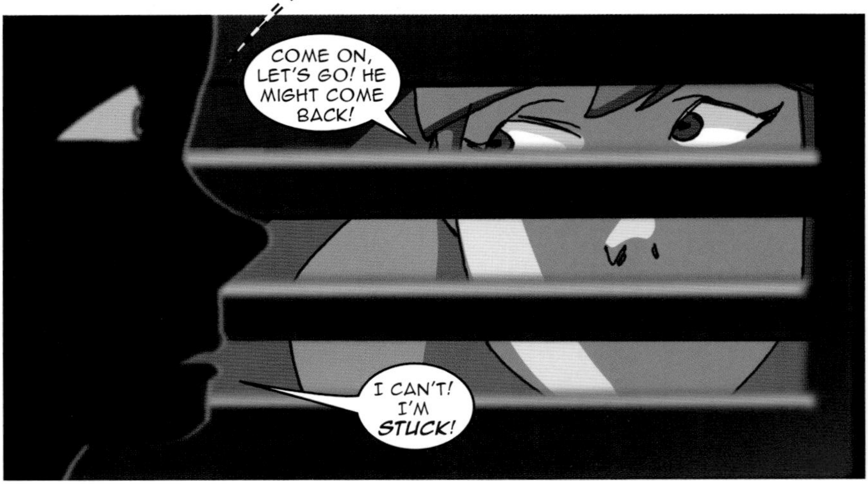
COME ON, LET'S GO! HE MIGHT COME BACK!
I CAN'T! I'M STUCK!

STUCK? HOW'D YOU GET IN? ~UNGH~
OW! I WENT IN BACKWARDS SO I COULD WATCH WHAT WAS GOING ON! NOW I CAN'T GO FORWARD!
SO KEEP GOING BACKWARDS! IT'S GOT TO COME OUT SOME-WHERE!
EASIER SAID THAN DONE! THERE'S SOME KIND OF DROP BEHIND ME! IT PROBABLY LEADS TO THE BASEMENT!
YOU LET GO AND I'LL TRY TO WRIGGLE DOWN. I'LL MEET YOU DOWN-STAIRS!
WAIT! WHAT IF YOU GET STUCK AGAIN ALONG THE WAY?

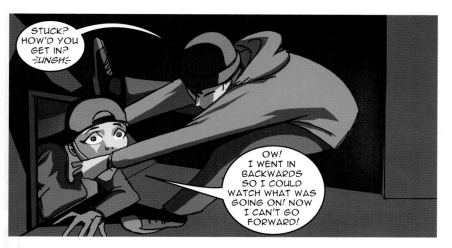

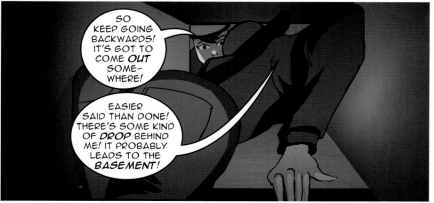

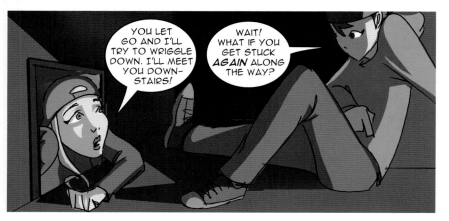

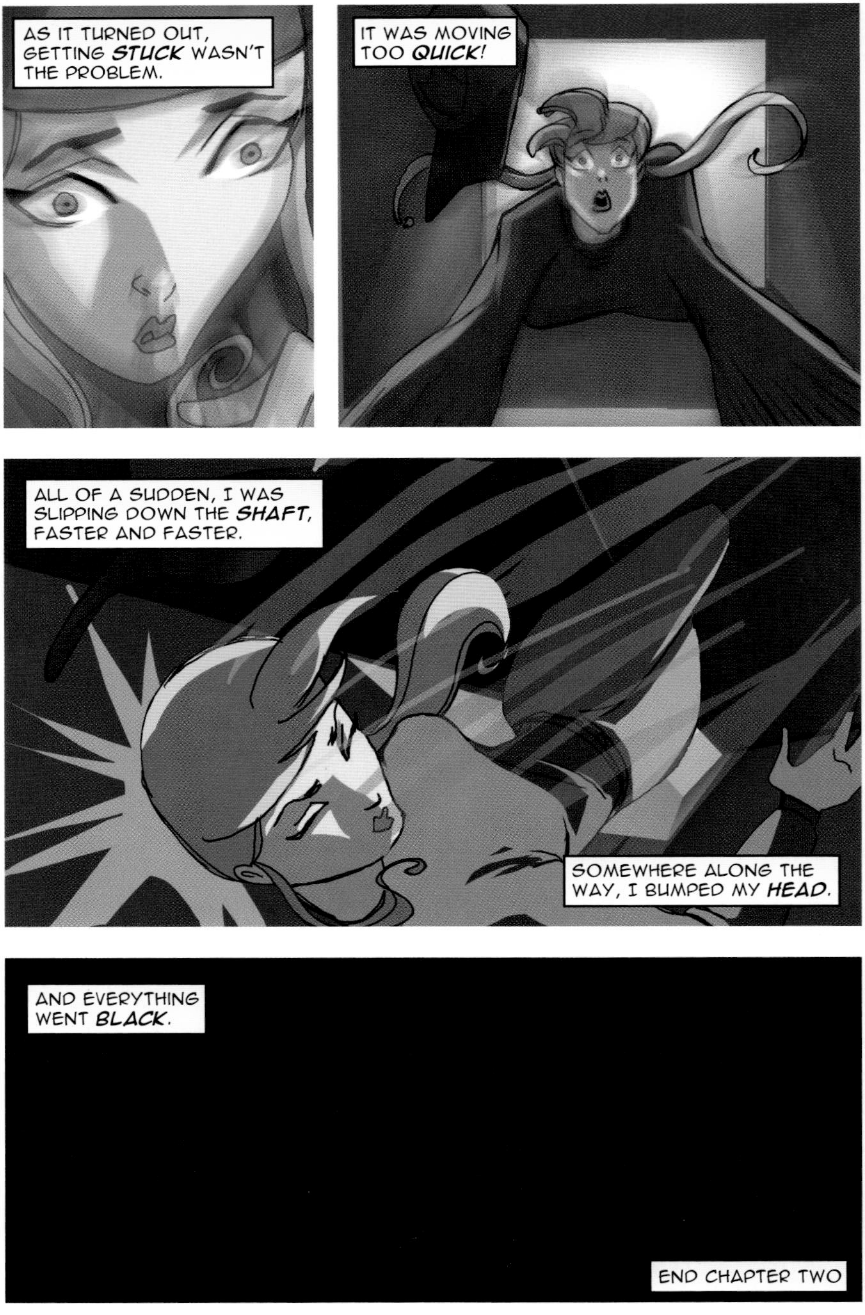
AS IT TURNED OUT, GETTING STUCK WASN'T THE PROBLEM.
IT WAS MOVING TOO QUICK!
ALL OF A SUDDEN, I WAS SLIPPING DOWN THE SHAFT, FASTER AND FASTER.
SOMEWHERE ALONG THE WAY, I BUMPED MY HEAD.
AND EVERYTHING WENT BLACK.
END CHAPTER TWO

CHAPTER THREE: OUT OF THE VENT, INTO THE FIRE

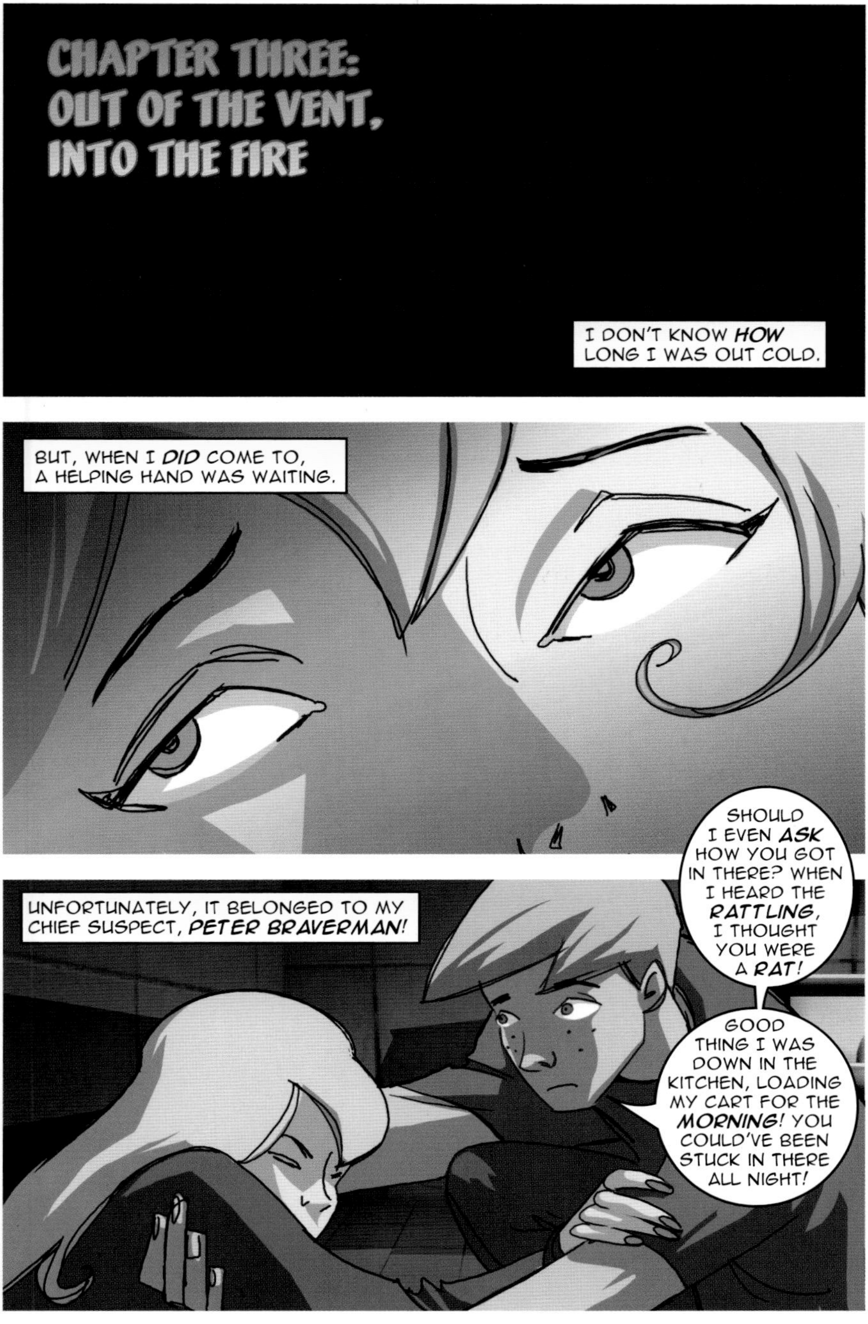
I DON'T KNOW *HOW* LONG I WAS OUT COLD.
BUT, WHEN I *DID* COME TO, A HELPING HAND WAS WAITING.
UNFORTUNATELY, IT BELONGED TO MY CHIEF SUSPECT, *PETER BRAVERMAN*!
SHOULD I EVEN *ASK* HOW YOU GOT IN THERE? WHEN I HEARD THE *RATTLING*, I THOUGHT YOU WERE A *RAT*!
GOOD THING I WAS DOWN IN THE KITCHEN, LOADING MY CART FOR THE *MORNING*! YOU COULD'VE BEEN STUCK IN THERE ALL NIGHT!

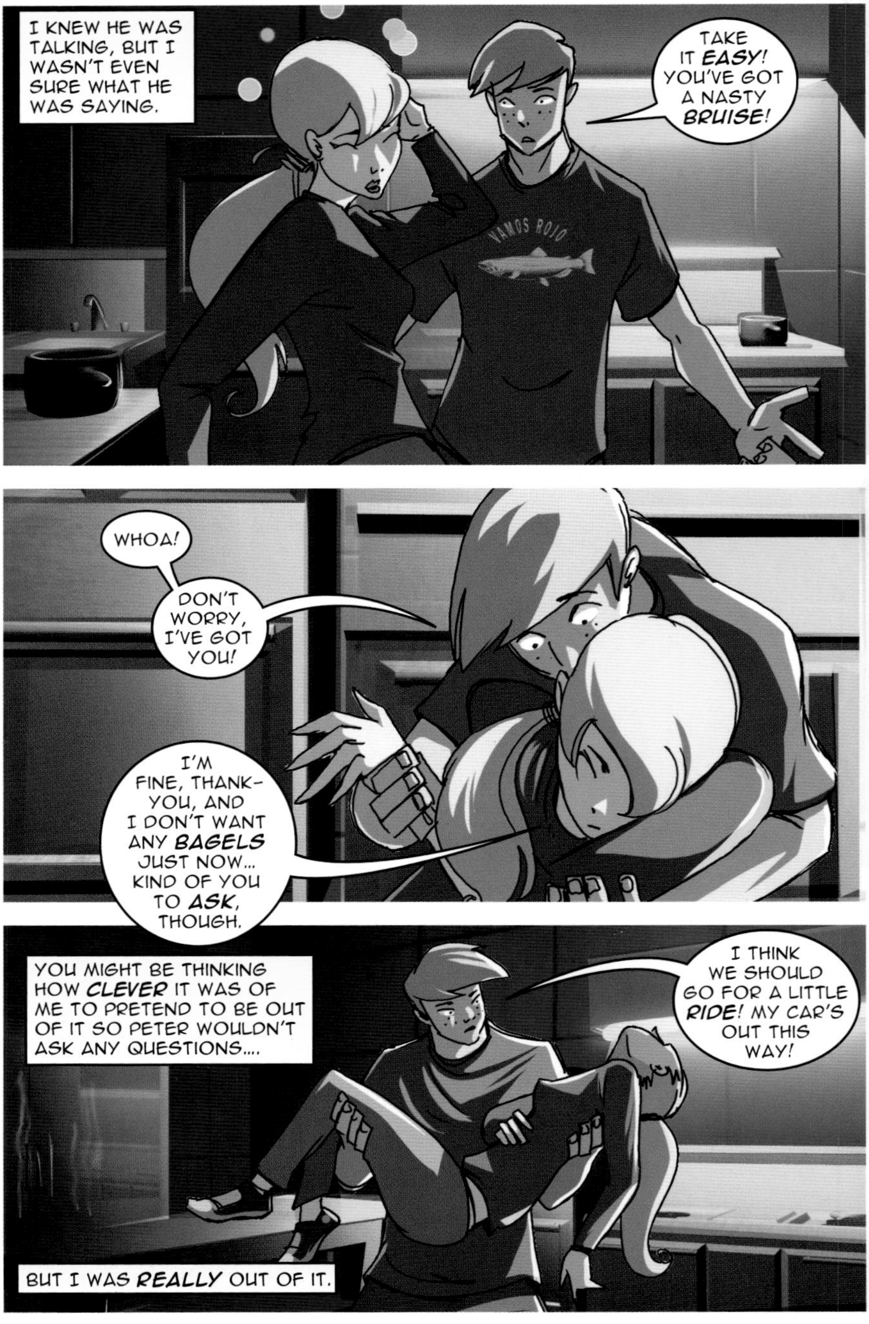
I KNEW HE WAS TALKING, BUT I WASN'T EVEN SURE WHAT HE WAS SAYING.
TAKE IT EASY! YOU'VE GOT A NASTY BRUISE!
VAMOS ROJO
WHOA!
DON'T WORRY, I'VE GOT YOU!
I'M FINE, THANK-YOU, AND I DON'T WANT ANY BAGELS JUST NOW... KIND OF YOU TO ASK, THOUGH.
YOU MIGHT BE THINKING HOW CLEVER IT WAS OF ME TO PRETEND TO BE OUT OF IT SO PETER WOULDN'T ASK ANY QUESTIONS....
I THINK WE SHOULD GO FOR A LITTLE RIDE! MY CAR'S OUT THIS WAY!
BUT I WAS REALLY OUT OF IT.

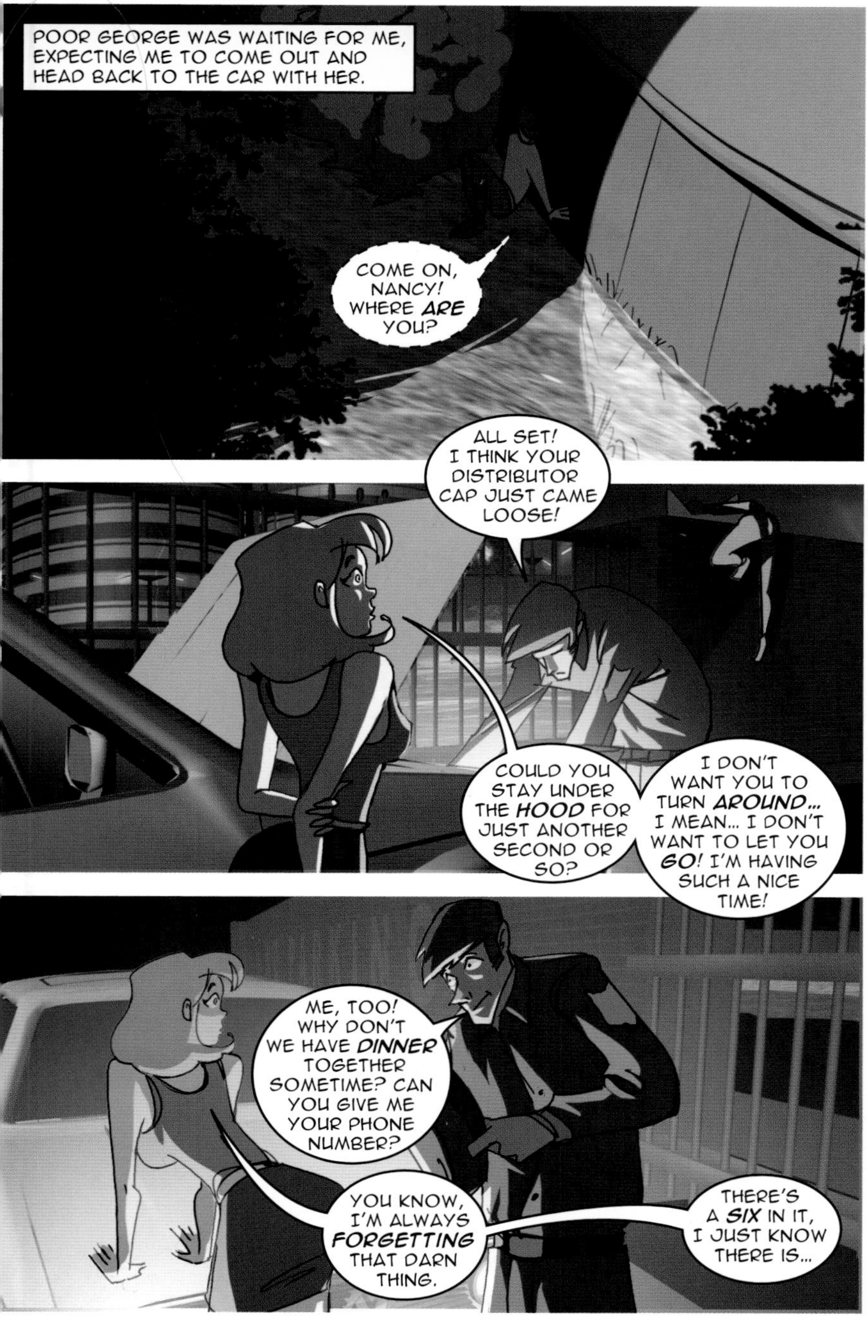
POOR GEORGE WAS WAITING FOR ME, EXPECTING ME TO COME OUT AND HEAD BACK TO THE CAR WITH HER.
COME ON, NANCY! WHERE ARE YOU?
ALL SET! I THINK YOUR DISTRIBUTOR CAP JUST CAME LOOSE!
COULD YOU STAY UNDER THE HOOD FOR JUST ANOTHER SECOND OR SO?
I DON'T WANT YOU TO TURN AROUND... I MEAN... I DON'T WANT TO LET YOU GO! I'M HAVING SUCH A NICE TIME!
ME, TOO! WHY DON'T WE HAVE DINNER TOGETHER SOMETIME? CAN YOU GIVE ME YOUR PHONE NUMBER?
YOU KNOW, I'M ALWAYS FORGETTING THAT DARN THING.
THERE'S A SIX IN IT, I JUST KNOW THERE IS...

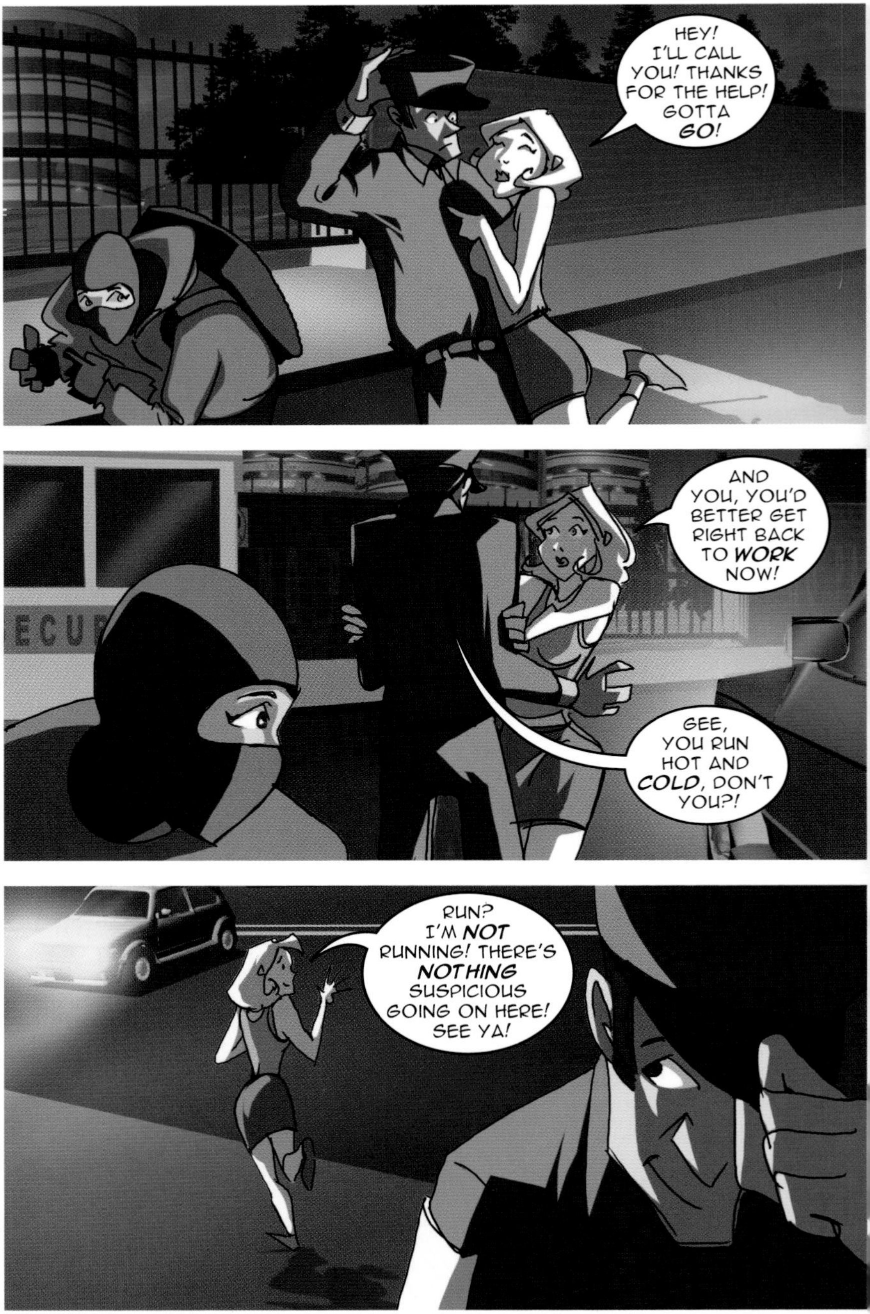
HEY! I'LL CALL YOU! THANKS FOR THE HELP! GOTTA **GO**!
AND YOU, YOU'D BETTER GET RIGHT BACK TO **WORK** NOW!
GEE, YOU RUN HOT AND **COLD**, DON'T YOU?!
RUN? I'M **NOT** RUNNING! THERE'S **NOTHING** SUSPICIOUS GOING ON HERE! SEE YA!

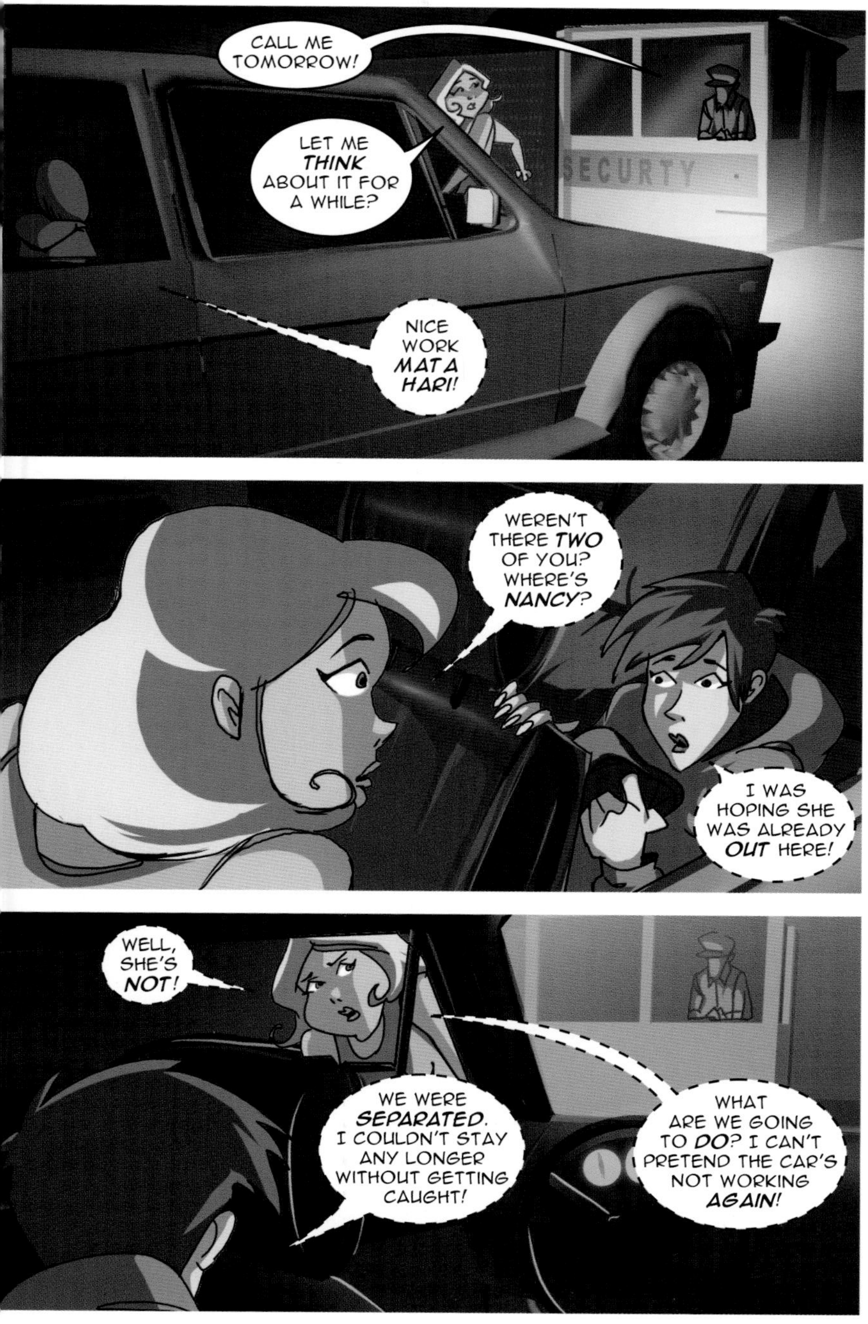
CALL ME TOMORROW!
LET ME THINK ABOUT IT FOR A WHILE?
NICE WORK MATA HARI!
SECURTY
WEREN'T THERE TWO OF YOU? WHERE'S NANCY?
I WAS HOPING SHE WAS ALREADY OUT HERE!
WELL, SHE'S NOT!
WE WERE SEPARATED. I COULDN'T STAY ANY LONGER WITHOUT GETTING CAUGHT!
WHAT ARE WE GOING TO DO? I CAN'T PRETEND THE CAR'S NOT WORKING AGAIN!

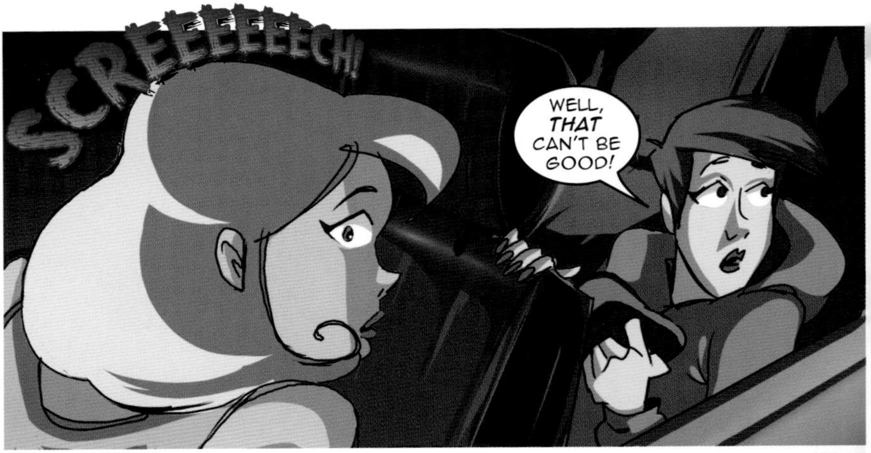
SCREEEEEECH!
WELL, THAT CAN'T BE GOOD!

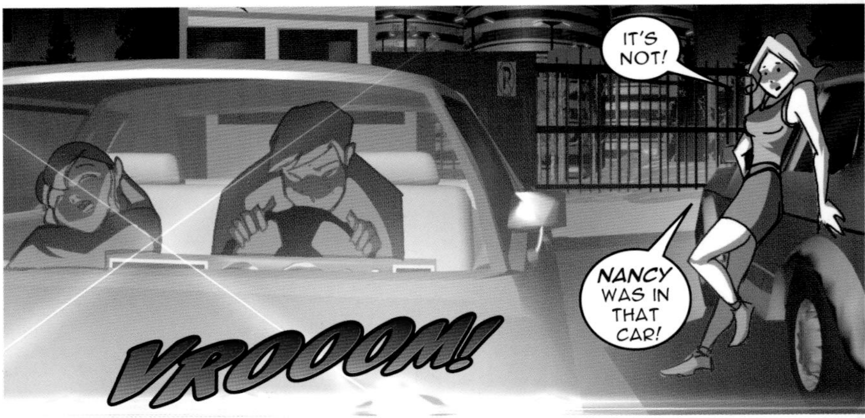
IT'S NOT!
NANCY WAS IN THAT CAR!
VROOOM!

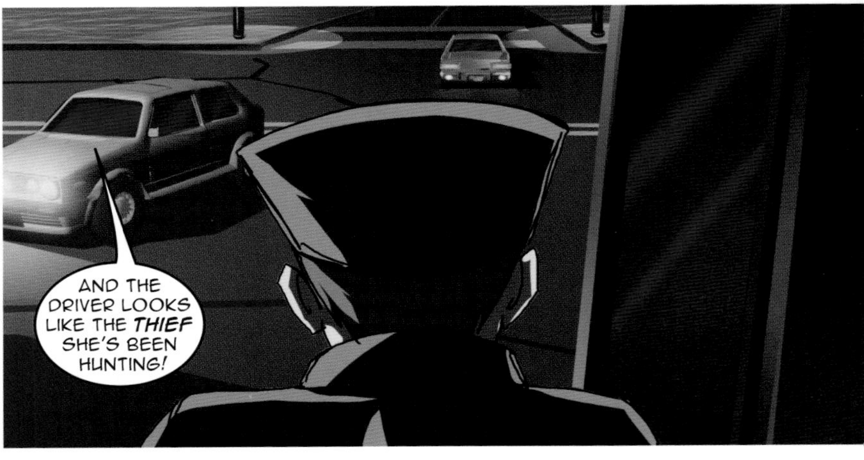
AND THE DRIVER LOOKS LIKE THE THIEF SHE'S BEEN HUNTING!

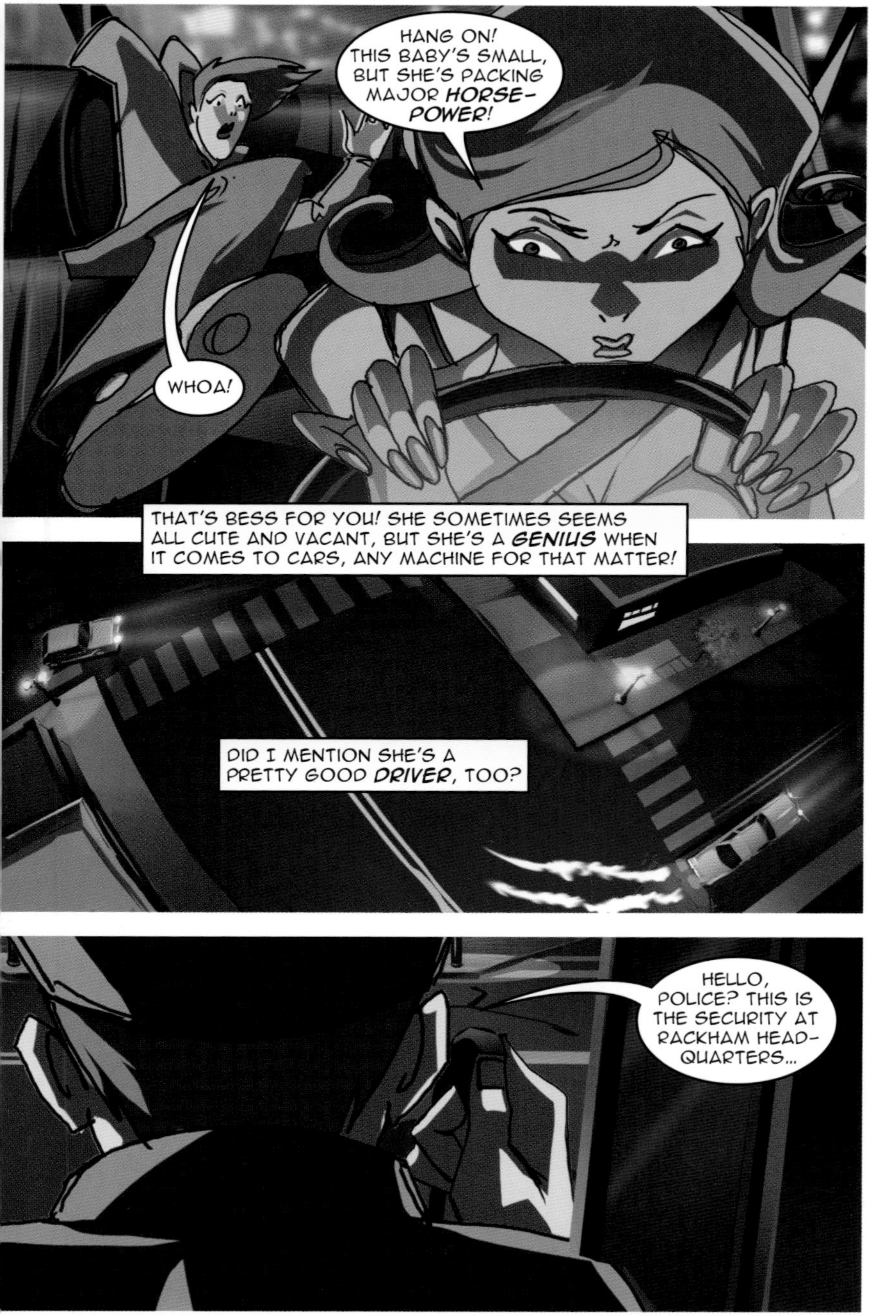
HANG ON! THIS BABY'S SMALL, BUT SHE'S PACKING MAJOR HORSE-POWER!
WHOA!
THAT'S BESS FOR YOU! SHE SOMETIMES SEEMS ALL CUTE AND VACANT, BUT SHE'S A GENIUS WHEN IT COMES TO CARS, ANY MACHINE FOR THAT MATTER!
DID I MENTION SHE'S A PRETTY GOOD DRIVER, TOO?
HELLO, POLICE? THIS IS THE SECURITY AT RACKHAM HEAD-QUARTERS...

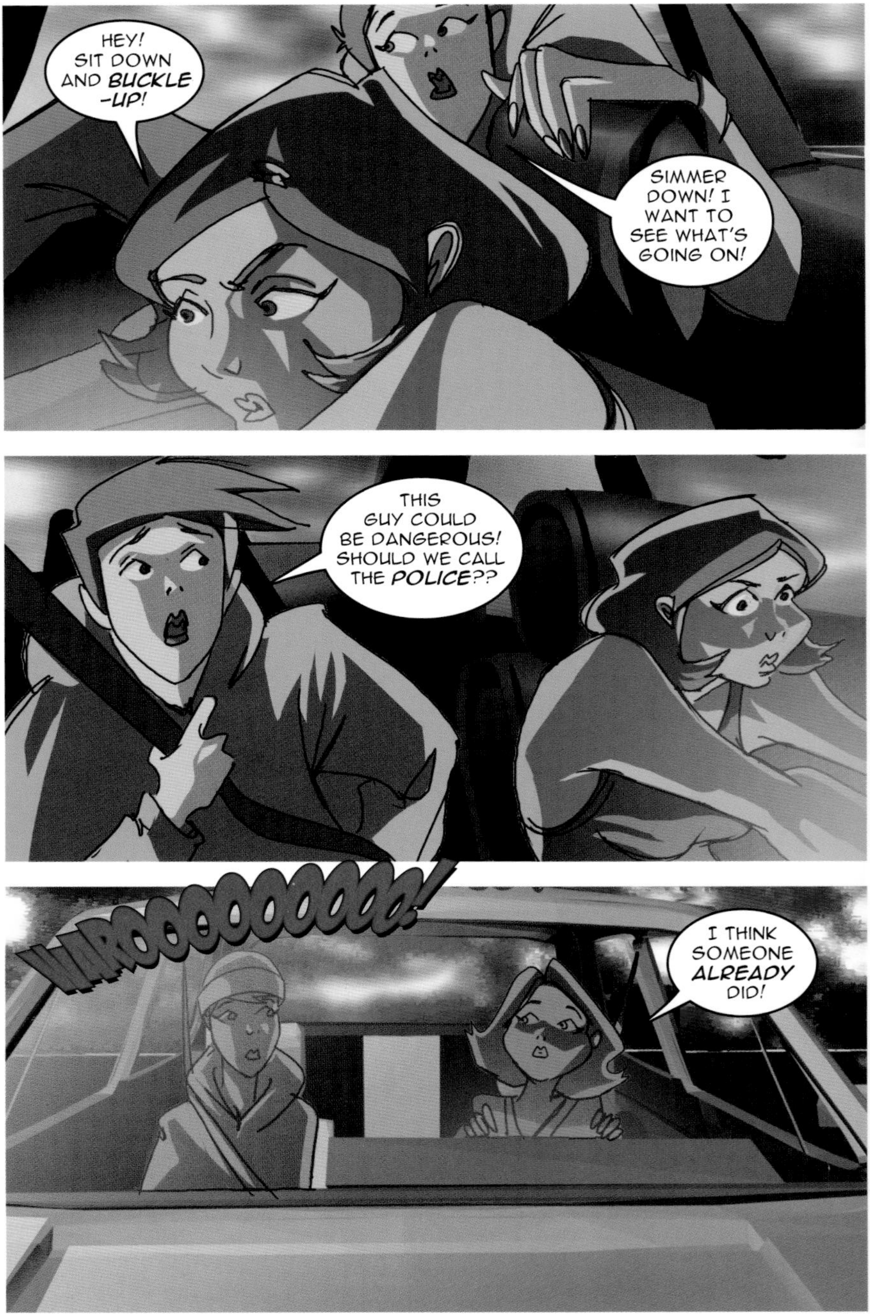
HEY! SIT DOWN AND BUCKLE -UP!
SIMMER DOWN! I WANT TO SEE WHAT'S GOING ON!
THIS GUY COULD BE DANGEROUS! SHOULD WE CALL THE POLICE??
WHROOOOOOOOOO!
I THINK SOMEONE ALREADY DID!

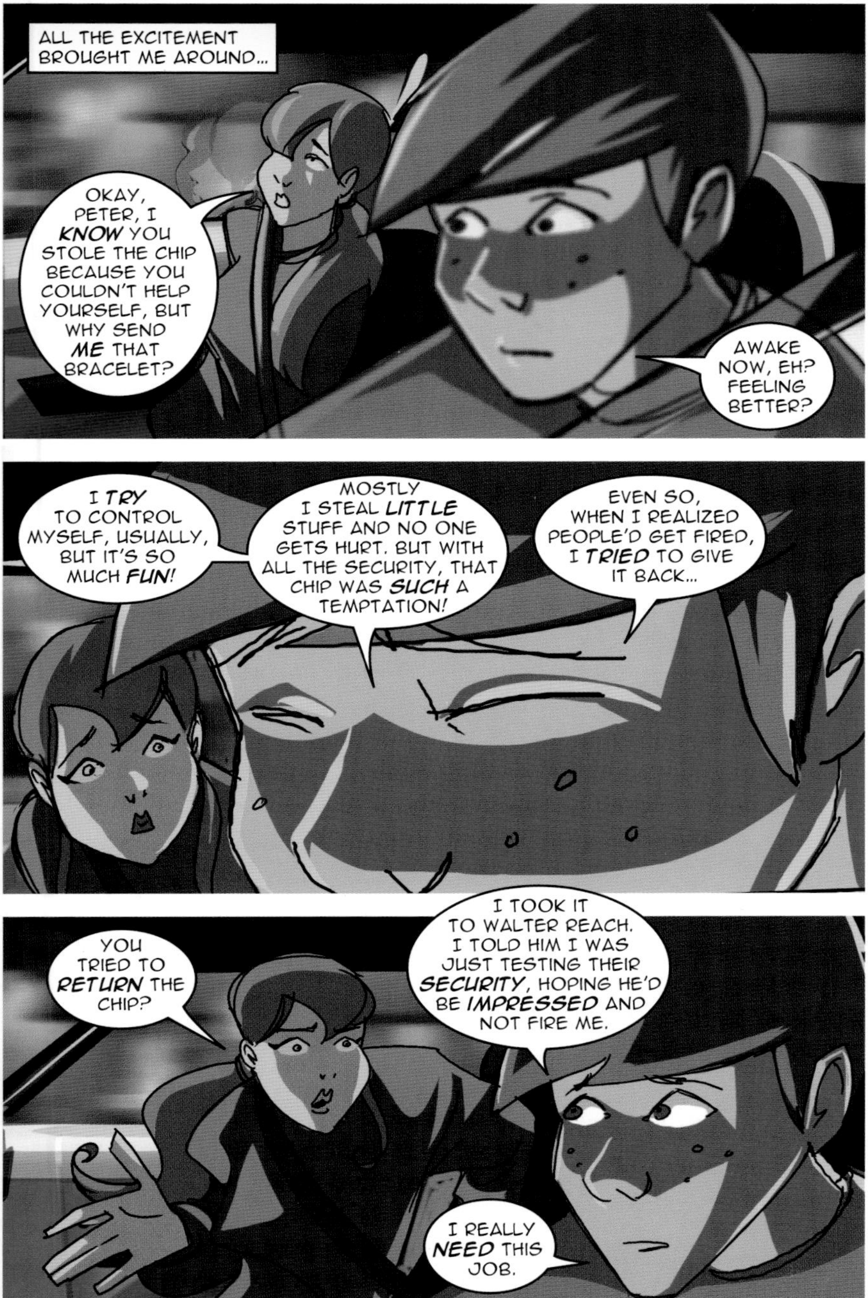
ALL THE EXCITEMENT BROUGHT ME AROUND...
OKAY, PETER, I KNOW YOU STOLE THE CHIP BECAUSE YOU COULDN'T HELP YOURSELF, BUT WHY SEND ME THAT BRACELET?
AWAKE NOW, EH? FEELING BETTER?
I TRY TO CONTROL MYSELF, USUALLY, BUT IT'S SO MUCH FUN!
MOSTLY I STEAL LITTLE STUFF AND NO ONE GETS HURT. BUT WITH ALL THE SECURITY, THAT CHIP WAS SUCH A TEMPTATION!
EVEN SO, WHEN I REALIZED PEOPLE'D GET FIRED, I TRIED TO GIVE IT BACK...
YOU TRIED TO RETURN THE CHIP?
I TOOK IT TO WALTER REACH. I TOLD HIM I WAS JUST TESTING THEIR SECURITY, HOPING HE'D BE IMPRESSED AND NOT FIRE ME.
I REALLY NEED THIS JOB.

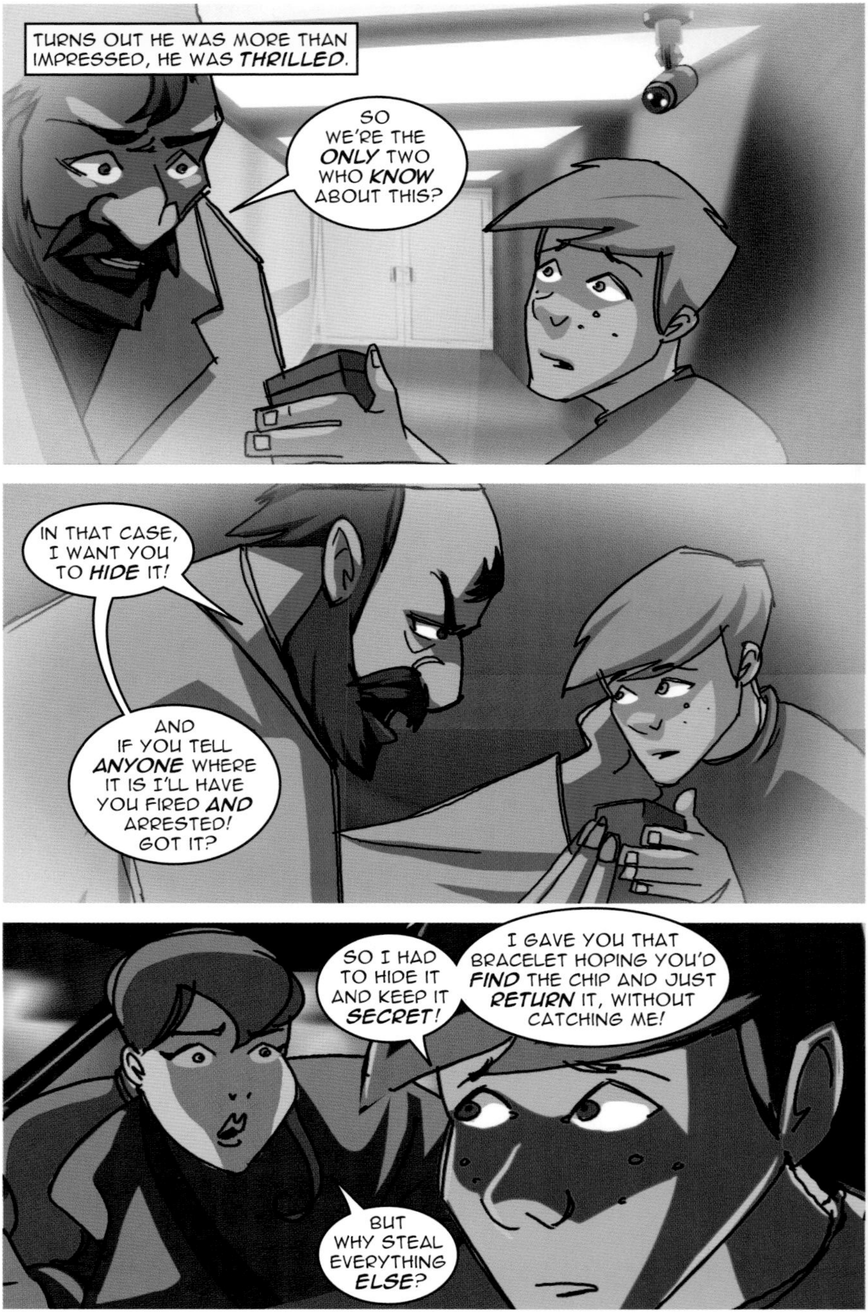
TURNS OUT HE WAS MORE THAN IMPRESSED, HE WAS THRILLED.
SO WE'RE THE ONLY TWO WHO KNOW ABOUT THIS?
IN THAT CASE, I WANT YOU TO HIDE IT!
AND IF YOU TELL ANYONE WHERE IT IS I'LL HAVE YOU FIRED AND ARRESTED! GOT IT?
SO I HAD TO HIDE IT AND KEEP IT SECRET!
I GAVE YOU THAT BRACELET HOPING YOU'D FIND THE CHIP AND JUST RETURN IT, WITHOUT CATCHING ME!
BUT WHY STEAL EVERYTHING ELSE?

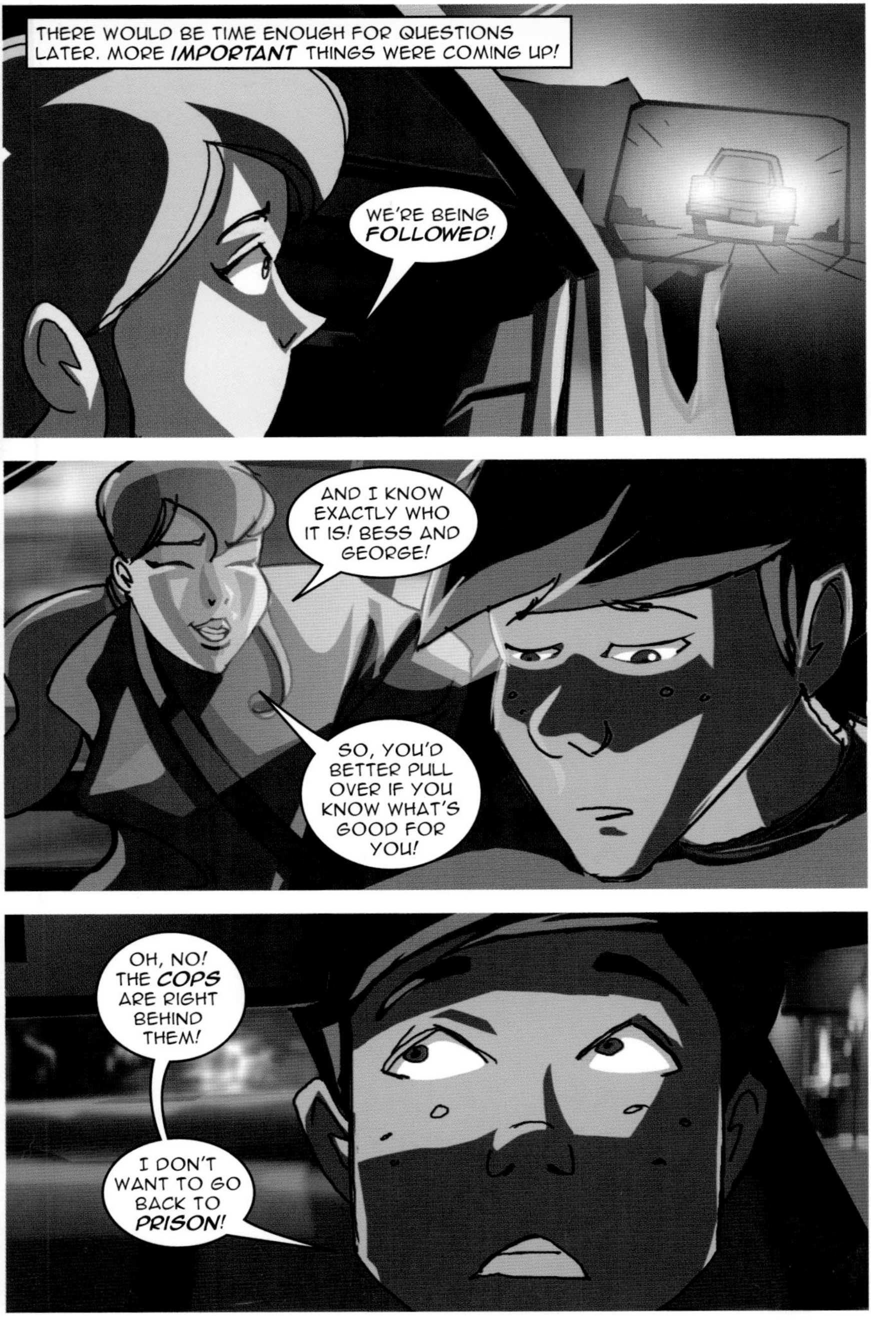
THERE WOULD BE TIME ENOUGH FOR QUESTIONS LATER. MORE IMPORTANT THINGS WERE COMING UP!
WE'RE BEING FOLLOWED!
AND I KNOW EXACTLY WHO IT IS! BESS AND GEORGE!
SO, YOU'D BETTER PULL OVER IF YOU KNOW WHAT'S GOOD FOR YOU!
OH, NO! THE COPS ARE RIGHT BEHIND THEM!
I DON'T WANT TO GO BACK TO PRISON!

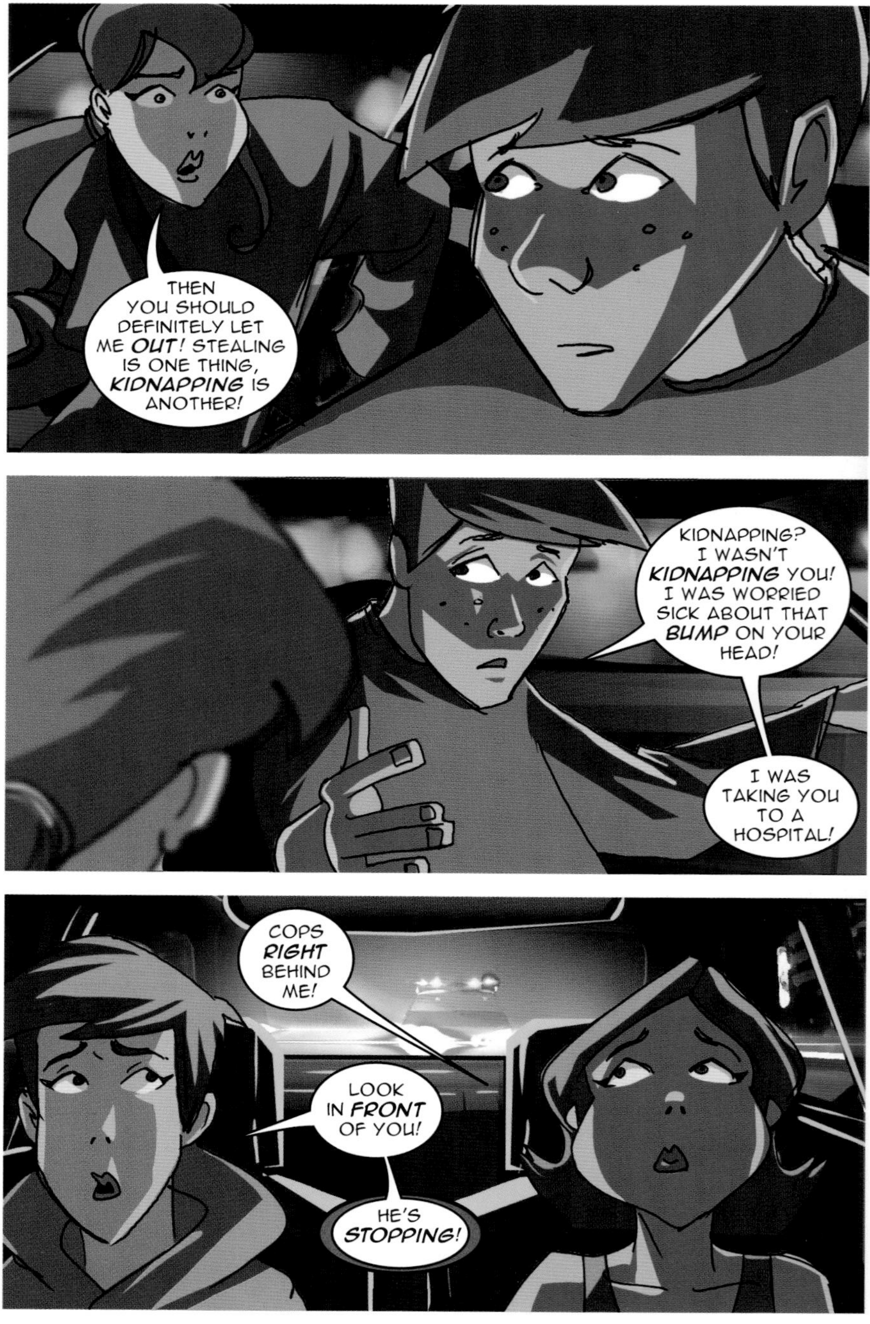
THEN YOU SHOULD DEFINITELY LET ME OUT! STEALING IS ONE THING, KIDNAPPING IS ANOTHER!
KIDNAPPING? I WASN'T KIDNAPPING YOU! I WAS WORRIED SICK ABOUT THAT BUMP ON YOUR HEAD!
I WAS TAKING YOU TO A HOSPITAL!
COPS RIGHT BEHIND ME!
LOOK IN FRONT OF YOU!
HE'S STOPPING!

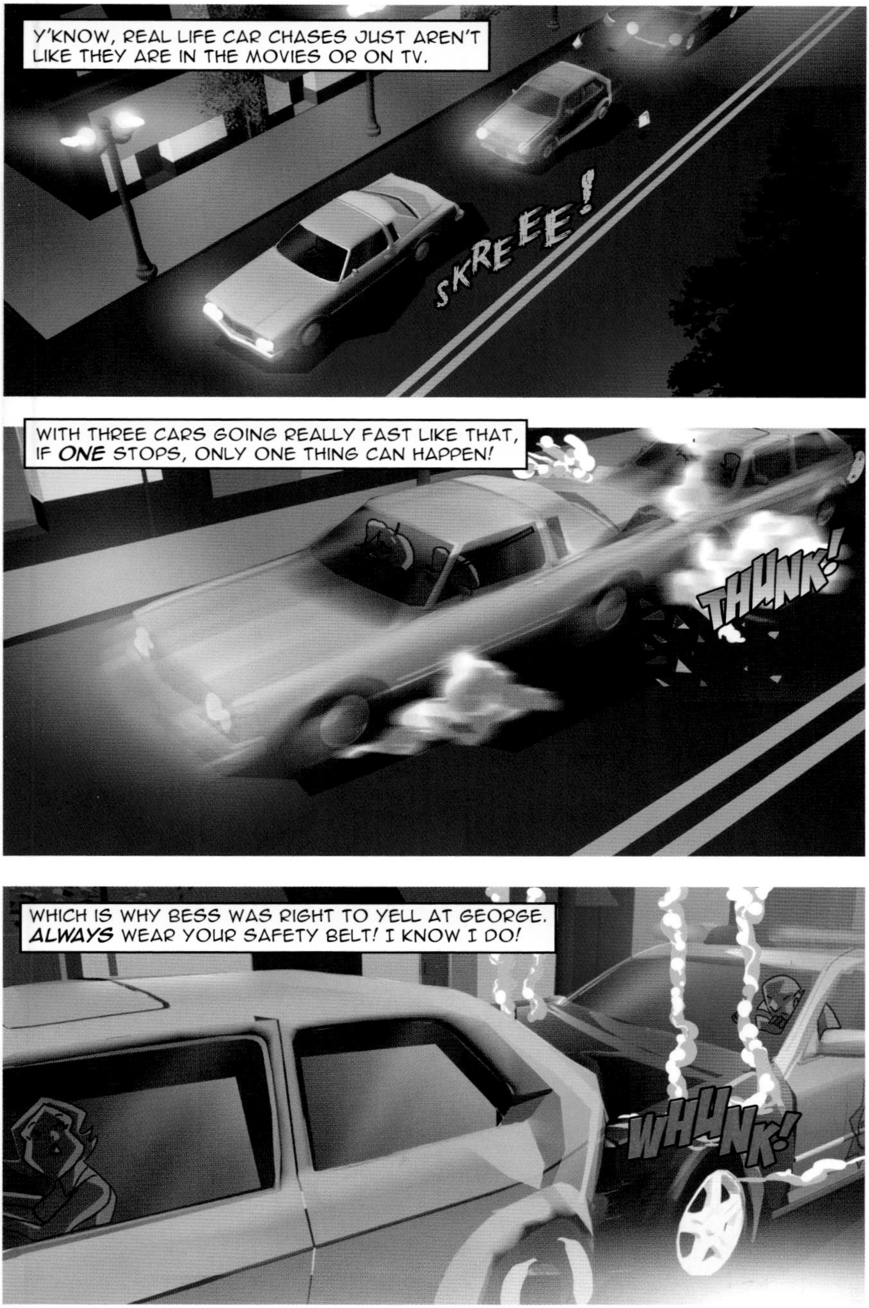
Y'KNOW, REAL LIFE CAR CHASES JUST AREN'T LIKE THEY ARE IN THE MOVIES OR ON TV.
SKREEEE!
WITH THREE CARS GOING REALLY FAST LIKE THAT, IF ONE STOPS, ONLY ONE THING CAN HAPPEN!
THUNK!
WHICH IS WHY BESS WAS RIGHT TO YELL AT GEORGE. ALWAYS WEAR YOUR SAFETY BELT! I KNOW I DO!
WHUNK!

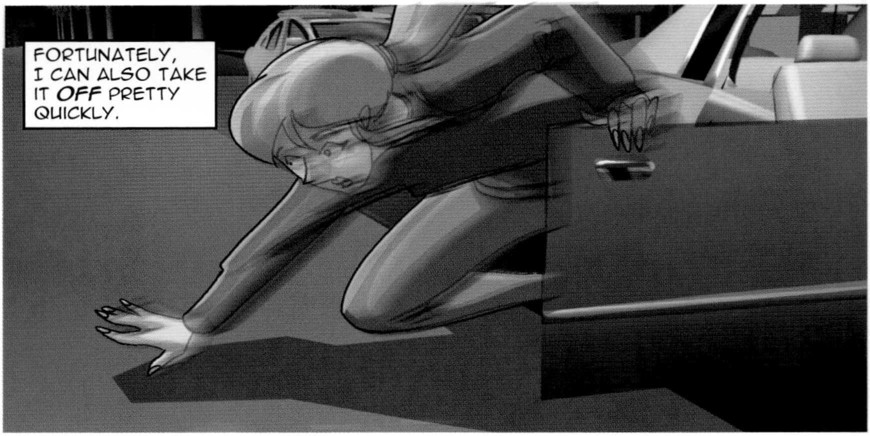
FORTUNATELY, I CAN ALSO TAKE IT *OFF* PRETTY QUICKLY.

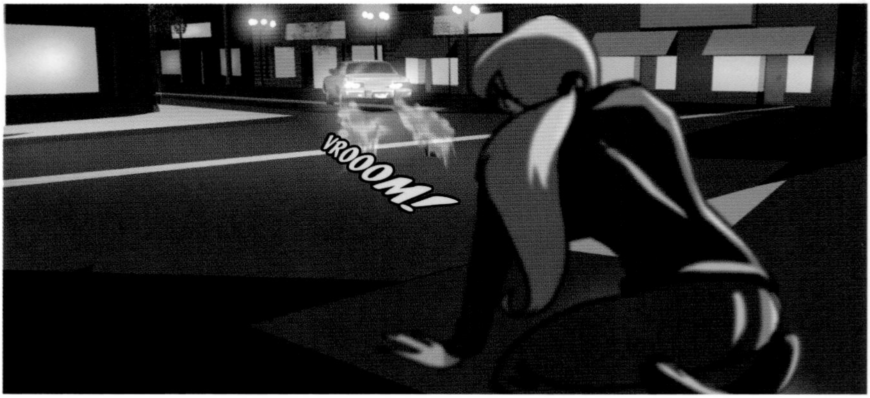
VROOOM!

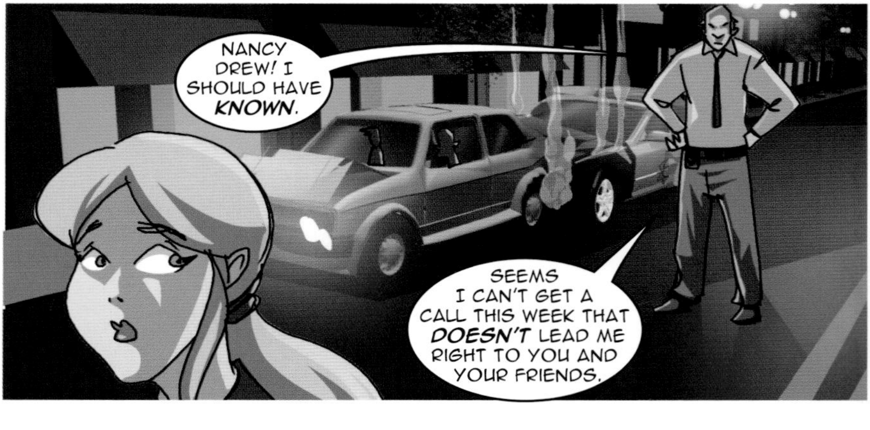
NANCY DREW! I SHOULD HAVE *KNOWN*.
SEEMS I CAN'T GET A CALL THIS WEEK THAT *DOESN'T* LEAD ME RIGHT TO YOU AND YOUR FRIENDS.

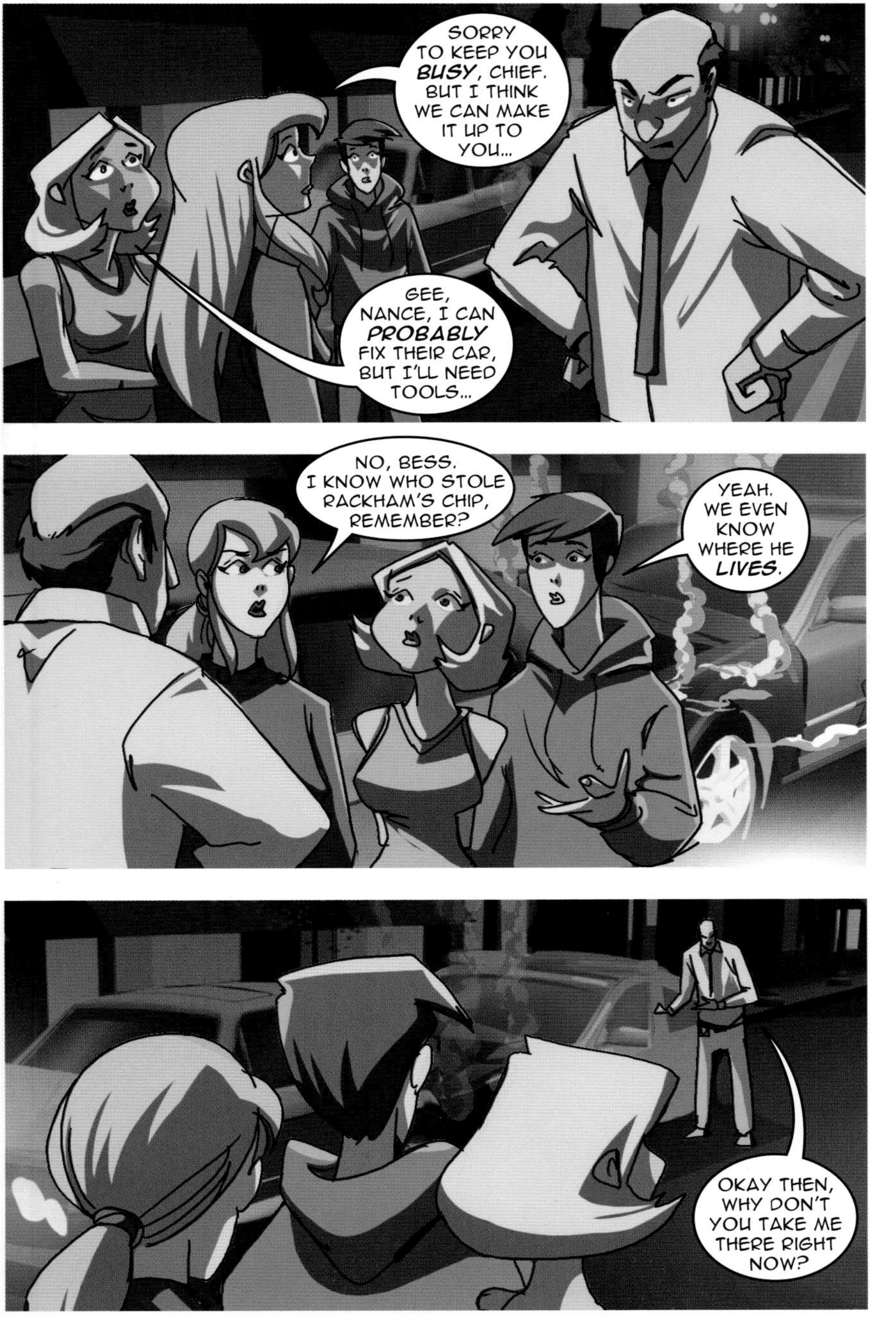
SORRY TO KEEP YOU *BUSY*, CHIEF. BUT I THINK WE CAN MAKE IT UP TO YOU...
GEE, NANCE, I CAN *PROBABLY* FIX THEIR CAR, BUT I'LL NEED TOOLS...
NO, BESS. I KNOW WHO STOLE RACKHAM'S CHIP, REMEMBER?
YEAH. WE EVEN KNOW WHERE HE *LIVES*.
OKAY THEN, WHY DON'T YOU TAKE ME THERE RIGHT NOW?

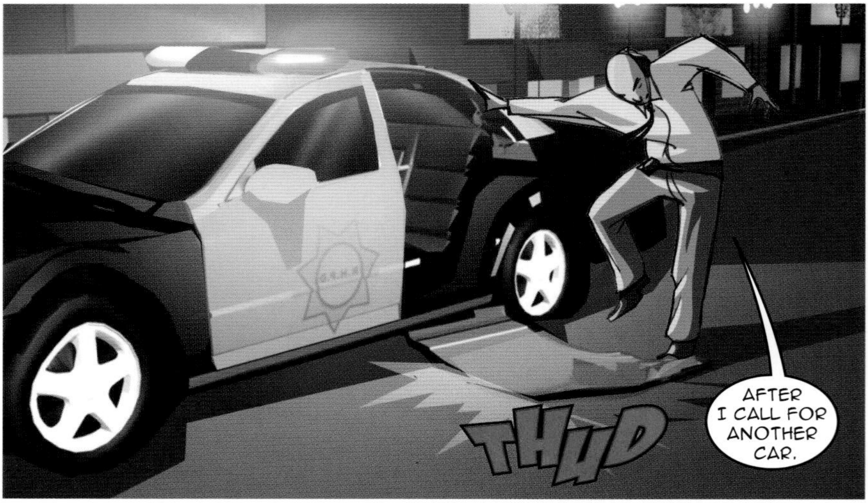
AFTER I CALL FOR ANOTHER CAR.
THUD

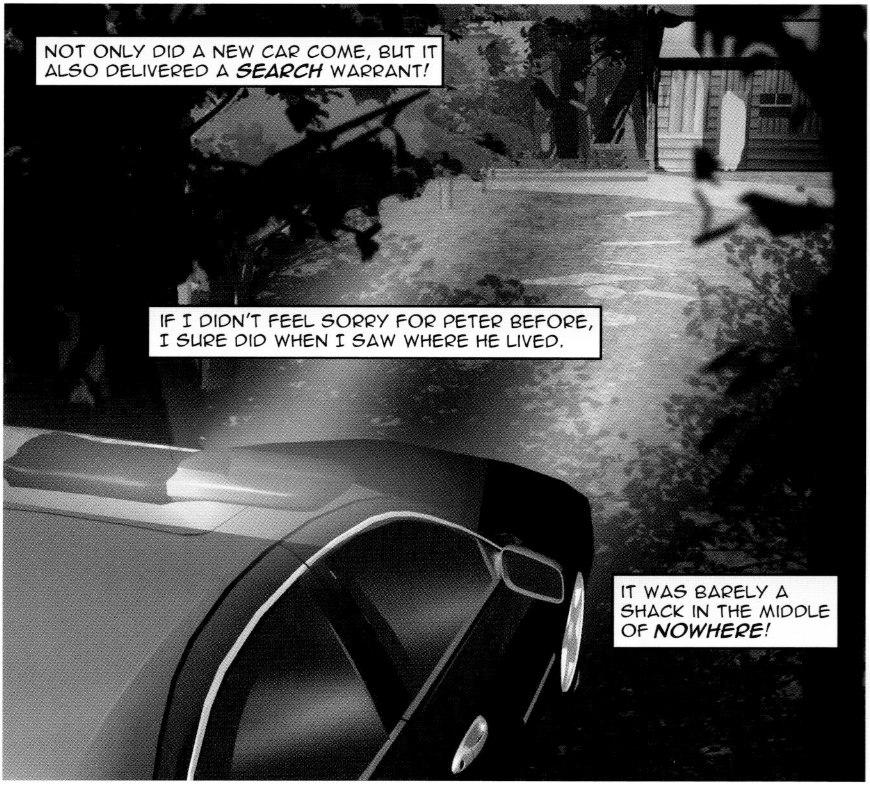
NOT ONLY DID A NEW CAR COME, BUT IT ALSO DELIVERED A ***SEARCH*** WARRANT!
IF I DIDN'T FEEL SORRY FOR PETER BEFORE, I SURE DID WHEN I SAW WHERE HE LIVED.
IT WAS BARELY A SHACK IN THE MIDDLE OF ***NOWHERE***!

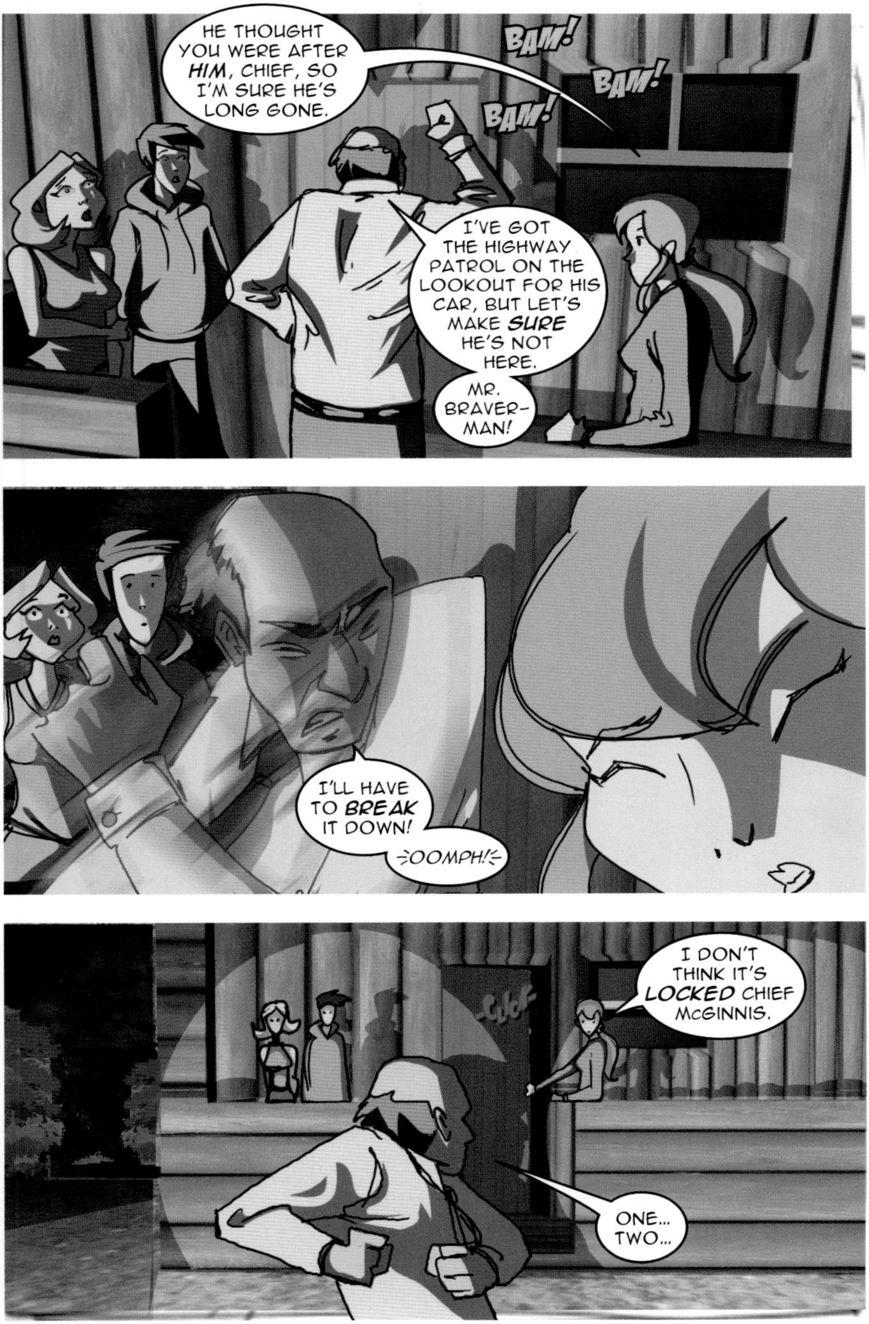
HE THOUGHT YOU WERE AFTER *HIM*, CHIEF, SO I'M SURE HE'S LONG GONE.
BAM!
BAM!
BAM!
I'VE GOT THE HIGHWAY PATROL ON THE LOOKOUT FOR HIS CAR, BUT LET'S MAKE *SURE* HE'S NOT HERE.
MR. BRAVER-MAN!
I'LL HAVE TO ***BREAK*** IT DOWN!
OOMPH!
-CLICK-
I DON'T THINK IT'S ***LOCKED*** CHIEF McGINNIS.
ONE... TWO...

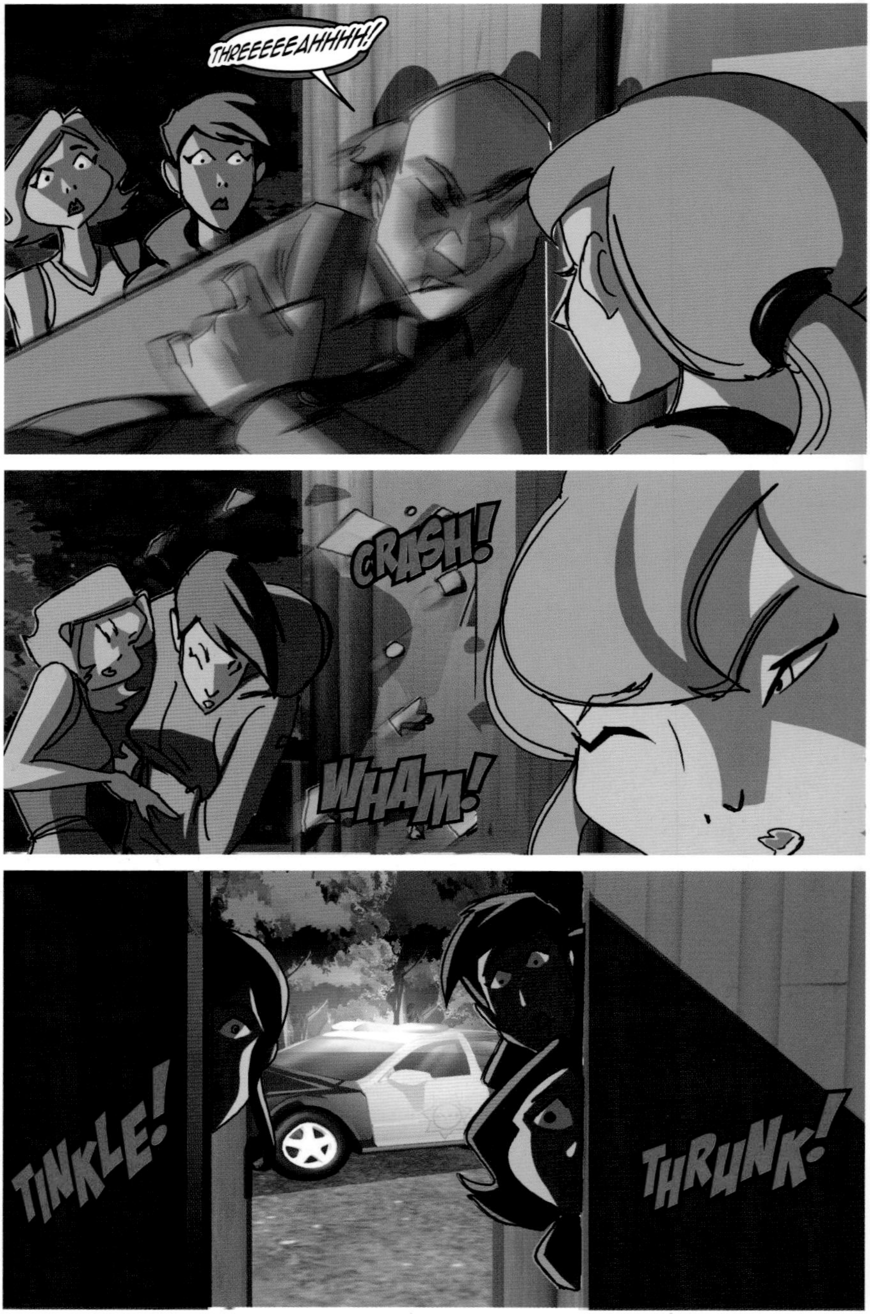
THREEEEEAHHHH!
CRASH!
WHAM!
TINKLE!
THRUNK!

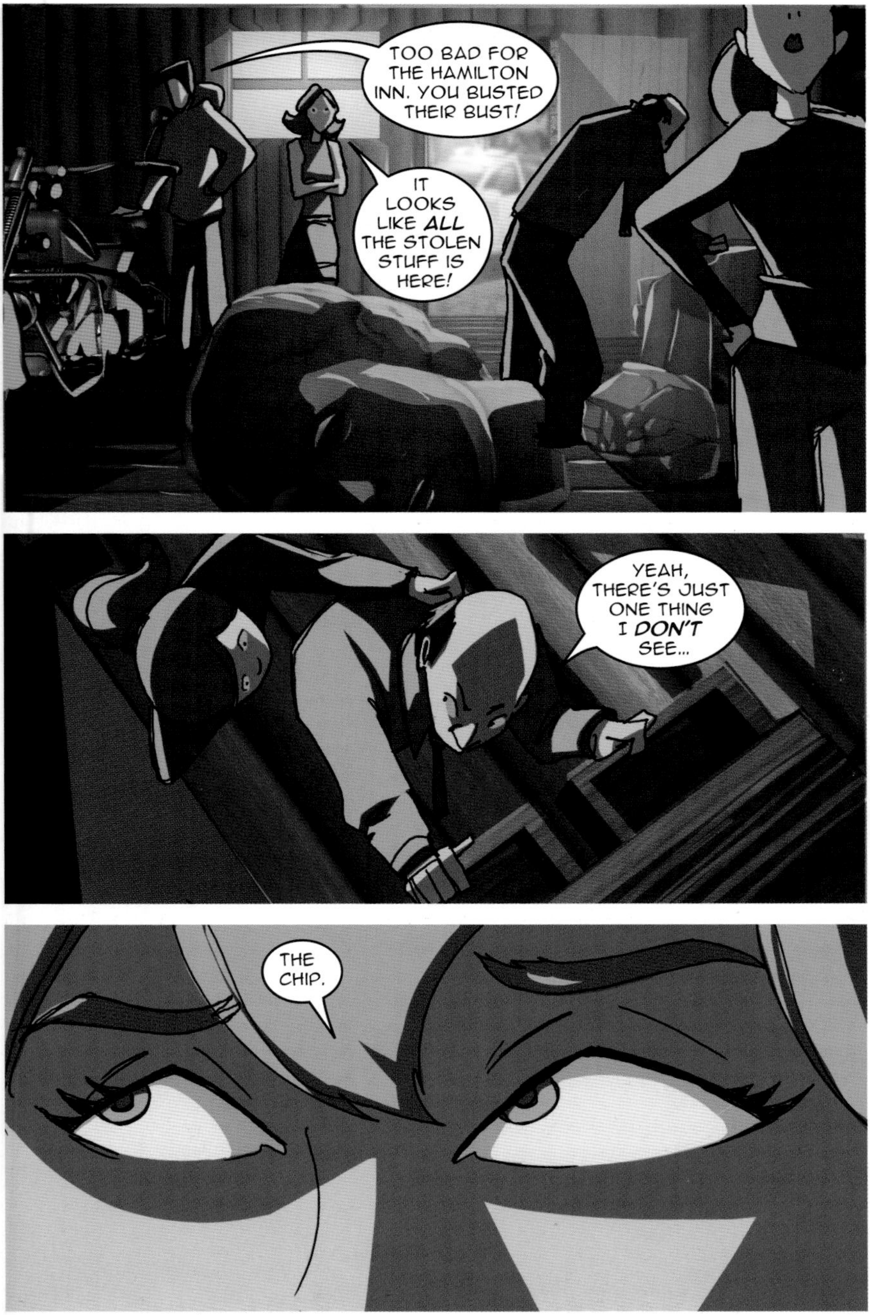
TOO BAD FOR THE HAMILTON INN. YOU BUSTED THEIR BUST!
IT LOOKS LIKE ALL THE STOLEN STUFF IS HERE!
YEAH, THERE'S JUST ONE THING I DON'T SEE...
THE CHIP.

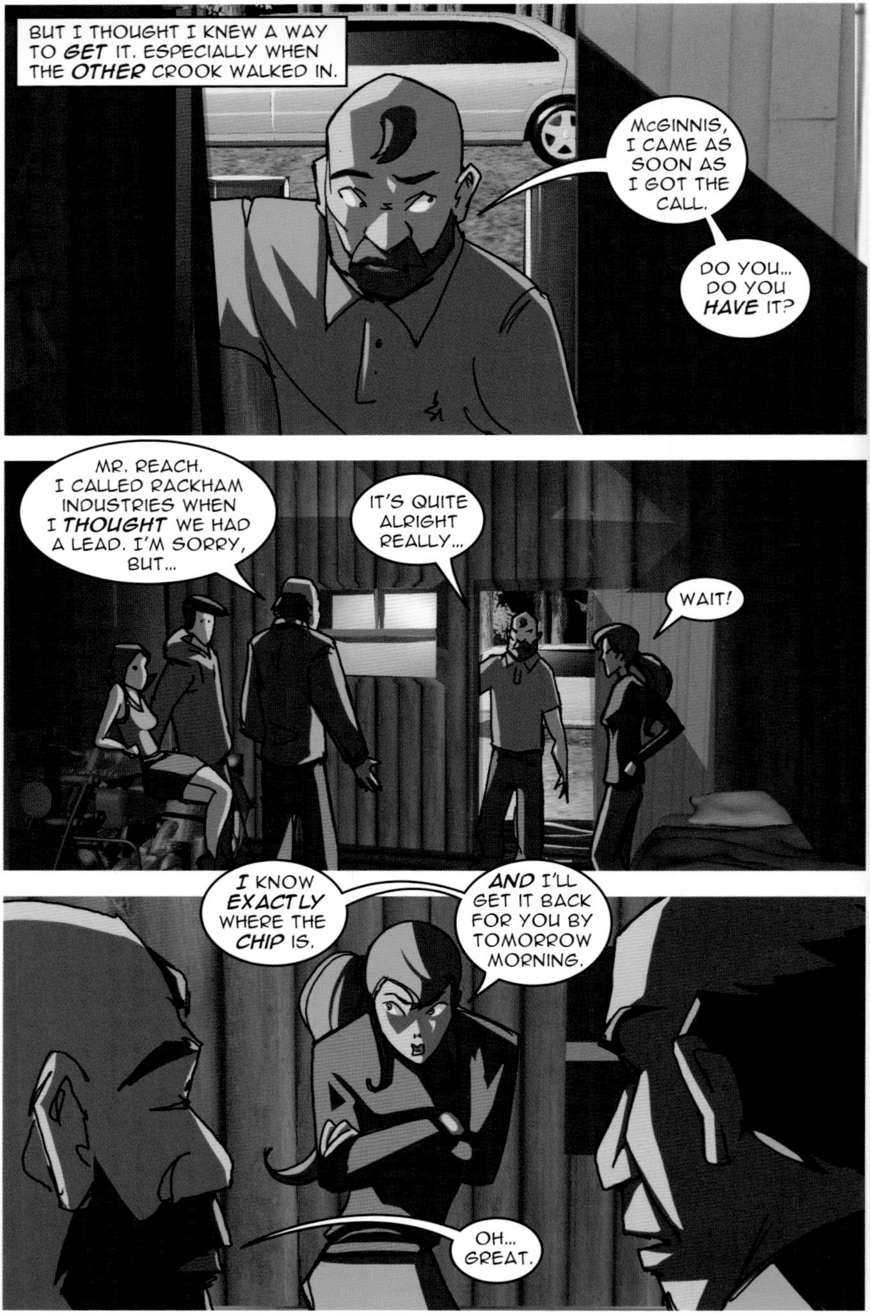
BUT I THOUGHT I KNEW A WAY TO GET IT. ESPECIALLY WHEN THE OTHER CROOK WALKED IN.
McGINNIS, I CAME AS SOON AS I GOT THE CALL.
DO YOU... DO YOU HAVE IT?
MR. REACH. I CALLED RACKHAM INDUSTRIES WHEN I THOUGHT WE HAD A LEAD. I'M SORRY, BUT...
IT'S QUITE ALRIGHT REALLY...
WAIT!
I KNOW EXACTLY WHERE THE CHIP IS.
AND I'LL GET IT BACK FOR YOU BY TOMORROW MORNING.
OH... GREAT.

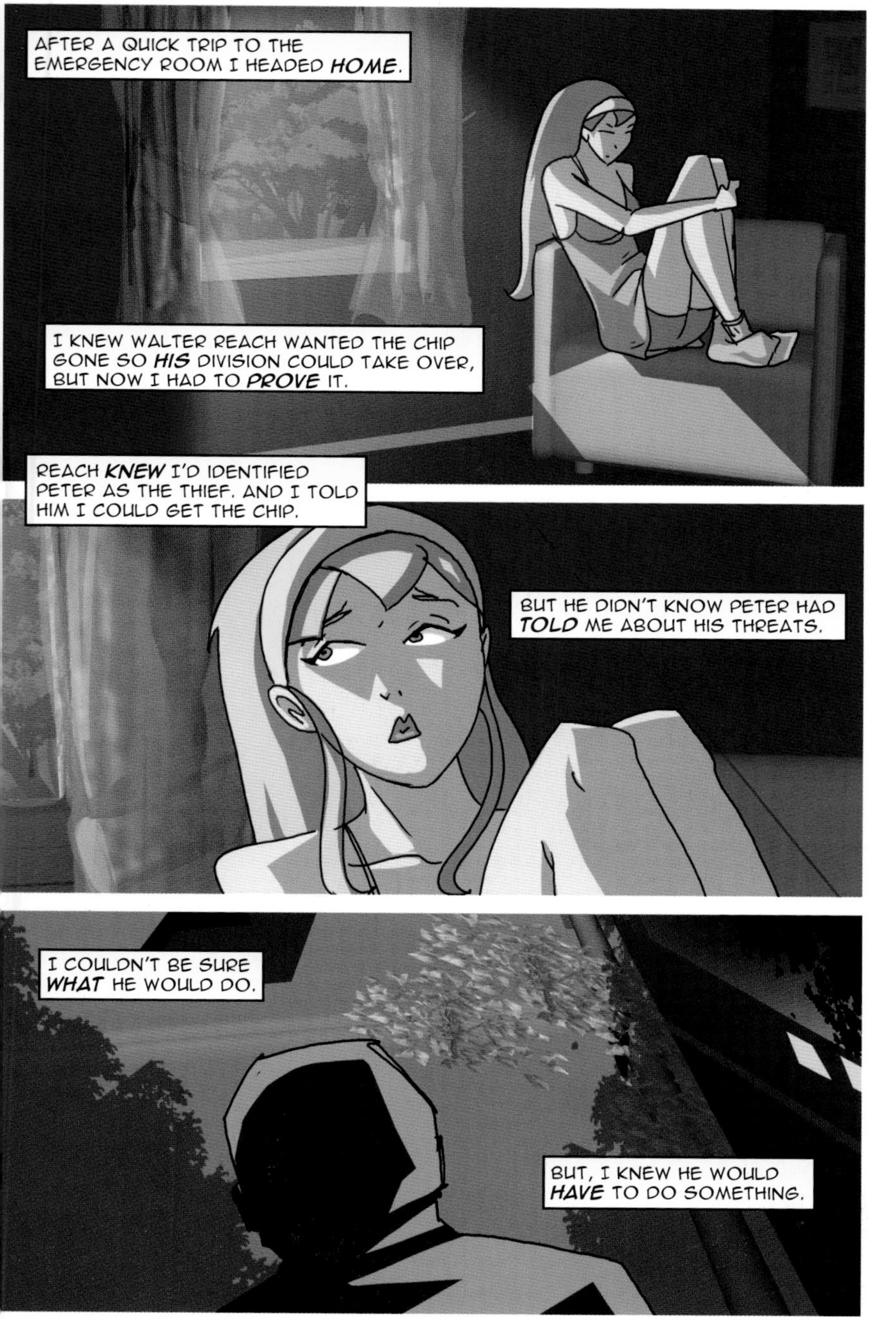
AFTER A QUICK TRIP TO THE EMERGENCY ROOM I HEADED **HOME**.
I KNEW WALTER REACH WANTED THE CHIP GONE SO **HIS** DIVISION COULD TAKE OVER, BUT NOW I HAD TO **PROVE** IT.
REACH **KNEW** I'D IDENTIFIED PETER AS THE THIEF. AND I TOLD HIM I COULD GET THE CHIP.
BUT HE DIDN'T KNOW PETER HAD **TOLD** ME ABOUT HIS THREATS.
I COULDN'T BE SURE **WHAT** HE WOULD DO.
BUT, I KNEW HE WOULD **HAVE** TO DO SOMETHING.

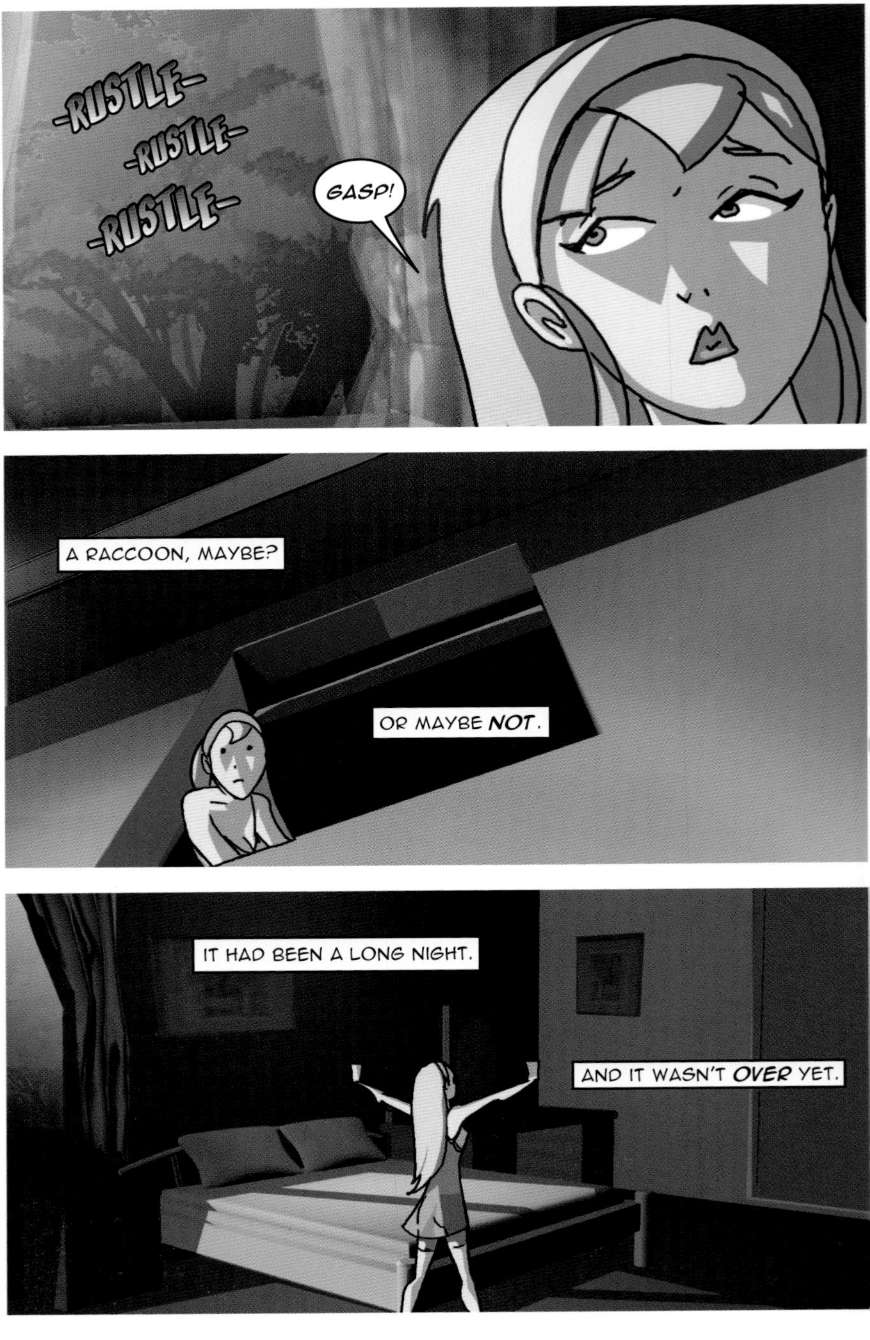
-RUSTLE-
-RUSTLE-
-RUSTLE-
GASP!
A RACCOON, MAYBE?
OR MAYBE NOT.
IT HAD BEEN A LONG NIGHT.
AND IT WASN'T OVER YET.

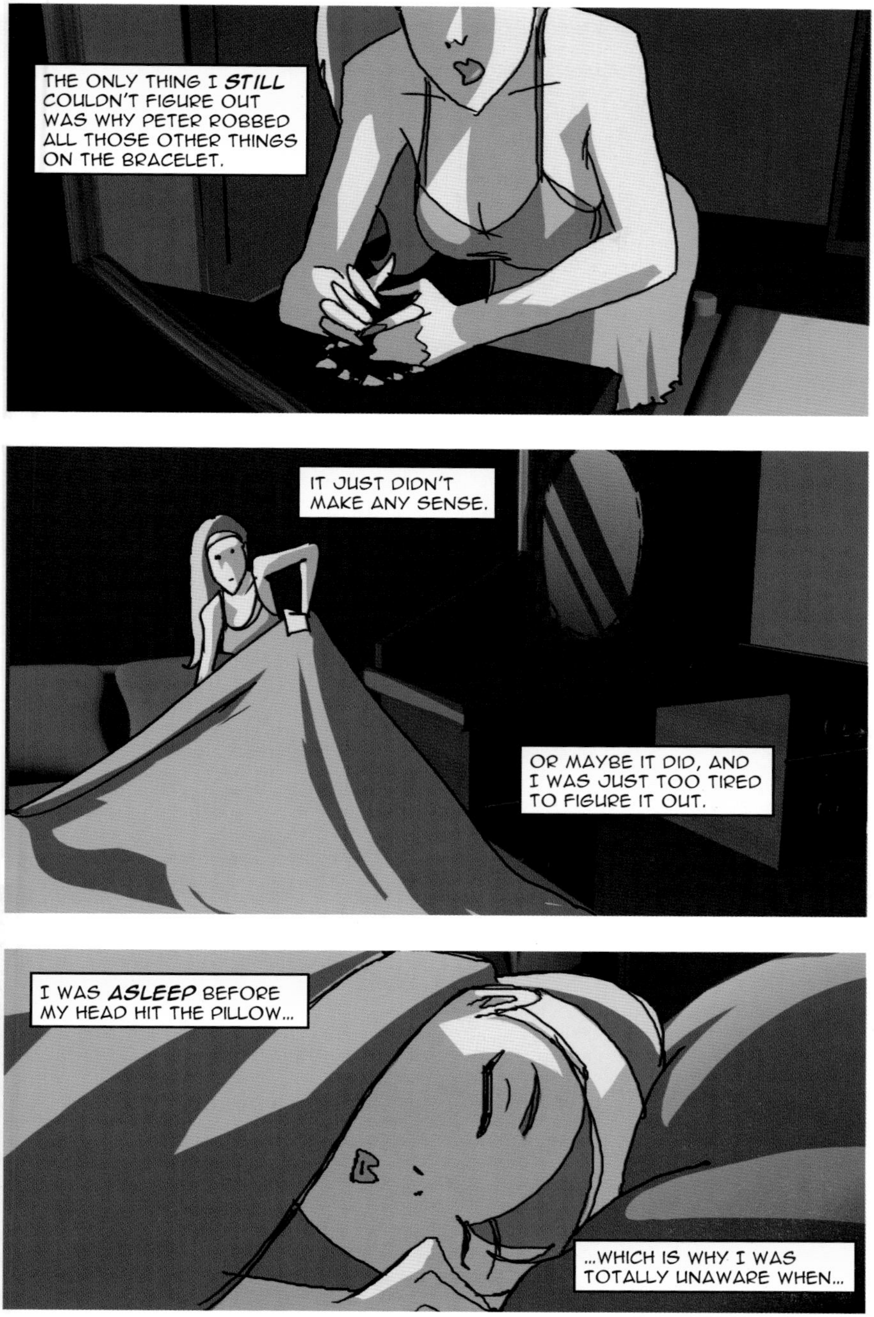
THE ONLY THING I *STILL* COULDN'T FIGURE OUT WAS WHY PETER ROBBED ALL THOSE OTHER THINGS ON THE BRACELET.
IT JUST DIDN'T MAKE ANY SENSE.
OR MAYBE IT DID, AND I WAS JUST TOO TIRED TO FIGURE IT OUT.
I WAS *ASLEEP* BEFORE MY HEAD HIT THE PILLOW...
...WHICH IS WHY I WAS TOTALLY UNAWARE WHEN...

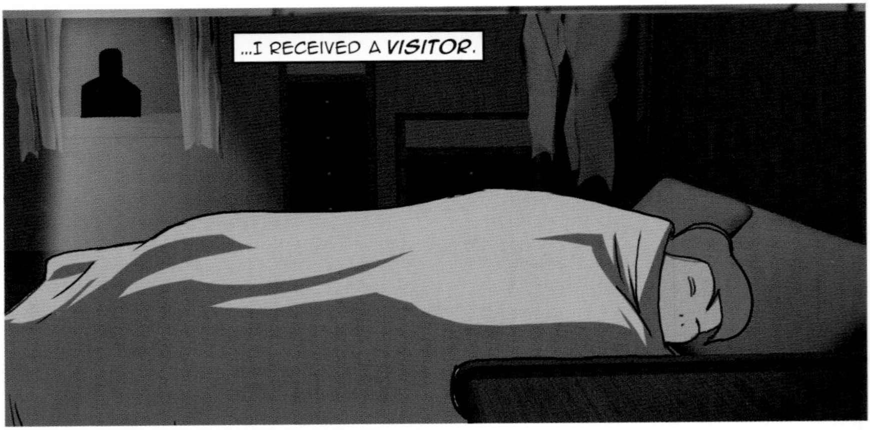
...I RECEIVED A VISITOR.

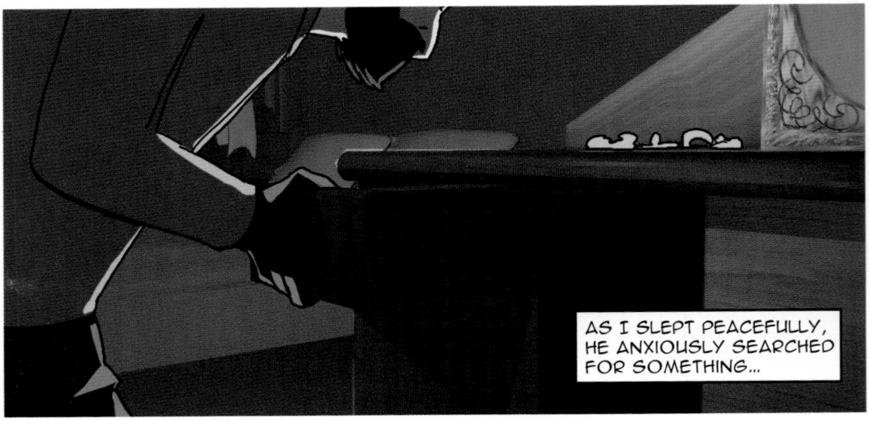
AS I SLEPT PEACEFULLY, HE ANXIOUSLY SEARCHED FOR SOMETHING...

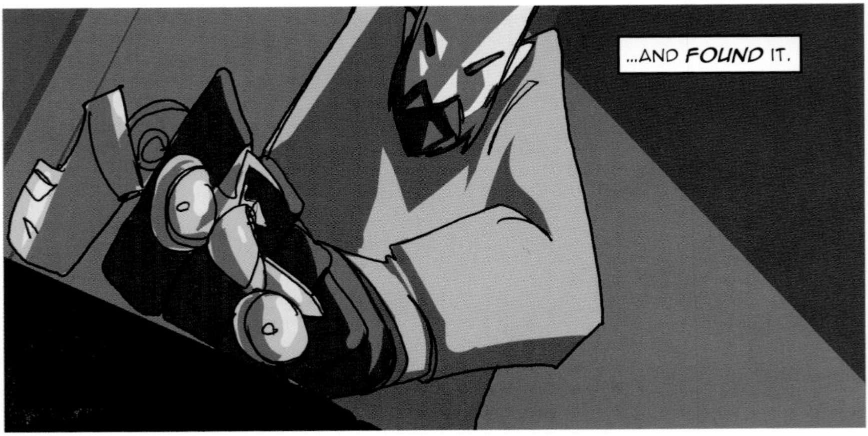
...AND FOUND IT.

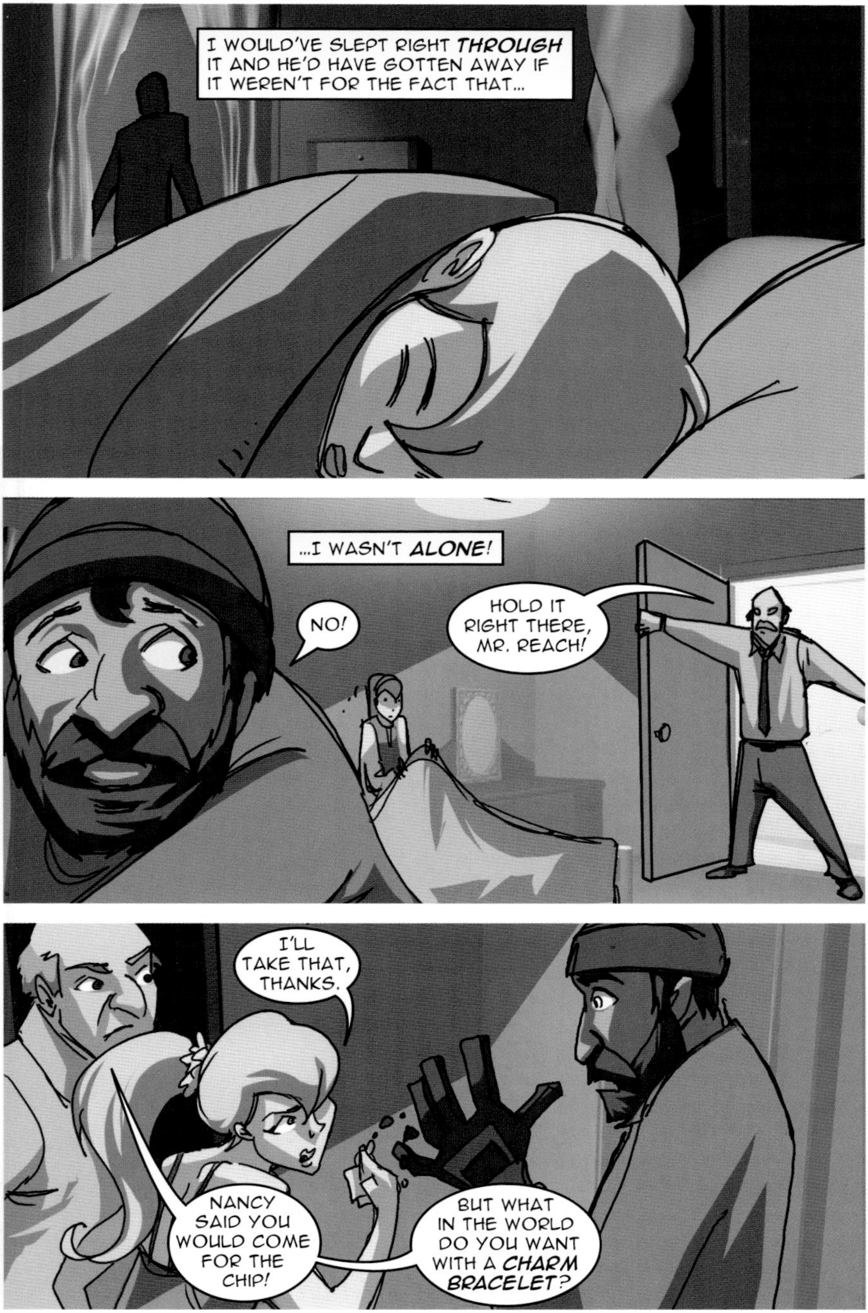
I WOULD'VE SLEPT RIGHT THROUGH IT AND HE'D HAVE GOTTEN AWAY IF IT WEREN'T FOR THE FACT THAT...
...I WASN'T ALONE!
HOLD IT RIGHT THERE, MR. REACH!
NO!
I'LL TAKE THAT, THANKS.
NANCY SAID YOU WOULD COME FOR THE CHIP!
BUT WHAT IN THE WORLD DO YOU WANT WITH A CHARM BRACELET?

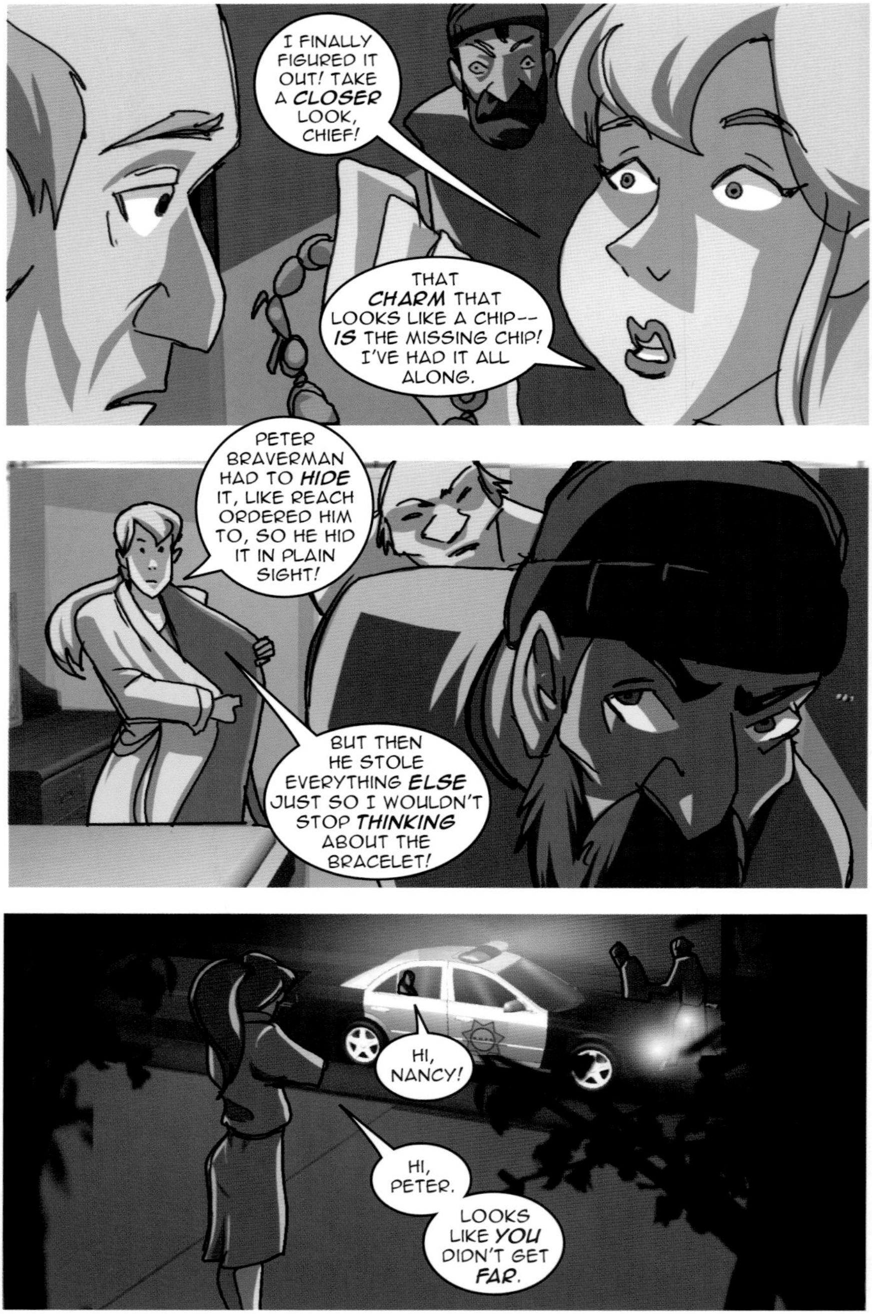
I FINALLY FIGURED IT OUT! TAKE A CLOSER LOOK, CHIEF!
THAT CHARM THAT LOOKS LIKE A CHIP-- IS THE MISSING CHIP! I'VE HAD IT ALL ALONG.
PETER BRAVERMAN HAD TO HIDE IT, LIKE REACH ORDERED HIM TO, SO HE HID IT IN PLAIN SIGHT!
BUT THEN HE STOLE EVERYTHING ELSE JUST SO I WOULDN'T STOP THINKING ABOUT THE BRACELET!
HI, NANCY!
HI, PETER.
LOOKS LIKE YOU DIDN'T GET FAR.

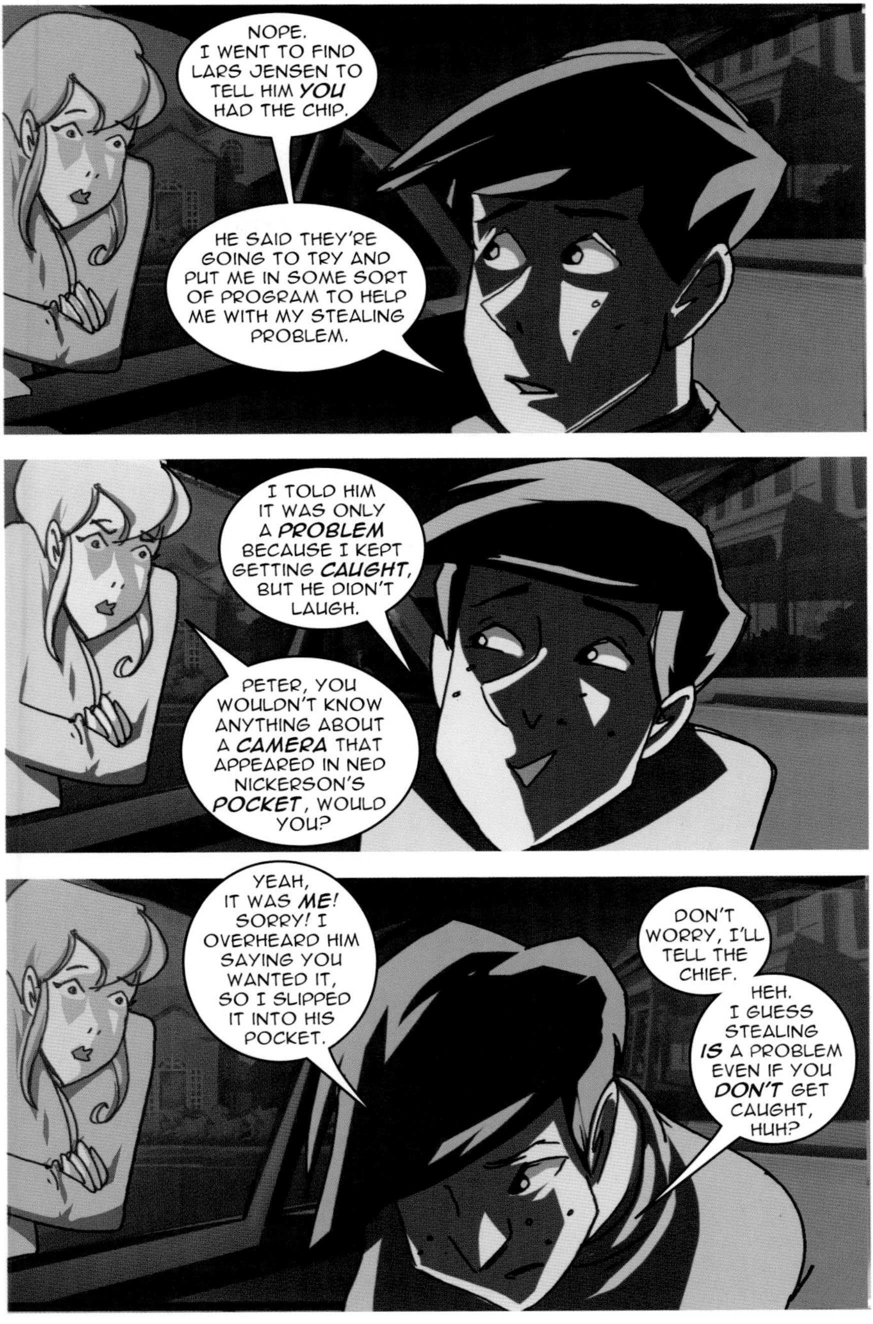
NOPE. I WENT TO FIND LARS JENSEN TO TELL HIM *YOU* HAD THE CHIP.
HE SAID THEY'RE GOING TO TRY AND PUT ME IN SOME SORT OF PROGRAM TO HELP ME WITH MY STEALING PROBLEM.
I TOLD HIM IT WAS ONLY A *PROBLEM* BECAUSE I KEPT GETTING *CAUGHT*, BUT HE DIDN'T LAUGH.
PETER, YOU WOULDN'T KNOW ANYTHING ABOUT A *CAMERA* THAT APPEARED IN NED NICKERSON'S *POCKET*, WOULD YOU?
YEAH, IT WAS *ME*! SORRY! I OVERHEARD HIM SAYING YOU WANTED IT, SO I SLIPPED IT INTO HIS POCKET.
DON'T WORRY, I'LL TELL THE CHIEF.
HEH. I GUESS STEALING *IS* A PROBLEM EVEN IF YOU *DON'T* GET CAUGHT, HUH?

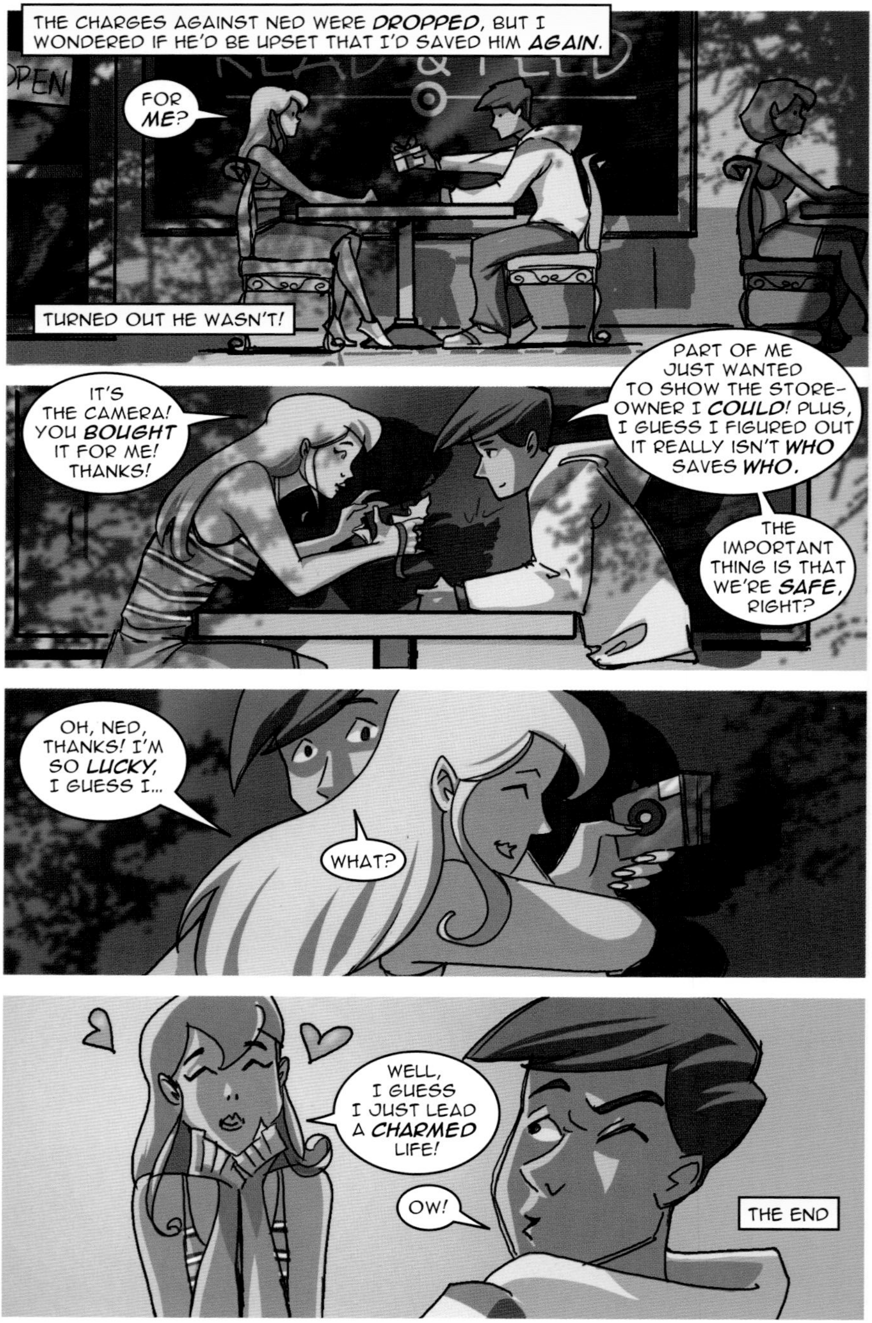
THE CHARGES AGAINST NED WERE DROPPED, BUT I WONDERED IF HE'D BE UPSET THAT I'D SAVED HIM AGAIN.
OPEN
FOR ME?
TURNED OUT HE WASN'T!
IT'S THE CAMERA! YOU BOUGHT IT FOR ME! THANKS!
PART OF ME JUST WANTED TO SHOW THE STORE-OWNER I COULD! PLUS, I GUESS I FIGURED OUT IT REALLY ISN'T WHO SAVES WHO.
THE IMPORTANT THING IS THAT WE'RE SAFE, RIGHT?
OH, NED, THANKS! I'M SO LUCKY, I GUESS I...
WHAT?
WELL, I GUESS I JUST LEAD A CHARMED LIFE!
OW!
THE END

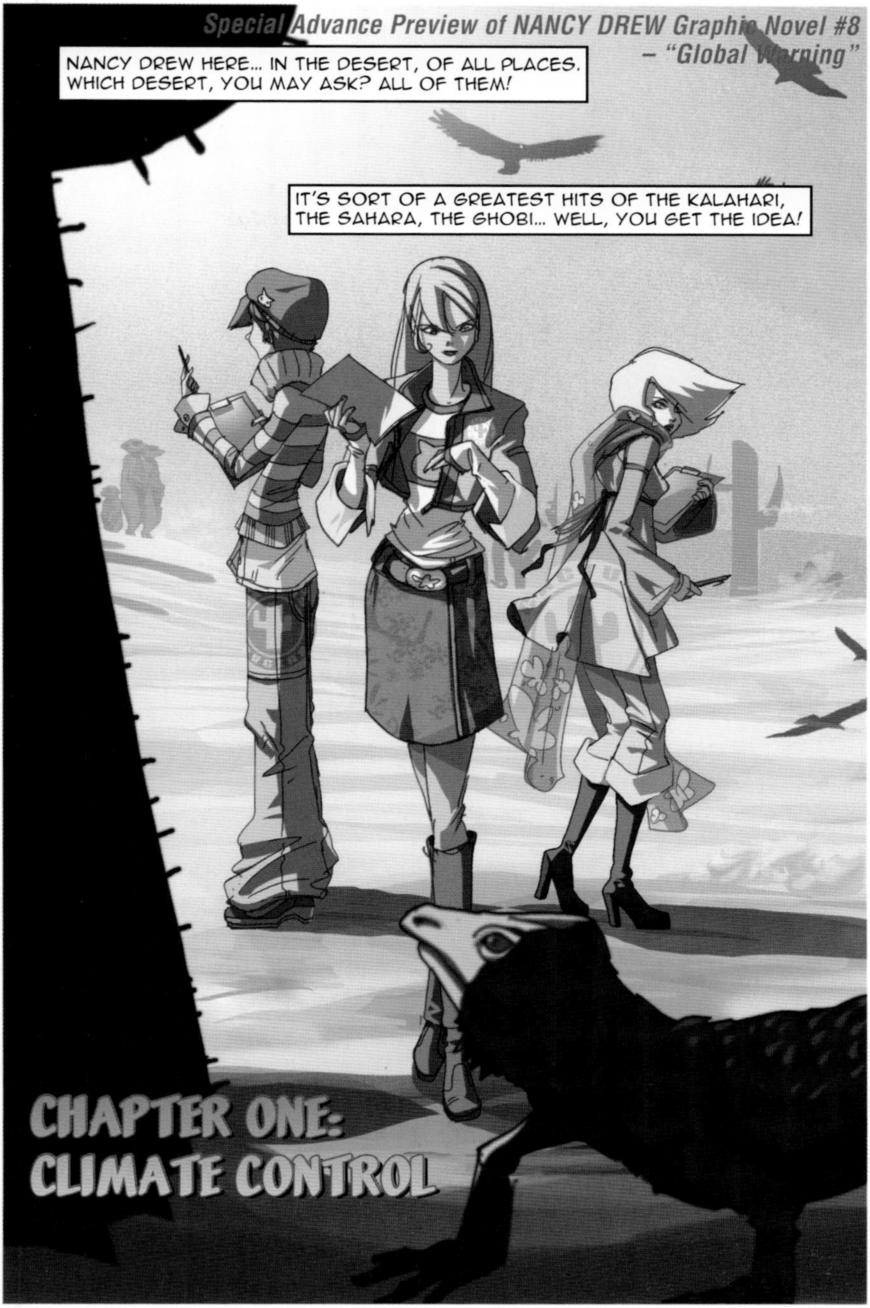
Special Advance Preview of NANCY DREW Graphic Novel #8
– "Global Warning"
NANCY DREW HERE... IN THE DESERT, OF ALL PLACES. WHICH DESERT, YOU MAY ASK? ALL OF THEM!
IT'S SORT OF A GREATEST HITS OF THE KALAHARI, THE SAHARA, THE GHOBI... WELL, YOU GET THE IDEA!
CHAPTER ONE: CLIMATE CONTROL

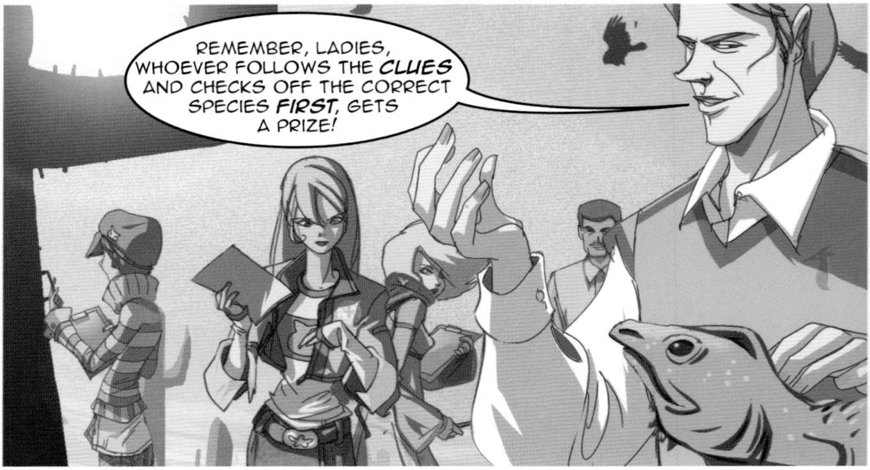
REMEMBER, LADIES, WHOEVER FOLLOWS THE CLUES AND CHECKS OFF THE CORRECT SPECIES FIRST, GETS A PRIZE!

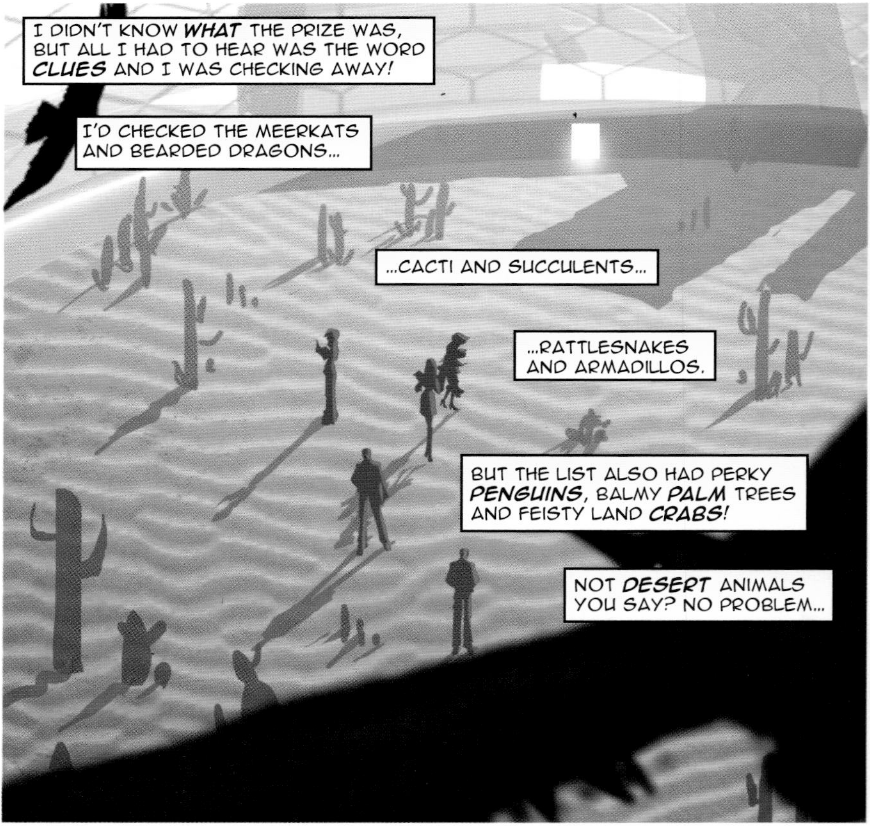
I DIDN'T KNOW WHAT THE PRIZE WAS, BUT ALL I HAD TO HEAR WAS THE WORD CLUES AND I WAS CHECKING AWAY!
I'D CHECKED THE MEERKATS AND BEARDED DRAGONS...
...CACTI AND SUCCULENTS...
...RATTLESNAKES AND ARMADILLOS.
BUT THE LIST ALSO HAD PERKY PENGUINS, BALMY PALM TREES AND FEISTY LAND CRABS!
NOT DESERT ANIMALS YOU SAY? NO PROBLEM...

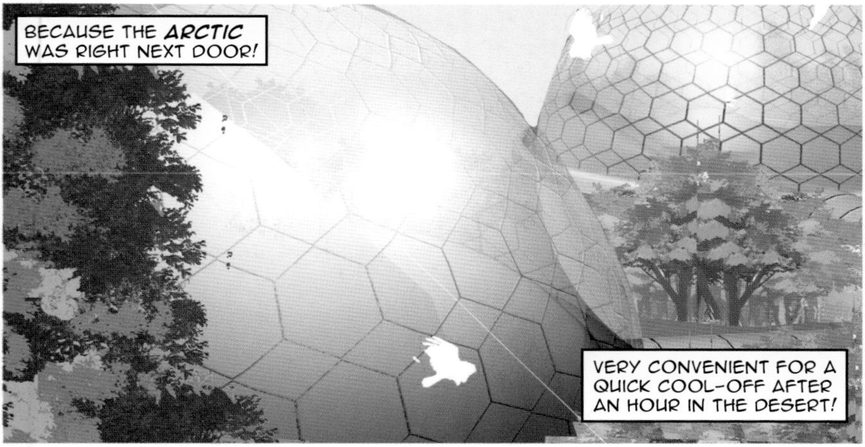
BECAUSE THE ARCTIC WAS RIGHT NEXT DOOR!
VERY CONVENIENT FOR A QUICK COOL-OFF AFTER AN HOUR IN THE DESERT!

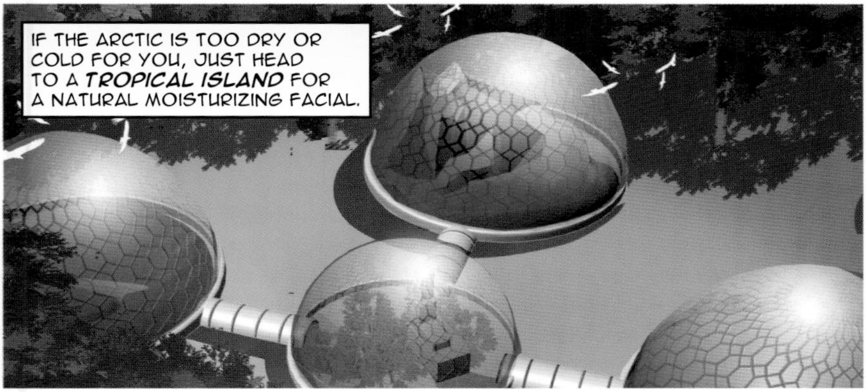
IF THE ARCTIC IS TOO DRY OR COLD FOR YOU, JUST HEAD TO A TROPICAL ISLAND FOR A NATURAL MOISTURIZING FACIAL.

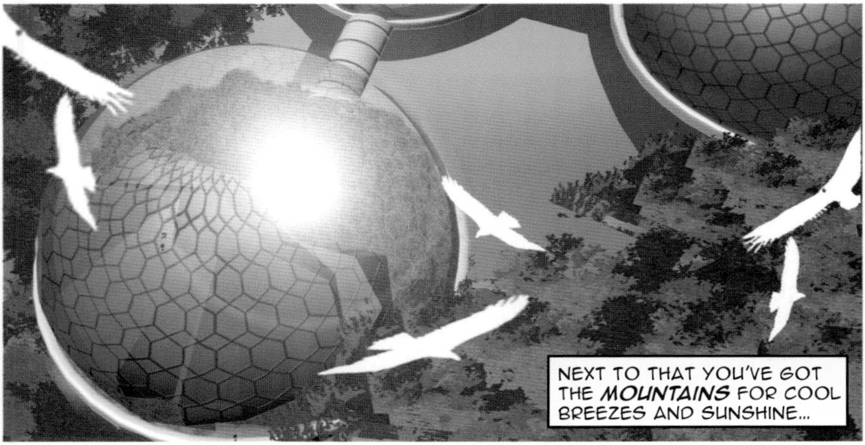
NEXT TO THAT YOU'VE GOT THE MOUNTAINS FOR COOL BREEZES AND SUNSHINE...

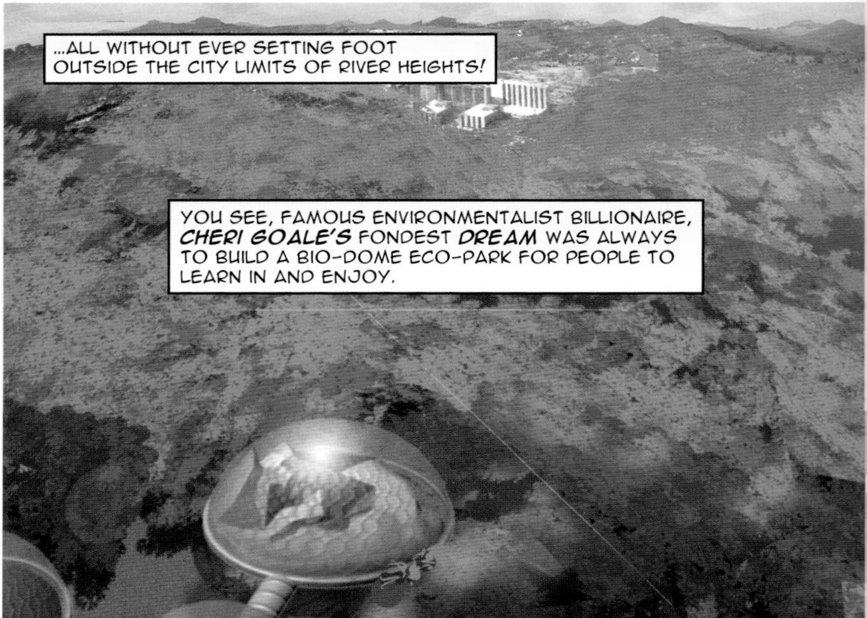
...ALL WITHOUT EVER SETTING FOOT OUTSIDE THE CITY LIMITS OF RIVER HEIGHTS!
YOU SEE, FAMOUS ENVIRONMENTALIST BILLIONAIRE, CHERI GOALE'S FONDEST DREAM WAS ALWAYS TO BUILD A BIO-DOME ECO-PARK FOR PEOPLE TO LEARN IN AND ENJOY.
AND IN SOME WAYS, BILLIONAIRES HAVE AN EASIER TIME MAKING THEIR DREAMS COME TRUE!

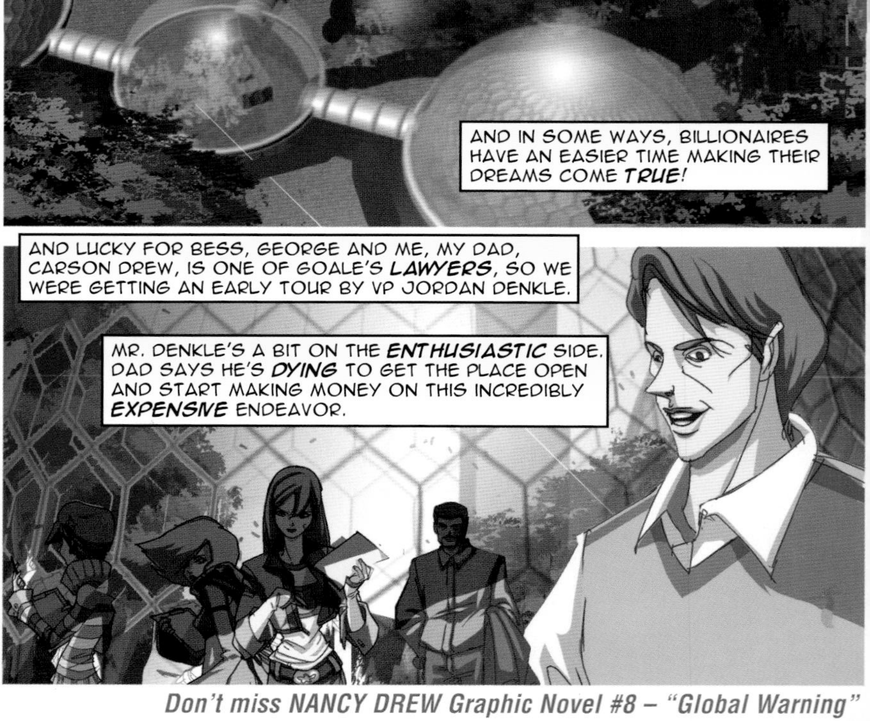
AND LUCKY FOR BESS, GEORGE AND ME, MY DAD, CARSON DREW, IS ONE OF GOALE'S LAWYERS, SO WE WERE GETTING AN EARLY TOUR BY VP JORDAN DENKLE.
MR. DENKLE'S A BIT ON THE ENTHUSIASTIC SIDE. DAD SAYS HE'S DYING TO GET THE PLACE OPEN AND START MAKING MONEY ON THIS INCREDIBLY EXPENSIVE ENDEAVOR.

Don't miss NANCY DREW Graphic Novel #8 – "Global Warning"

Go Undercover in Paris as Nancy Drew® in

Danger by Design

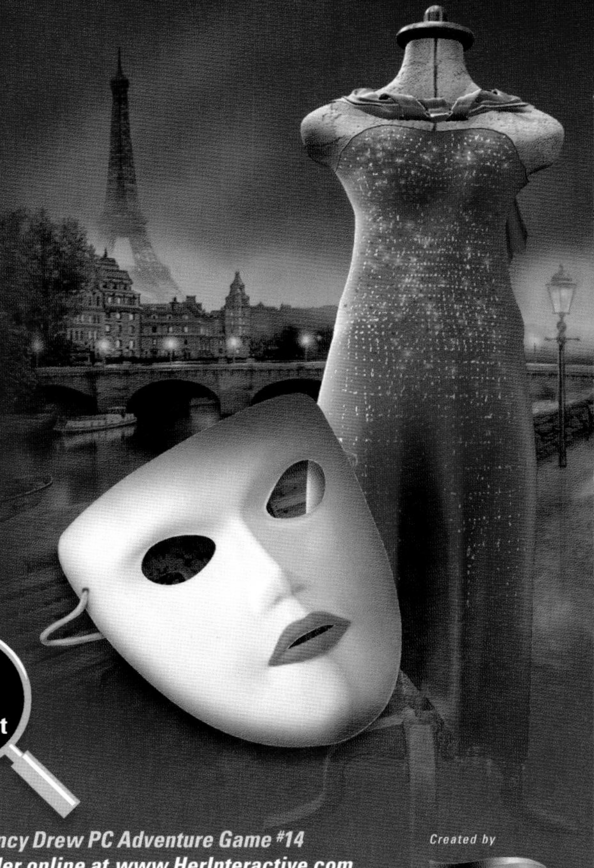

You, as Nancy Drew, are in Paris to work undercover for a prestigious fashion designer. Minette is all the rage in the fashion world, but strange threats and unwelcome guests are causing her to unravel. It's up to you to stitch the clues together and unmask the mystery in this PC adventure game.

dare to play™

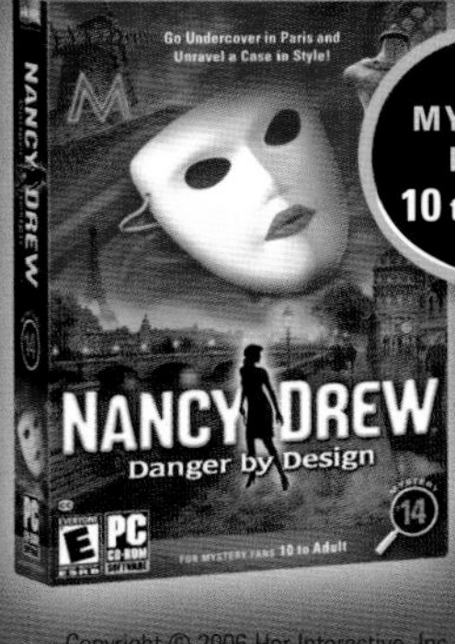

Go Undercover in Paris and Unravel a Case in Style!
NANCY DREW
Danger by Design
PC

FOR MYSTERY FANS 10 to Adult

Nancy Drew PC Adventure Game #14
Order online at www.HerInteractive.com or call 1-800-461-8787. Also in stores!

Compatible with WINDOWS® 98/2000/Me/XP/Vista

Created by

HeR interactive

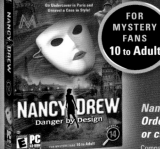

THE HARDY BOYS

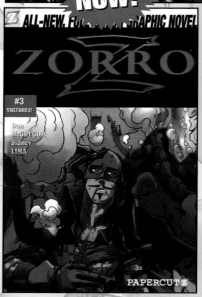

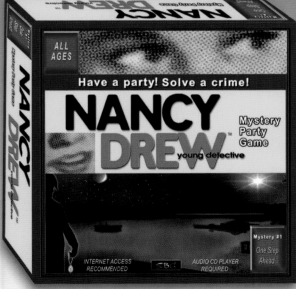

WATCH OUT FOR PAPERCUTZ™

The publisher of graphic novels created just for YOU!

Hi, Papercutz people! It's me, Jim Salicrup - the happiest graphic novel editor in the whole wide world. Why am I so happy? There's a gazillion reasons, here's just a few:

Nancy Drew graphic novel #1, "The Demon of River Heights," has won the prestigious 2006 Benjamin Franklin Award for graphic novels! For details, check out our full report on page 98.

To help celebrate, we've got interviews with writer Stefan Petrucha (page 99) and artist Sho Murase (page 103), the creative team responsible for our award-winning Nancy Drew graphic novel.

We also know we've got really talented fans, and now we're hoping to showcase some of your work in our Papercutz backpages. See page 108 to find out how to submit your artwork.

We're also thrilled about what's been going on in The Hardy Boys. Just to see if you've been paying attention, we challenge you to take our special Hardy Boys Trivia Quiz on page 110.

There is one thing that can make me even happier, and that's to hear from you. Tell us what you think of Papercutz - our characters, our writers and artists -- and tell us which characters you'd like to see Papercutz publish in the future. You can email me at salicrup@papercutz.com or write to me at Jim Salicrup, c/o Papercutz, 40 Exchange Place, Ste. 1308, New York, NY 10005.

And until we meet again--be sure to tell your friends all about Papercutz! Share the fun!

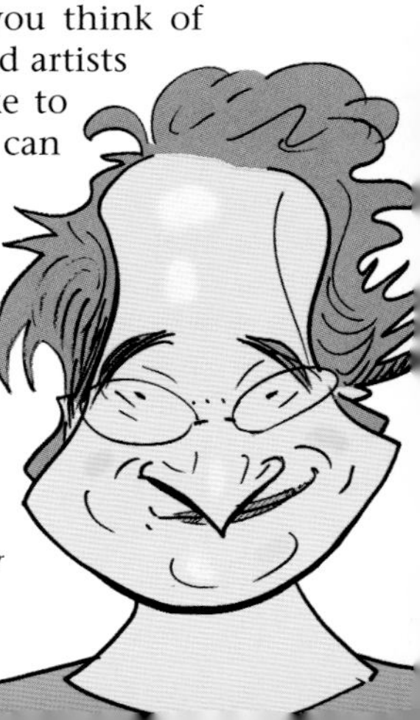

Caricature drawn by Steve Brodner at the 2005 MoCCA Art Fest.

Nancy Drew Wins Benjamin Franklin Award™

Papercutz is proud to announce that Nancy Drew graphic novel #1 ("The Demon of River Heights") has received the 2006 Benjamin Franklin Award for best graphic novel. The Benjamin Franklin Awards are the best known awards in the independent book publishing field. They are given out by the Publishers Marketing Association, the independent publishers association which has thousands of members, at the annual Benjamin Franklin Award Gala held just before the BEA, Book Expo America, the book publishing industry's convention. This is the first year the Benjamin Franklin Awards added a category for Graphic Novels.

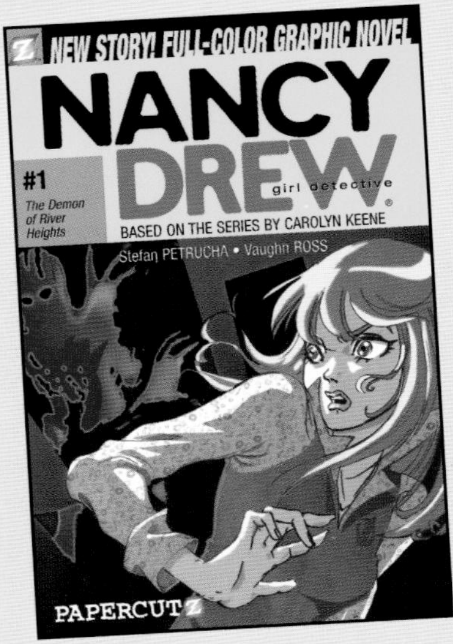
NEW STORY! FULL-COLOR GRAPHIC NOVEL
NANCY
DREW
girl detective
#1
The Demon of River Heights
BASED ON THE SERIES BY CAROLYN KEENE
Stefan PETRUCHA • Vaughn ROSS
PAPERCUTZ

Named in honor of America's most cherished publisher/printer, the Benjamin Franklin Awards recognizes excellence in independent publishing. Publications are judged on editorial and design merits by top practitioners in each field. The trophies are awarded to the best books in several categories and are presented to the publishers during a gala awards ceremony on the last evening of the Publishing University, just before the opening of Book Expo America.

The Nancy Drew graphic novel is one of the first graphic novels published by Papercutz, the independent graphic novel publishing company founded by publisher Terry Nantier and Editor-in-Chief Jim Salicrup. "For one of our first efforts," Salicrup says, "to win such an important award is a tribute to the talents of writer Stefan Petrucha and artist Sho Murase, not to mention the enduring popularity and charm of America's favorite girl detective, Nancy Drew. Everyone at Papercutz is truly honored and thankful."

The Write Stuff

Meet Stefan Petrucha -
the writer of the award-winning
Nancy Drew graphic novels from Papercutz

Whenever Papercutz publishes a graphic novel, every effort is made to find the right talent to craft the most compelling and entertaining stories and artwork possible. Stefan Petrucha is one of the very best writers working in comics today, with a reputation of creating smart stories, and perfectly capturing characters' personalities. With the first Nancy Drew graphic novel, "The Demon of River Heights," winning the 2006 Benjamin Franklin Award, we thought now would be a great time for Papercutz people to get to know Stefan a little bit better...

Stefan Petrucha

Papercutz: Tell us, Stefan, where are you from?
Stefan: I was born in the Bronx, New York, where, about a decade later, I met my lifelong chum and editor extraordinaire, Jim Salicrup. Since then I've spent about half my time living in Westchester County and the other half living in parts of New York City. August 2006 actually brought about the biggest move in my life, to Amherst, Massachusetts.

Papercutz: How did you become a writer?

Stefan: Ever since about 5th grade, I received a lot of compliments for the ease with which I could sling together a sentence - and I always kinda liked it. I attempted my first movie script in the 6th grade, and writing's been it for me ever since.

Papercutz: Who are your favorite writers?

Stefan: The list is huge! In comics, it'd be Stan Lee and Alan Moore, in prose, Steinbeck and Kafka, and, more recently, M.T. Anderson (who wrote the wonderful novel "Feed.")

Papercutz: Did you read all the original Nancy Drew books by Carolyn Keene? Which is your favorite?

Stefan: Nope! My mom had a few of the old hardcovers on her shelf and I remember as a child looking at the pictures. When I was asked to write the Nancy Drew graphic novels, though, I did go back and read the first few, and several of the new series. I'd have to say my favorite, so far, is the first, "The Secret of the Old Clock" - I just love the old style language in it.

Papercutz: How would you describe Nancy Drew?

Stefan: Smart, feisty and driven by a strong sense of right and wrong! Also a bit on the obsessive side - when she's on a case, she can forget everything from wearing the same color socks to filling her gas tank!

Papercutz: Where do you get your ideas?

Stefan: Everywhere! I keep an eye out for interesting news stories (like the one about a missing lake that I wound up using in "The Fake Heir") and whenever I watch a movie or TV show or read a book I'm

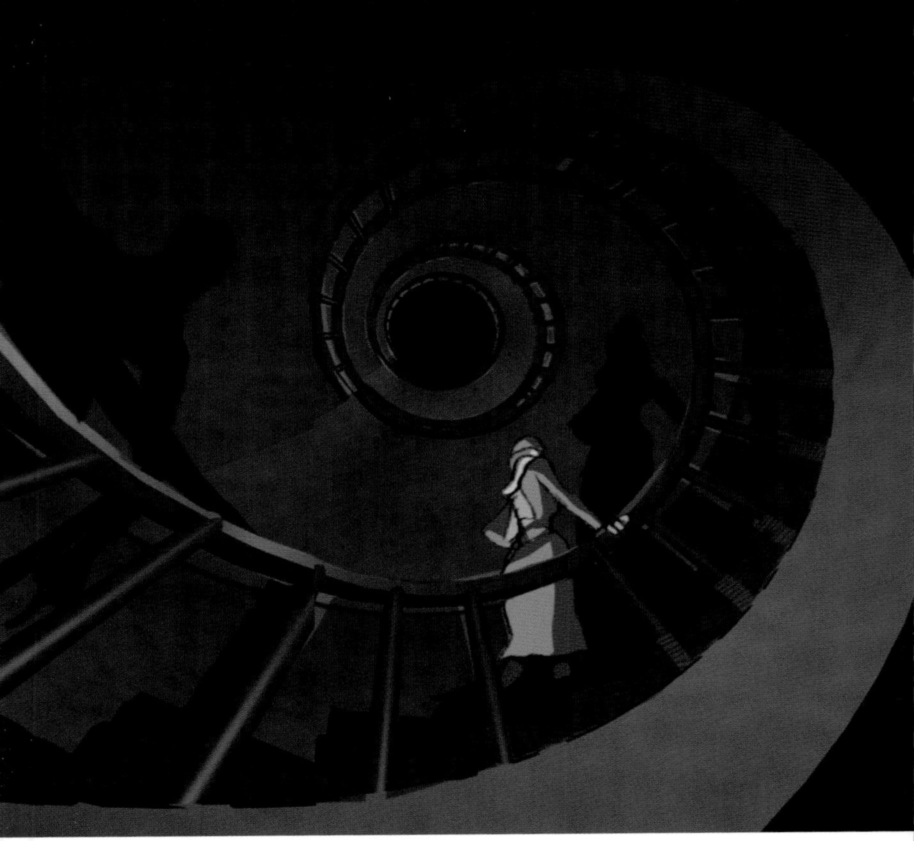

really enjoying, I try to figure out just why it works for me, so I can do something like that in my own writing.

Papercutz: How do you like working for Papercutz?
Stefan: It's been terrific! Jim and Terry are the best, and the folks at Simon & Schuster like the stories I'm doing - so what could be better?

Papercutz: What do you think of how Sho Murase and Vaughn Ross handle your stories?
Stefan: I like them both a lot. I think Sho really managed to design a Nancy Drew that works fantastically for today's savvy kids, and Vaughn brings a nice comic/cartoon touch to the characters.

Papercutz: What else do you write?
Stefan: TimeTripper from Penguin, a series of teen novels about a

high school student who can transcend time. The first two books, "Yestermorrow" and "InRage" are in bookstores and going over great with critics. Then there's my latest adult novel, "The Shadow of Frankenstein," a sequel to the Universal movie classic "Bride of Frankenstein," now also in bookstores. And Halloween 2007 will see the launch of a new series of teen horror books from Harper Collins, "Wicked Dead," written with co-author Thomas Pendleton.

Papercutz: What can you tell us about future Nancy Drew graphic novels?

Stefan: In #8, "Global Warning," Nancy visits a bio-dome park about to open in River Heights - featuring different environments - an arctic world, a jungle world, a desert world and so on. Only someone, dressing as various mythic monsters, is out to destroy it! This is a particularly exciting story, since we worked on it with HER Interactive, the makers of the great Nancy Drew Computer games - so in our story Nancy runs into some of the characters she originally met in a computer mystery game. After that, Nancy will have a series of adventures that tie together into one big three-book epic called "the High Miles Mystery," focusing on a secret engine developed decades ago and thought lost, until it's recovered (with Nancy's help) in an abandoned government plant outside River Heights. Great excitement ensues.

Sho and Tell

Meet Sho Murase - the artist behind Nancy Drew's makeover as a Papercutz graphic novel star

When Papercutz won the rights to present Nancy Drew in comics form for the very first time ever, we searched to find the right artist to create the new look for everyone's favorite girl detective. Once we saw Sho Murase's amazing artwork, we knew we found our artist.

Papercutz: Where are you from?
Sho: I'm half Japanese, half Korean, grew up in Spain.

Papercutz: How did you become an artist?
Sho: I was drawing since I was a kid. I did fine arts, went to animation school and went off to work as an animator.

Papercutz: How exactly do you draw Nancy Drew, and who are the artists you work with, and what do they do?
Sho: I draw everything directly on my Cintiq tablet in the computer, I work with

Sho Murase
Photo: Bosco Ng

two excellent artists, Rachel Ito, who models all the CG elements on the environments, and CJ Guzman, who does all the coloring. They do an awesome job, specially under some really tight deadlines.

Papercutz: Who are your favorite artists?
Sho: Mucha, Leyendecker, Egon Schiele, Klimt. Contemporary: Yoshitaka Amano, Yumi Tada, Claire Wendling, and Joshua Middleton.

Papercutz: Did you read all the original Nancy Drew books by Carolyn Keene? Which is your favorite?
Sho: I haven't read them all, because I started reading them when I first started drawing her, but I love what I have read. My favorite one is "The Secret of the Old Clock."

Papercutz: How would you describe Nancy Drew?
Sho: She is feminine without being too girlie, strong, clever, really cares for her friends and family, and she is a bit obsessed with clues and mysteries.

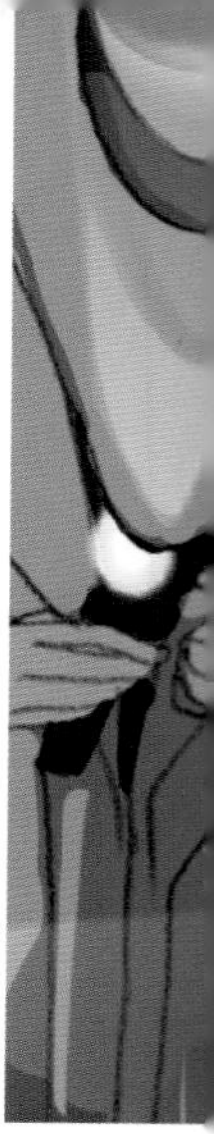

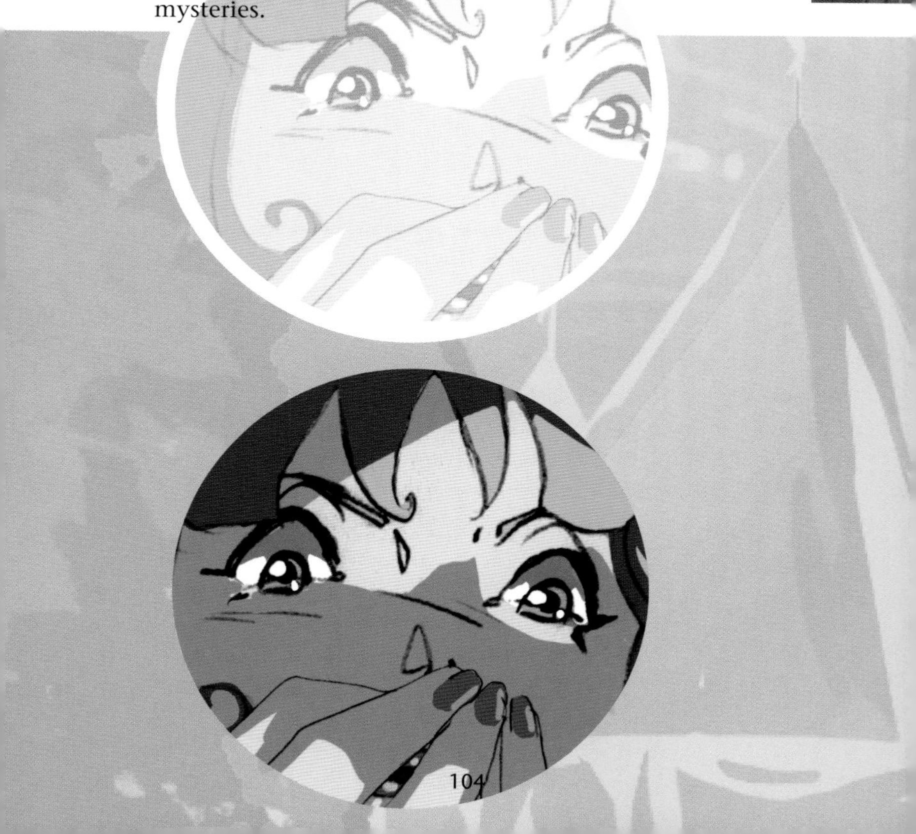

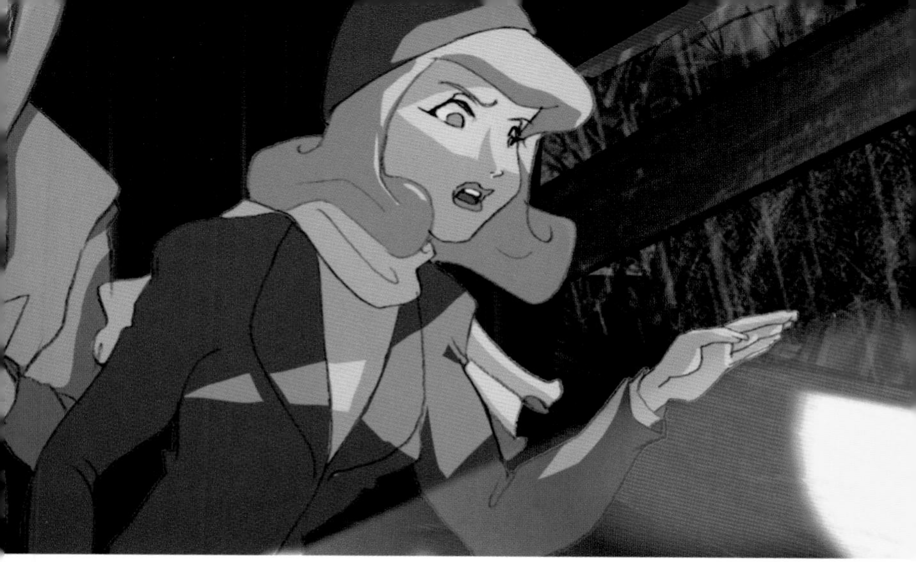

Papercutz: How do you like working for Papercutz?
Sho: Except for the sometime crazy deadlines, it's great. Jim and Terry are very pleasant persons and I do my work from my studio in San Francisco.

Papercutz: What do you think of Stefan Petrucha's stories?
Sho: He does a really great job keeping to the original Nancy Drew spirit.

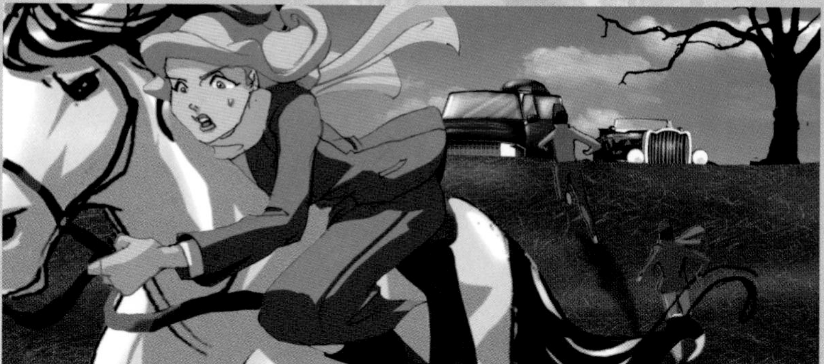

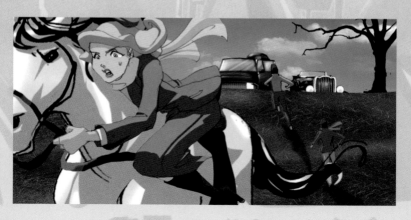

Papercutz: What else do you draw?

Sho: ME2 for Tokyopop, SEI "Death and Legend," for Image -- currently working on #2 -- fashion design illustrations, "Uberbabe" for the Uberbabe ninja ladies in Canada. Lots of animation designs, storyboards and I also do some animation.

A Cintiq tablet, like what Sho uses to draw Nancy Drew.

Papercutz: What can you tell us about future Nancy Drew graphic novels?

Sho: #8 is by far my best one as far as drawings go, and also a really good one from Stefan. There are lots of cute animals and as always, a great mystery to be solved. Can't say much 'cause I don't wanna spoil it.

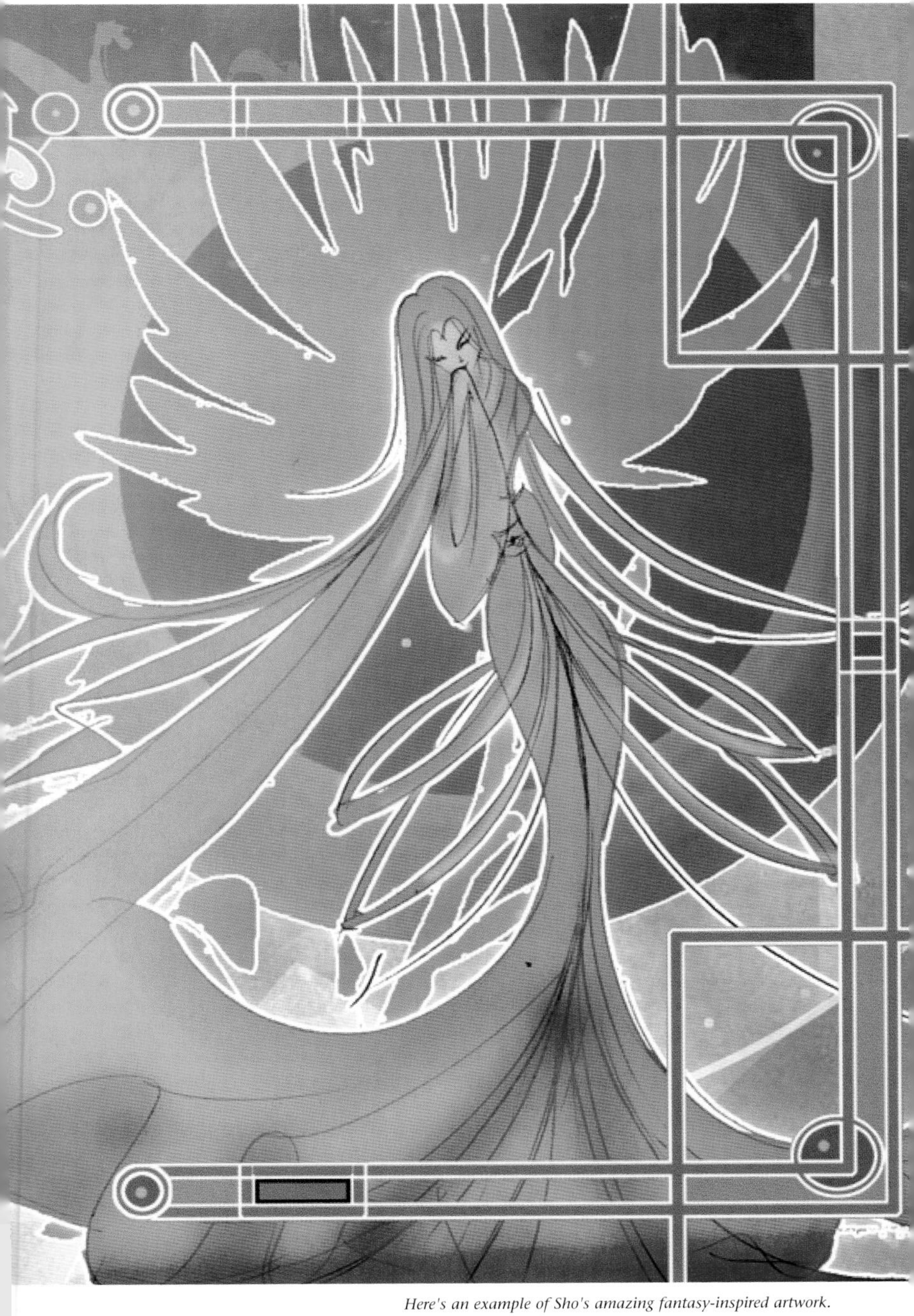

Here's an example of Sho's amazing fantasy-inspired artwork.

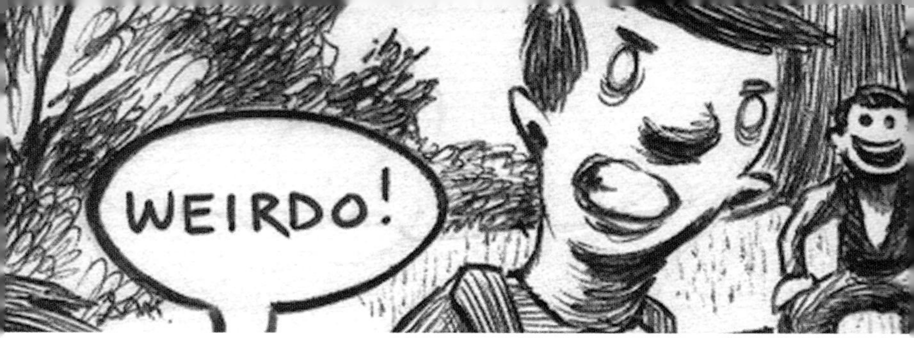
WEIRDO!

Calling All Artists!

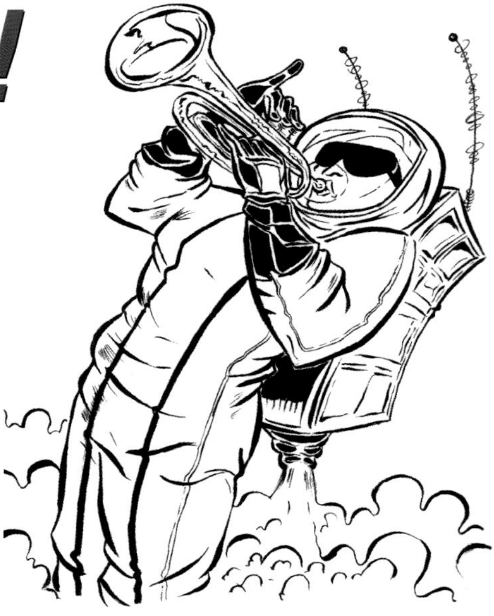
Art by and ©2006 Thomas Pitilli

Our Papercutz fans are not only a sophisticated and charming bunch, but it turns out many of them are also very talented. We've been getting so many great pics of Nancy Drew, The Hardy Boys, Zorro, and Alex, Clover, and Samantha (from Totally Spies!), that we've decided to showcase some of the best ones, right here in future Papercutz backpages, as we like to call this little section. So, if you'd like to contribute some of your artwork, send copies of your work - please don't send your originals - to Jim Salicrup, Papercutz, 40 Exchange Place, Ste. 1308, New York, NY 10005 or to salicrup@papercutz.com. Be sure to include your name, age, and address.

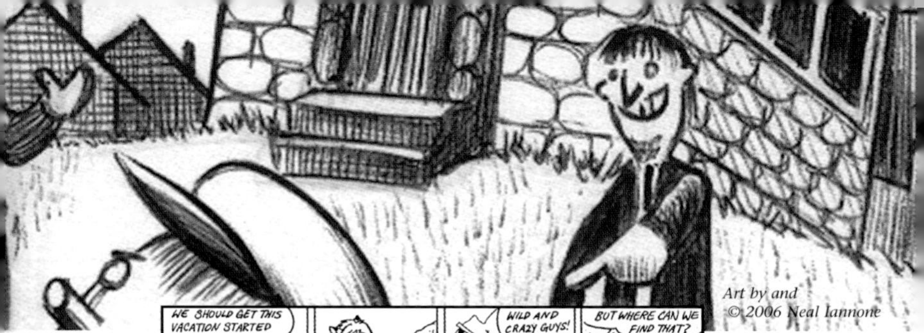

Art by and © 2006 Neal Iannone

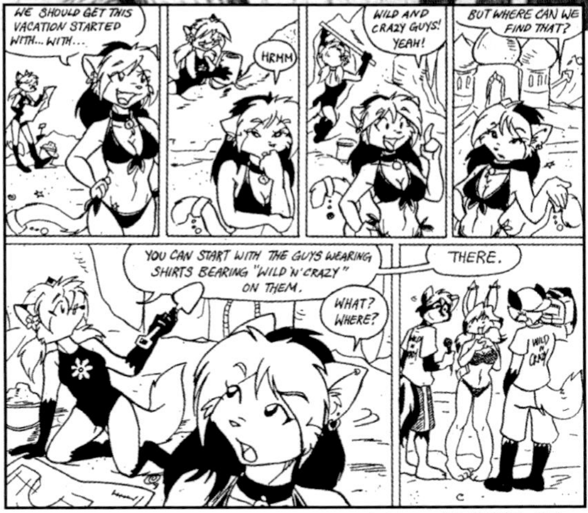
WE SHOULD GET THIS VACATION STARTED WITH... WITH...
HRMM
WILD AND CRAZY GUYS! YEAH!
BUT WHERE CAN WE FIND THAT?
YOU CAN START WITH THE GUYS WEARING SHIRTS BEARING "WILD 'N' CRAZY" ON THEM.
WHAT? WHERE?
THERE.

Art by and © 2006 Jodi Tong

Recently, Papercutz Editor-in-Chief Jim Salicrup, was asked to join other representatives from such top comics publishing companies as Marvel, DC, First Second, and others, at an event called Fresh Meat, to review the art portfolios of students from New York City's School of Visual Arts who hope to break into comics.

The students were all very talented as these samples clearly show.

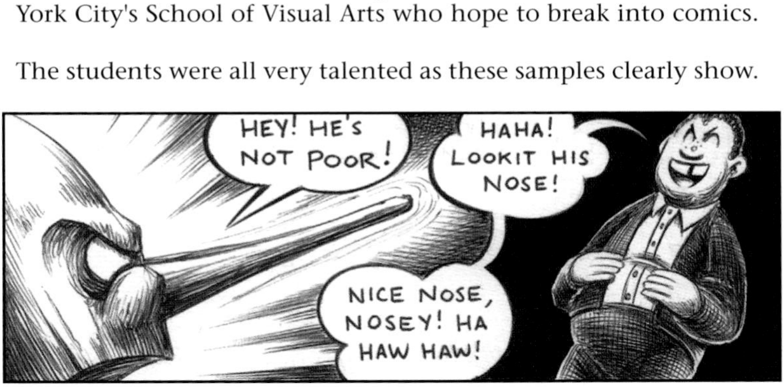
HEY! HE'S NOT POOR!
HAHA! LOOKIT HIS NOSE!
NICE NOSE, NOSEY! HA HAW HAW!

Art by and © 2006 Neal Iannone

Watching the Teen Detectives

A Hardy Boys Trivia Quiz

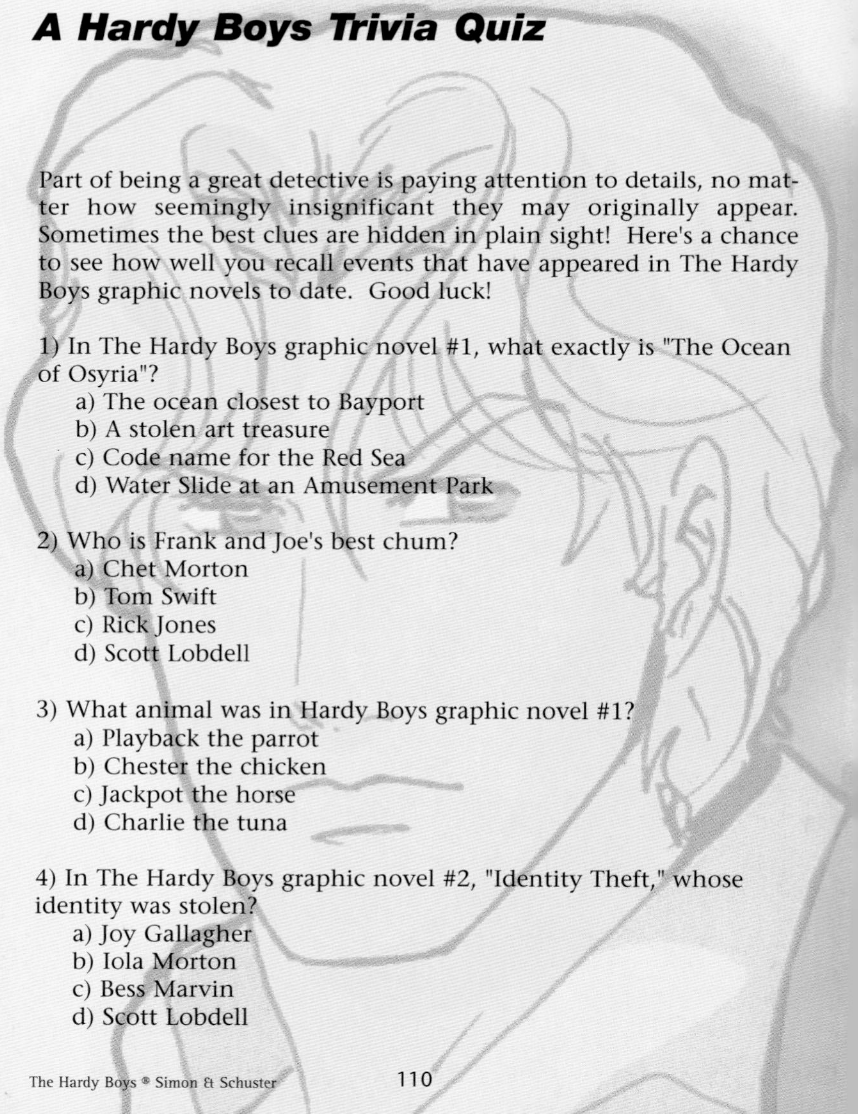

Part of being a great detective is paying attention to details, no matter how seemingly insignificant they may originally appear. Sometimes the best clues are hidden in plain sight! Here's a chance to see how well you recall events that have appeared in The Hardy Boys graphic novels to date. Good luck!

1) In The Hardy Boys graphic novel #1, what exactly is "The Ocean of Osyria"?
   a) The ocean closest to Bayport
   b) A stolen art treasure
   c) Code name for the Red Sea
   d) Water Slide at an Amusement Park

2) Who is Frank and Joe's best chum?
   a) Chet Morton
   b) Tom Swift
   c) Rick Jones
   d) Scott Lobdell

3) What animal was in Hardy Boys graphic novel #1?
   a) Playback the parrot
   b) Chester the chicken
   c) Jackpot the horse
   d) Charlie the tuna

4) In The Hardy Boys graphic novel #2, "Identity Theft," whose identity was stolen?
   a) Joy Gallagher
   b) Iola Morton
   c) Bess Marvin
   d) Scott Lobdell

5) What animal was in Hardy Boys graphic novel #2?
   a) Playback the parrot
   b) Mr. Snuggles the dog
   c) Scarlet the cat
   d) Tony the tiger

6) Which one of the following characters wasn't in The Hardy Boys graphic novel #3, "Mad House"?
   a) Joy Gallagher
   b) Jaye Long
   c) Malcolm Tate
   d) Brian Conrad

7) In Hardy Boys graphic novel #3, which object saved Joe Hardy from being hit by an arrow?
   a) A tractor
   b) A pack of cigarettes
   c) A surfboard
   d) A Nancy Drew graphic novel

8) In The Hardy Boys graphic novel # 4, "Malled," Fenton Hardy was considering...
   a) Moving back to their old house
   b) Becoming a teacher
   c) Shutting down A.T.A.C.
   d) Hanging out at the Bayport Mall

9) In Hardy Boys graphic novel #4, who was B. Emily Starr?
   a) A college journalism student
   b) An insurance adjuster
   c) A waitress in the Food Court
   d) Ringo's sister

10) In The Hardy Boys graphic novel #5, "Sea You, Sea Me," what's the name of the ship Frank and Joe work on?
   a) The Minnow
   b) The Franklin W. Dixon
   c) The Silver Lining
   d) The Titanic

Answers: 1b, 2a, 3c, 4a, 5b, 6a, 7c, 8c, 9a, 10c.
Congratulations! If you answered all the questions correctly, you really are paying attention! If you didn't, don't worry, these questions were tough! The best thing is just to re-read the graphic novels again -- that way you'll be ready for our next Hardy Boys Trivia Quiz!

111

Totally Spies!™

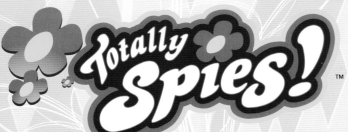

Graphic Novels available from

PAPERCUTZ™

At bookstores now:
Graphic Novel #1 "The O.P."
Graphic Novel #2 "I Hate the 80s"
Coming in December: Graphic Novel #3 "Evil Jerry"
$7.95 each in paperback
$12.95 each in hardcover
Please add $3.00 for postage and handling for the first book, add $1.00 for each additional book.
Send for our catalog:
Papercutz
40 Exchange Place, Suite 1308
New York, NY 10005
www.papercutz.com

New Full-Color Graphic Novel!
#1
Totally Spies!
THE OP
PAPERCUTZ

New Full-Color Graphic Novel!
#2
Totally Spies!
I HATE THE 80s!
PAPERCUTZ

New Full-Color Graphic Novel!
#3
Totally Spies!
EVIL JERRY
PAPERCUTZ

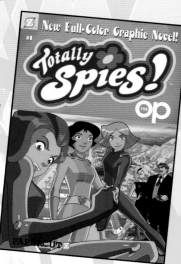

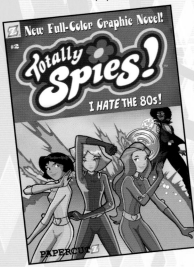

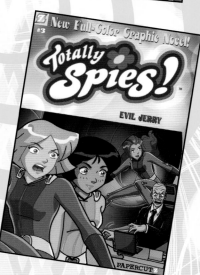

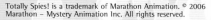